SUSAN MALLERY

"If you haven't read Susan Mallery, you must!"
—*USA TODAY* bestselling author Suzanne Forster

"Susan Mallery is warmth and wit personified.
Always a fabulous read."
—*New York Times* bestselling author Christina Dodd

CHRISTINE RIMMER

"Ms. Rimmer has developed into a major, major talent."
—*Romantic Times*

"Appealing characters, comfortable pacing
and plenty of passion demonstrate just why
Christine Rimmer is such a fan favorite."
—*Romantic Times*

LAURIE PAIGE

"Laurie Paige doesn't miss..."
—Bestselling author Catherine Coulter

"Consummate craftsman Laurie Paige
entertains with exquisite stories. It is always a joy to
savor the consistent excellence of this outstanding author."
—*Romantic Times*

SUSAN MALLERY

Susan Mallery is the bestselling and award-winning author of over sixty-five books. Even after all those stories, she swears that writing romance novels is the best job in the world! After all, there's always a happy ending in the making. She makes her home in sunny Southern California with her handsome prince of a husband and her two adorable-but-not-bright cats.

CHRISTINE RIMMER

A reader favorite whose books consistently top the Waldenbooks romance bestseller list, Christine Rimmer has written fifty novels for Silhouette Books. Her stories have been nominated for numerous awards, including Romance Writers of America's RITA® and *Romantic Times'* Series Storyteller of the Year Award. Christine has written for a number of Silhouette imprints including Silhouette Special Edition, Silhouette Desire and Silhouette Single Title. Her latest Silhouette Single Title novel, *The Man Behind the Mask,* will also be out this month.

LAURIE PAIGE

When not writing or reading or viewing landscaping shows on TV, Laurie Paige is avidly learning to create rock gardens in the volcanic soil of her Northern California home. She recently joined a hiking group that goes on excursions into the mountains once a week, winter and summer. Having reached the top of Black Butte, she is now eyeing Mount Shasta's fourteen-thousand-foot spire. Well, maybe not…

SUSAN MALLERY

CHRISTINE RIMMER

LAURIE PAIGE

MOTHER BY DESIGN

Silhouette Books

Published by Silhouette Books

America's Publisher of Contemporary Romance

Special thanks and acknowledgment are given to Susan Mallery, Christine Rimmer and Laurie Paige for their contribution to the LOGAN'S LEGACY series.

 SILHOUETTE BOOKS

MOTHER BY DESIGN
Copyright © 2004 by Harlequin Books S.A.

ISBN 0-373-21823-0

The publisher acknowledges the copyright holder of the individual works as follows:

LILY'S EXPECTING
Copyright © 2004 by Harlequin Books S.A.

RACHEL'S BUNDLE OF JOY
Copyright © 2004 by Harlequin Books S.A.

JENNA'S HAVING A BABY
Copyright © 2004 by Harlequin Books S.A.

This edition published by arrangement with Harlequin Books S.A.

® and TM are trademarks of Harlequin Books S.A., used under license. Trademarks indicated with ® are registered in the United States Patent and Trademark Office, the Canadian Trade Marks Office and in other countries.

Visit Silhouette Books at www.eHarlequin.com

Printed in U.S.A.

CONTENTS

LILY'S EXPECTING
Susan Mallery

Chapter 1

Any woman who'd been left at the altar had the perfect right—maybe even an obligation—to go a little crazy. Who wouldn't understand a wild weekend in the Caribbean or an inappropriate relationship with a much younger man? Lily Tyler chose to handle her public humiliation by getting pregnant and then buying a house.

"What do you think?" she asked eagerly. As she spoke, she tucked her right hand behind her back and crossed her fingers. Jake Stone was many things: best friend, all-around great guy and honest to a fault. The closest he came to lying was not saying anything. If he thought the house was a disaster, he would tell her—even if the news broke her heart.

He glanced around the dining room, taking in the hardwood floors, the crown molding and the bay window that offered a view of the Willamette River.

"Good-sized rooms," he said slowly. "You had the roof inspected?"

She nodded, trying not to bounce with excitement. "Uh-huh. And the wiring and the pipes. I know the place is old, but the owner before the last one did a lot of refurbishing." Unfortunately the previous owner had done squat, except apply some incredibly ugly paint and even worse wallpaper.

"The building inspector gave me a big thumbs-up," she added hopefully.

Jake turned his attention from the window to her. His dark gaze didn't give anything away—not a surprise, and one of his more annoying habits, she thought affectionately.

"Tell me the truth," she said, then winced.

He grinned. "Say it like you mean it."

"I do mean it. I'm just nervous."

"You want the house."

"More than chocolate."

He raised his eyebrows. "I didn't know there was anything you wanted more than chocolate."

"I mean it, Jake," she told him. "Am I crazy?"

He looped an arm around her shoulders and squeezed. "Lil, you've always been crazy. Lately, though, your impulses have gotten a lot more expensive."

She stepped back and socked his arm. "I'm serious."

"So am I. If you love the house that much, buy it."

She grabbed his hand. "Really? But it needs a lot of work."

"All cosmetic. You've had the inspections, you know it's sound. From my experience, you don't have any structural issues. So go for it. You can afford it." His eyes narrowed. "Can't you?"

"Of course." She flung herself at him. "I'm so glad you approve. Not that I need your approval."

He pulled her close and kissed her forehead. "Of course not. That's why you were crossing your fingers behind your back."

She laughed. "You saw that?"

"I see everything."

"Oh, right." Lily stepped back and sighed. "Okay, I'm going ahead with the deal. Which means I have three months to get the place all fixed up."

Jake shook his head. "That's not gonna happen."

"Of course it is." She touched her stomach. "I'm not going to wait until after the baby's born."

"You're six months pregnant."

"Actually, I'm aware of that."

"You know what I mean, Lily. Have you checked with your doctor? Is it safe for you to be stripping wallpaper and painting?"

"The stripping is fine. I'll be using a steamer. As for painting…" She let her voice trail off and looked at him from under her lashes. "It could be difficult."

Jake groaned. "Let me guess. You thought I could pitch in and help."

She blinked. "If it's not too much trouble."

"Great. So you expect me to paint the place."

"Just the inside. I'm hiring a crew to do the outside."

"Gee, thanks," he grumbled. "What else?"

"I want to put down tile in the master bath. You've done that before, right? Maybe you could give me a few pointers."

"Anything else?"

She beamed. "Not right now."

Jake gave the sigh of the long-suffering. "I need to get my tape measure from the truck. I'll be right back."

While he was gone, Lily crossed to the bay window and stared out at the trees at the edge of her property and the way the yard sloped down to the river.

After four years of small apartments and student loan payments, she was finally buying her first-ever house. The fact that it was the old O'Malley place— a house she'd loved since she'd been a teenager— made the moment even more special. The pain of the past had finally faded. She could think about Michael Carson—wormy weasel dog—and not even flinch. She still had a little trouble when she remembered being all dressed up in her white wedding gown with no groom, but even *that* humiliation had faded a lot. She'd gotten on with her life, which made this a very good day.

She heard footsteps. Before she could turn around, she felt Jake's hand on the small of her back.

"You okay?" he asked, his voice low and concerned.

"Of course. I'm excited about the house."

"And Sam?"

She reached for his hand and brought it around to rest on the mound of her stomach. "I am *not* naming the baby Sam."

"Why not?" he asked. "It's the perfect name. Samantha if it's a girl and Samuel if it's a boy."

"I see." She smiled. "And I should listen to you why?"

"Because I'm always right."

"I can think of several occasions when your judgment was called into question. There was your entire six-month relationship with a girl named Buffy, and she did not come close to living up to her television namesake."

"She liked kickboxing."

"*There's* a recommendation."

"You could solve the problem by letting them tell you the gender at your next ultrasound," he reminded her.

"I know and I'm really tempted, but I want the surprise."

"Fair enough."

Jake rubbed her back for a couple more seconds, then stepped away. "I need to measure the rooms."

"Have at it."

Lily watched him walk into the living room and unclip the tape measure from his belt. In his worn jeans and work boots he looked like a sexy carpenter. The kind women fantasize about showing up at their door. He was tall, lean and good-looking enough to turn heads when he went out in public. He was also her rock.

"I owe you," she called to him.

"Sure. You say that now but do you ever pay up?"

"I'm waiting for the right moment."

Not that she *could* repay him. Not for the past

eight months. When Michael had left her at the altar, Jake had been there to pick up the pieces. He'd held her while she'd cried, offered to beat up the guy, gone out at midnight to buy her double chocolate chunk fudge brownie ice cream and had promised it would eventually stop hurting so bad. He'd put his own impressive social life on hold to hang out with her, even after she'd told him she'd gone ahead with artificial insemination and was pregnant.

She glanced down at her stomach. ''You were a bit of a surprise,'' she told her baby. ''Everyone told me it was unlikely to happen the very first time, but they were wrong, huh?''

Not that Lily minded. She'd always wanted a ton of kids and had assumed there would be a husband to go along with her fantasy. Unfortunately she hadn't found anyone she loved enough to stay with forever, until Michael. Then he'd turned out to be a class-A jerk. Which had left her with a limited amount of time in which to start her family.

She and her girlfriends Rachel and Jenna had always joked about getting artificial insemination for their thirty-fourth birthdays if there were no men in their pictures. Lily had actually gone ahead with it. There might not be a Mr. Right hanging around, but she had everything else she'd ever wanted. It was enough, she told herself. She was content.

She walked out of the dining room and headed upstairs where she found Jake standing in the middle of the master bath. As always, the sight of the gold foil bamboo-and-palm-frond wallpaper made her wince.

"What were they thinking?" she asked.

"Maybe it was some kind of punishment."

"What scares me is that someone at the wallpaper company presented this design as one that would sell, and the committee or whoever decides what goes in the books agreed it was a good idea. Then someone bought it." She shuddered. "It has to go."

Jake leaned against the Formica-covered counter. "Lil, you have to prioritize for both time and money. You have three months until the baby comes. What do you want done before then and what can wait? I agree with the painting, even though I'm going to be the one doing it. You'll get a lot of bang for your buck. The tile will be pretty easy, too. Just a lot of cutting to make it all fit."

She smiled. "How convenient that your work schedule gives you a lot of time off."

"Yeah. Lucky me."

Jake was a firefighter. His schedule required him to work twenty-four hours at a time, but there was plenty of non-work time in compensation.

"You're right about the list," she said. "Let me

look around and come up with the most important items. We can do them first.''

He raised his eyebrows. ''We? I don't think so, Lil. I've agreed to the painting and tile, but that's it.''

She pretended to pout. ''We're friends and you adore me, right? So pleasing me is the most important part of your day?''

Jake stared into Lily's green eyes and knew this was one time he was going to have to keep his mouth shut. Adore her? That didn't begin to describe his feelings.

''You're okay,'' he said. ''Make me a list and we'll talk. Also, I need you to pick out paint and tile. And no, I'm not coming to the paint store with you. I remember when you wanted to paint your apartment bathroom. It took you four hours to pick out a single gallon of paint.''

She planted her hands on her hips. ''That is *so* not fair. The yellows were all either too bright or had too much green in them. I wanted a pale yellow with a hint of…''

He shook his head as he backed up a step. ''This would be my point. You choose it and I'll cart it over here. Fair enough?''

''Absolutely.'' Her humor faded. ''Seriously, Jake,

you're being amazing. I owe you big time. Just tell me what you want and it's yours.''

What he wanted? That was a whole different conversation.

''Don't sweat it, Lil. You've been there for me in the past. Consider this a chance to even the score.''

''I don't think so. You've needed me for advice about women—which you never take—and a couple of shopping trips. You're watching over me like this baby is yours, and now you're signing on to help me with the house.''

He noticed they were getting into dangerous territory and decided to sidestep the potential trouble.

''You forget you also get free access to my wit and charm,'' he said. ''There are a lot of women who would gladly trade places with you.''

''I know. They send me daily e-mails. Come on. You ready to get out of here?''

''Sure.''

He followed her through the old house to the front door, where she looked around one last time before fishing the key out of her purse and pulling the door shut behind her.

''You don't have to buy this house right now,'' he told her. ''You could wait.''

She smiled at him. ''As usual, you're reading my mind. But I'm going to keep telling myself to feel the fear and do it anyway. I want this, Jake. I'm done putting my life on hold waiting for Mr. Right to show up. I've proven time and time again that I have lousy taste when it comes to men.'' She turned the lock. ''Present company excluded.''

''We're not romantically involved.''

''Exactly. You're the only decent guy I know and we've never gone out. Why is that?''

Before he could answer, she laughed. ''Oh, yeah. I remember. Because you only date girls under the age of twenty-five who used to be either cheerleaders or beauty contestants. Mind telling me why?''

''Because they say yes when I ask them out.''

''Gee, how about asking out someone with a brain or a little ambition?''

''Maybe. For a change.''

Someone like her? he wondered. Was that the solution to his problem? To find a woman exactly like Lily? Was that possible? Or would he just spend his time comparing her to Lily and watching her fall short of what he really wanted?

''I'm a mess,'' Lily said cheerfully. ''A mess whose days of seeing her feet are numbered.''

''But a homeowner,'' he reminded her.

''Soon.''

They walked to his truck.

Jake gave her a hand up into the seat and did his

best not to react when her fingers closed around his. Heat flashed through him, making him want to pull her close and brush his mouth against hers. Telling himself she was pregnant didn't seem to decrease his libido, so he settled on the cold hard truth that she wasn't interested in him. Not that way.

"Did I tell you I had loan approval?" she asked as he slid behind the wheel.

"No. That's a big step."

"About the final one. Apparently I'm the first lottery winner the mortgage company has had to deal with." Humor brightened her green eyes. "If we'd won millions I wouldn't have needed the loan at all. As it is I had to send them a letter explaining where the down-payment money came from. There were many questions."

"I'll bet."

He put the truck in reverse. As he glanced behind him to check for oncoming traffic, he saw her shoulders slump. He had a feeling he knew the reason.

After years of playing the lottery, Lily, Rachel and Jenna had finally scored a five-hundred-thousand dollar jackpot. It had come on the heels of Lily being left at the altar by that jerk she'd nearly married. The money hadn't mended her broken heart, but it had provided a distraction. Unfortunately, the three friends had had a falling out and hadn't spoken in months.

"Rachel and Jenna?" he asked gently.

She swatted his arm. "Stop knowing what I'm thinking."

"I can't help it."

She sighed. "I know. Sorry. Yes, it's them. I miss them."

"So call."

"I want to, it's just…" she shrugged "…complicated."

"You miss them. You care about them. Call."

"Stop making it sound so easy."

"It is," he said. "With push-button phones you don't even have the trouble of dialing anymore."

"Oh, sure. But you're assuming I'm ready to act maturely."

"You are."

She reached across the bench seat and grabbed his hand. "Thanks, Jake. You're the best. You know that, right?"

"Of course."

He laced his fingers with hers and knew he couldn't read anything into the act. To Lily, they were best friends. He'd been the one to change the rules without telling her. He'd been the one to wake up one morning and realize he'd loved her for years.

Unfortunately, the revelation had come about six months too late. She'd already been in love with Michael Carson. When the guy had proposed and Lily had accepted, Jake had vowed to keep his feelings to himself forever.

Then Michael hadn't bothered showing up at the church. He'd sent a note telling Lily that he'd never intended for things to get this far. Worse, he'd lied about getting a divorce and was still married. Lily had been heartbroken, and Jake had been there to lend a shoulder to cry on.

He'd known there was no point in telling her about his feelings. Not until she'd gotten over Michael. Talk about timing. He'd planned a casual dinner at his house, complete with wine, candlelight and a confession of love on his part. Two days before their scheduled rendezvous, Lily had called to tell him she was pregnant.

The good news had been there wasn't a guy involved. Lily had used artificial insemination and a sperm donor. But her announcement had put a crimp in his confession plans. If he told her he loved her *after* she had told him she was pregnant, would she think he was simply reacting to the baby? Would she assume that his feelings were merely concern?

He didn't have a good answer to any of his questions and until he did, he kept his emotions to himself. It made life hell, but he'd learned to endure that a lot in the past few months. Besides, there was no guarantee Lily wanted to change things between them. As far as he could tell, she was happy just being friends.

"Are you all packed for the move?" he asked.

"Pretty much. I left the books like you made me promise."

"Good. I'll be by in a couple of days to finish things up."

She glanced at him. "I could box up my books just fine, you know. I can move a few at a time. All the extra walking back and forth would be good exercise for me."

"No way. I know you, Lil. You'll get a box all loaded then decide you don't like where it is. The next thing you know you'll be moving it by yourself and straining something. Leave the books for me."

"Okay, but I have to tell you, you're getting kind of bossy."

"You like being told what to do."

"Actually I don't." She smiled. "But I like letting you think you're in charge."

"I *am* in charge."

She squeezed his hand. "Sure you are, big guy."

* * *

"Am I really doing this?" Lily asked as the burly men continued to load her belongings into the truck. "Is it too late to change my mind?"

Jake set down the box he'd been carrying and looked at her. "Do you really want an answer?"

"I'm serious." Panic overwhelmed her. "What was I thinking? This was a huge mistake." She covered her face with her hands. "I can't believe I bought a house."

"Hell of a time to be having buyer's remorse," Jake told her, then put his arm around her and gave her a hug. He was warm and strong and big and she decided to lean on him for the next sixty seconds or until her breathing returned to normal. Whichever came first.

"You're not making a mistake."

She dropped her hands to her side and sighed. "You're just saying that because you don't want me to burst into tears."

"That's part of it, but I'm telling the truth, too."

"How do you figure?"

He wrapped his other arm around her and stared into her eyes. They weren't exactly body-to-body, not with her belly jutting out between them, but the almost-contact still felt nice and safe. Plus he was really easy to look at.

"You have a job," he said.

"That's true. I'm employed and I have benefits. I even have a paid maternity leave from the hospital." She drew in a breath. "Nursing is the kind of career that's here to stay. I don't need to worry about being downsized or replaced by a computer."

"Exactly. You put a large down payment on the house, right?"

"Uh-huh." Despite the knot in her stomach she grinned. "With my lottery winnings."

"You have money budgeted for the remodeling you want to do?"

She nodded. "And savings and a small emergency fund."

He released her. "See? You have nothing to worry about."

She wasn't ready to be let go and grabbed his shirt front. "Wait a minute. This isn't just about money. What about me being a single parent? Can I do that? I don't know how to work a lawn mower. I grew up in apartments."

Jake stared at her. "I'm not getting the lawn mower–single parent linkage."

"They're not related. I went back to house worry."

"Could we pick a topic and stay on it for a while?"

"I don't think so." She clutched the front of her

stomach as her insides rolled around. "I'm going to be sick."

He frowned. "I thought you were long done with morning sickness."

"This has nothing to do with the baby. I'm ruining my life and I paid to do it."

Still holding onto her belly, she sank onto the grass in front of her apartment building.

"I used to be sensible," she murmured. "I used to have plans and be organized. Lately I'm impulsive and look at what it's gotten me. My life is a disaster."

Jake crouched in front of her. "Lily, snap out of it. Your life is great. You're healthy, pregnant and you just bought a terrific house. Nothing bad is going to happen."

She desperately wanted to believe him. "Promise?"

"Yeah, and if I'm wrong, I'll be right here to pick up the pieces."

The way he had after Michael had dumped her, she thought, and sniffed. And when he'd found out about the baby. Most people would have run screaming in the other direction but Jake had taken her announcement in stride.

"I don't deserve you," she whispered.

"You got that right. Now quit faking it and start

helping. You're still buying the pizza for dinner, and don't you forget it.''

The thought of food had her scrambling to her feet. ''You think there are any doughnuts left from breakfast?''

''What about staying healthy for the baby?'' he asked. ''Shouldn't you be eating bran muffins instead?''

She wrinkled her nose. ''I do great most of the time. I'll get a veggie pizza tonight, so get off me.''

Jake stood and stared at her. ''It's the hormones, right? That's why you can go from bone-crushing sadness to hungry in eight seconds?''

''Probably. You want another doughnut?''

''Only if it's a maple bar.''

She headed for the apartment building. ''Let me go check.''

''No way. You'll eat them all yourself then tell me there weren't any left.''

She tried not to smile as he caught up with her. ''Would I really do that?'' she asked innocently.

''In a heartbeat.''

Chapter 2

Jake stretched out on the sofa. He was tired from his day spent moving, but not inspired to go to bed. Not yet and sure as hell not alone.

There had been too many solo nights in the past eight or nine months. He'd tried dating, but no woman he'd asked out was Lily, and he couldn't seem to get interested in anyone else. Knowing he'd set up both himself and the woman in question for failure, he'd stopped asking and expecting the impossible.

Which left him alone, edgy and irritable.

There was a Mariner game on TV. He reached

for the remote, but before he could grab it, the phone rang.

"It's me," Lily said when he'd picked up the receiver. "Am I interrupting?"

"Sure. I have two coeds doing the dance of the seven veils right here in my living room."

He heard the smile in her voice as she spoke. "Yeah, I'm flaked out, too. Moving is a lot more work than I remembered. Of course, after college, everything I owned could fit in the back of a pickup truck. When did I get all this stuff? And why?"

"It seemed important at the time. Remember that oak bookcase you had to have? And the dining-room table? I nearly threw out my back with that one."

She sighed. "But it's beautiful and it looks great in my dining room. So when are you going to sell me that gorgeous hutch of yours? The one your grandmother left you? You know you don't appreciate it, and if she'd known how much I wanted it, she would have left it to me."

He grinned at the familiar argument. "But she didn't. Maybe one day, if you're really good, I'll let you make me an offer."

"Huh. Like I believe that. You just like having something to hold over me."

"That's true. So what's up? Is the house getting to you?"

Lily hesitated long enough for him to realize that he'd spoken the truth. One part concerned, two parts amused, he sat up.

"Let me guess," he said. "You're scared."

"I'm not scared. It's just the house is, you know. Big."

"I thought you liked that about it."

"I do. It's just there are weird noises. House noises. I'm not familiar with them yet."

He chuckled. "Are you going to make it through the night?"

"Of course." She sounded insulted. "I'm perfectly capable of surviving here by myself. In fact I like living alone. It's just so empty and some of the floors creak."

"By themselves or when you're walking?"

"When I'm walking. I'm not saying the place is haunted." Lily's breath caught. "You don't think it could be, do you? It's an old house. Who knows what happened here?"

He shifted so he could put his feet on the coffee table. "You're not seriously worried about ghosts are you?"

"No. Just first-night creeps. I'll be okay. Maybe I should get a dog. A really big one."

"Only if you want to be cleaning up after it."

"Oh. Good point. Maybe a cat, although I don't

think a cat would be much protection. Is it cold there? It's cold here."

Jake figured the outside temperature was all of fifty-five. "Turn on the heat."

"I guess. Or I could just get another blanket."

"You're in bed?"

"Uh-huh." Humor returned to her voice. "Want to know what I'm wearing? It's the cutting edge of maternity chic. There are barnyard animals dancing across my belly. Pretty sexy, huh?"

He knew she was joking and expected him to join in, but all he could think about was Lily curled up in a big bed and him sliding in beside her. He imagined himself spooning with her, his front against her back, his hand sliding around to cup her breasts while her tight, round fanny nestled against him. He could smell her soft skin and hear her breathing.

He closed his eyes and fought back a groan. For one thing, lusting after a pregnant woman was probably illegal. For another, if Lily knew he was having sexual fantasies about her she would cuff him, then call him a pervert. And the most pressing reason to knock it off was the sudden lack of blood in his brain and the hardness in his groin. Being tired and sore from moving wasn't enough. Now he had to deal with the physical manifestation of unfulfilled desire. Could the day get any worse?

"I grossed you out, huh?" she said, sounding resigned. "Sorry."

"Don't apologize. I'm sure you look great in barnyard animal PJs."

"You don't believe that for a second. The truth is I'm a cow myself. Huge and bovine-like. But I used to be sexy, right? I mean before the baby? And attractive. Although not attractive enough to keep Michael from standing me up at the altar."

"Don't go there, Lil," he told her. "Michael was an idiot and you're lucky to have him out of your life."

"I know and I'm really glad, it's just sometimes…" She sighed again. "I don't know. I wonder where it all went wrong. Why did I fall for him in the first place? Shouldn't I have seen the truth?"

"Sometimes we can't see what's right in front of us."

He hadn't figured out his feelings for Lily until it was too late, Jake thought grimly. A few months earlier and he could have told her *before* she'd met Michael. Maybe she wouldn't have been interested, but at least the information would have been out there and he wouldn't have spent the past nine months wondering.

"You're getting philosophical on me and that always makes me nervous,'' Lily said. ''I think you need to watch some sports or something because—''

A strange sound came through the phone line—a metallic ripping, then a huge crash. Jake sat up straight and clutched the receiver.

''Lily? Are you okay? What just happened?''

''I—I don't know. Something bad though. That was *not* a good sound. And I can hear a rushing noise. Like water. You don't suppose the Willamette River just flooded into my dining room, do you?''

''No, but be careful anyway.'' He stood, torn between staying on the phone with her and heading for her place. ''I'm going to call you right back from my cell.''

''Okay.''

He ran to the front of his house, grabbed his jacket and his keys, then raced toward his truck. As he started the engine, he hit the auto dial for her home number. She picked up instantly.

''There's water everywhere,'' she said, sounding more stunned than frantic. ''Like a real river through my dining room. I'm on the stairs and I'm kind of afraid to step into it. Where do you think it's coming from?''

''Broken pipe. Maybe the water heater.''

''This isn't good. I have to say, so far the home-owner experience isn't what I expected.''

Despite his concern, he smiled. "Just your luck, Lil. I'll be there in less than five minutes. Don't move off the stairs and if the water starts rising, head up to the second floor."

"Okay. You sound so confident and sure of yourself. It's the rescue thing, isn't it? You're comfortable in that role."

"Yeah, sure. I'm a hero to my bones. Hold on and I'll be there to get you."

"Thanks, Jake. You're the best."

He hung up. The best, huh? Best what? Friend? He wasn't interested in that. He wanted Lily to see him as the man of her dreams. What were the odds of that ever happening?

Lily stood watching two or three inches of water pouring through her downstairs. Whatever the cause, it couldn't be a good thing. Not when ancient carpeting and hardwood floors were getting soaked.

"My insurance agent is going to hate getting *this* call," she murmured, knowing there was no point in getting upset. Panicking wouldn't help either her or the baby and with Jake on the way, what was there to worry about? Still she couldn't help feeling that getting the house back to rights wasn't going to be easy.

The rush seemed to have slowed some. At least

the water wasn't rising. She took a step toward the main floor, then stopped. If the water heater had exploded or something, the water could be really hot. She was barefoot. And wearing really ugly pajamas.

"Oh, great," she muttered, knowing Jake had seen her at her worst, although not by much. She'd washed off her makeup and pulled her hair up on top of her head. To make matters more embarrassing, she had cows and pigs frolicking across her mid-section.

She heard a key in the front door. Thank goodness she'd given Jake a spare before he'd left.

"Lily?" he called as he opened the front door.

"Up here."

She took another step down as he walked into the foyer.

The entrance area was raised up, giving him a dry place to crouch and stare at the water. When he raised his gaze to hers, she wasn't sure what he was thinking. Then the corners of his mouth turned up.

"This would only happen to you," he said.

"Tell me about it. Any guesses?"

He tested the water with his fingers. "It's warm but not hot. I'm going to go with the water heater causing this. So where's the main shut-off?"

She folded her arms under her breasts and sniffed. "You probably think I don't know, but I do. It's in the mudroom behind the kitchen. Your key will open the back door if you don't want to wade through.''

"I've walked through worse," he told her as he crossed through to the kitchen. Before he disappeared, he turned back to her. "Stay there on the stairs until I see what's going on."

"Promise."

In less than five minutes he'd turned off the water and checked out the water heater, which was ripped open and on its side.

"Was it bolting for freedom?" Lily asked as she stared at the twisted hunk of metal. "Should I take the defection personally?"

"It was older than both of us. I think it simply fell apart from age."

"Something we can all look forward to," she murmured feeling more numb than upset. "What will the insurance cover?"

"Most of the damage. You'll need to call them first thing in the morning. We can get a crew out to dry the place. I'm guessing the hardwood floors will have to be refinished. The carpet's a goner."

"I'm glad I didn't like it."

He put an arm around her. "The good news is the water went through fast and didn't have a whole lot of time to soak in. I doubt the drywall will have to be replaced. You'll get a new water heater out of it."

She tried to get excited about that, but all she could think was that she'd owned the house for less than twenty-four hours and she'd already had a really big thing go wrong.

"You don't think this is a sign, right? I mean no one is trying to tell me I should have stayed in my apartment?"

He rubbed her back. "Are you okay?"

She tried to stay strong, but it was difficult when surveying the damage. "I haven't even been here a whole day."

"Come on." He led her through the kitchen to the stairs. "Go pack a few things. You can stay with me until this is all sorted out."

"You want me to leave?"

"I had to turn off the water. You don't have a water heater and your entire downstairs is soaked. Do you want to stay?"

She shook her head, afraid that if she tried to speak she would cry. This wasn't really happening. It couldn't be.

"Hey." Jake touched his index finger to her chin. "It's going to be okay. I've seen a lot worse."

"I know. I'm really lucky."

He smiled. "I don't think *lucky* describes your situation, but you're safe, this is all fixable and you've got a place to stay."

She sniffed. "You're a good friend."

"I'm a friend who expects you to cook me dinner while you're living with me."

She gave a strangled laugh that was perilously close to a sob. He wrapped his arms around her and pulled her against him. She settled against him, liking how strong he felt. Jake was solid—physically and emotionally. He always had been.

She pressed her nose against his shirt and inhaled the scent of his body. He smelled sexy and male. Her mood lifted as she thought about how horrified he would be if he knew she'd thought of him as sexy. Jake saw her as a sister—currently a very pregnant sister.

"Come on," he said, leading the way up the stairs. "I'll help you pack."

In less than an hour, she was tucked into his guest-room bed with a cup of hot chocolate on the night-stand. Despite what had happened, she felt safe, comfortable and optimistic. And guilty for dragging Jake out in the middle of the night.

"Better?" he asked from the doorway.

She nodded. "I know the house is going to be okay, once it's dry. My big worry is that I'm taking advantage of you. First you helped me with the painting and tile, then the move, now this."

He crossed to the bed and sat down next to her.

His dark hair fell across his forehead and his eyes crinkled as he smiled.

"Who goes with me every year to help me buy birthday presents for my sisters and my mom?"

She dismissed the question with a wave. "But that's shopping. I like to shop."

"Uh-huh. And who taught me how to cook the best chili in the firehouse?"

Lily thought about all the compliments Jake's fellow firefighters had given her and grinned. "That *was* pretty special."

"And who picked out my living-room furniture and helped me when I tore out the backyard to put in the big patio?"

"That would be me."

He shrugged. "That's what we do for each other. We're there at crunch time."

"I know, but things have felt inequitable since the whole Michael disaster. I don't want you to feel I'm taking advantage of you."

"I don't."

He probably didn't, she thought fondly. Jake was that kind of man. The good kind.

"You're very special," she said as she leaned forward and kissed his cheek. "One of these days you're going to meet someone amazing, get married and forget I even exist."

"That will never happen."

"Want to bet?"

He studied her face. "I'll never forget you, Lil. You know that."

Her throat got all tight and something unexpected quivered in her stomach. This wasn't the baby—she'd grown used to those fluttery feelings. This was something else. Something…erotic.

Horrified, Lily sank back against the pillow. What was wrong with her? Was this a hormonal reaction to her pregnancy? She hadn't had any serious food cravings. Couldn't she just want cookie dough ice cream or pound cake? Did she have to get the nibbles for Jake?

"I know," she said, going for cheerful and having a bad feeling the words came out kind of squished. "I'll see you in the morning."

He nodded and rose, then headed for the bedroom door. She watched him go.

When she was alone, she reached for the hot chocolate and considered the problem. Whatever was wrong with her, she had to get it fixed and pronto. Maybe she was just reacting to the whole rescue thing. Jake had experienced women wanting to go out with him after he'd saved them from a burning building. He was a fire fighter, which meant he had built-in hero potential.

Her water heater had committed suicide and he'd been there in a flash. Of course she was feeling stuff.

But what that ''stuff'' might be and what it could mean was better left unexplored. She and Jake had been friends forever. She didn't want anything to mess that up.

Jake had a bad feeling that living with Lily was going to be a unique brand of hell, so he was grateful when he had to work the next day. Twenty-four hours away from her would go a long way to restoring his equilibrium. At least that was the plan. When he walked into his house the following morning and found her cooking breakfast in his kitchen, he had to re-evaluate his strategy.

She stood in front of the stove, turning bacon. She wore brightly colored scrubs—teal pull pants and a print shirt, white shoes and no jewelry. Her still-damp hair had been pulled back into a braid. She looked beautiful.

As he paused in the utility room to pull off his boots, she called out a greeting.

''I can't remember the last time I got up early enough to cook eggs and bacon, so be sure to put a star by this day on the calendar.''

''I'll do that,'' he said, hating how just the sound of her voice made his chest tighten. A midnight call to a car fire might have robbed him of several hours of sleep but it had done nothing to impede his libido. Damn it all to hell if he didn't want Lily just as much this second as he had when he'd left.

"How was your shift?" she asked.

"Good. Busy." He walked into the kitchen and headed for the sink to wash up. "Nobody got dead."

She smiled at him. "I'm glad."

"Me, too."

He scrubbed his hands, splashed water on his face and reached for a towel. From there it was a short walk to the coffee.

"Did you get any sleep?" she asked.

"A few hours."

"You could go to bed for a few more," she pointed out as he filled a mug to the very top.

"Too much to do. What happened yesterday? Did you get everything lined up?"

"I did." She motioned to the table, then served the breakfast. "Even as we speak, large fans are drying out the floor. The carpet is completely destroyed, but the hardwood seems okay and because the water went through so quickly, most of the sub flooring was spared. I have a new water heater coming in and if all goes well, I'll be back in my house in about ten days."

He was torn between needing her gone for the sake of his sanity and never wanting her to leave.

"Sounds good," he said as he picked up his fork. "You got a lot done."

"You left me the names of really good people. After my insurance agent got over the shock of what had happened, she sent out an adjuster and we're all set to go."

Lily sat opposite him and picked up a piece of bacon. "Once again I owe you."

Jake scooped up eggs and shook his head. "We're even. I can't remember the last time anyone cooked me breakfast."

"If you dated women who were old enough to cook, that would be a start. Or you could go over to your mom's house. She would be delighted to have you around."

"No thanks," he said. "It's enough that I live across the street and two houses down from my mother. I don't need to be running over there every morning. She already thinks I don't have enough of a life."

Lily smiled. "You love the attention."

"Sometimes."

His dad had passed away ten years ago, leaving Jake the man of the family. He'd been in his twenties and more than willing to take on the responsibility.

After all, how much could there be? He was the baby of the family. His three sisters were happily married and his mother had been ruling the world since before his birth.

But upon the death of his father, she'd alternated between fiercely independent and a need to cling. In a moment of weakness, Jake had made an offer on the house he now lived in and had set himself up for a lifetime of living within shouting distance of his mother.

"She's terrific," Lily said. "It's not as if she ever just bursts in on you."

"Right. She always calls to say she's on her way over. Never mind that I might want to go out or have company."

Lily raised her eyebrows. "Ooh, sleepovers. That could be a shock. After a night of amazing passion you wake up to find your mother in the doorway."

"It's never happened."

"Gotten close?"

He grinned. "A couple of times."

Lily's humor faded. "What is she going to say when she finds out about me?"

"She's going to think my taste in women has improved."

"Are you sure she won't be upset?"

"Of course not. She adores you."

"And I adore her. Along with your sisters."

Lily had been an only child. He had always thought one of the reasons the two of them had stayed friends was his family. Lily loved the big, noisy holiday celebrations, the excess of kids running around.

He glanced at her stomach. "They're counting the days until Sam is born."

She rolled her eyes. "You haven't said anything about me naming the baby Sam, have you? I don't want them to think I have lousy taste."

"It's a great name. But they don't know about it."

"That's a relief." She sipped her tea, then looked at him over the rim. "We need to talk."

Four words every man dreaded hearing. "What about?"

"Me moving to a hotel. I can't stay here for a couple of weeks."

If he had his way, she could stay forever.

"Want to tell me why not?"

She set down her tea. "It wouldn't be right. You have a life. I don't want to get in the way of that."

"Meaning what? You're going to put a crimp in my dating style?"

"You have to admit that bringing your latest conquest home to a pregnant friend isn't going to ensure a smooth evening."

"No problem. I'm not seeing anyone right now."

"But—"

He shook his head. "Lily, you're welcome to stay. We have a good time together and we get along. Plus, you'll feel guilty and do a lot of cooking. What's not to like?"

She touched his hand. "I don't want you to end up resenting me for invading your life."

"That's not going to happen." If only it would, then he would know he was finally getting over her.

She took another bite of bacon, chewed, then swallowed. "Okay, but I want you to promise you'll tell me the second I start to be a pain."

"Done."

"I mean it."

"So do I. When you start really bugging me, I'll let you know and then help you move into my mom's place."

Lily winced. "I adore your mother, but I think I'd prefer a hotel. A week in her house and I'd gain about fifty pounds from all the rich food."

"Plus she'd talk your ear off."

"I don't know that I'd mind that." She reached for the bowl of cut-up fruit she'd set in the center of the table. "Any other house rules you want to discuss?"

"How about no sleepover dates?"

"I don't want to crimp your style."

"I mean for you."

She froze with a spoonful of fruit half way between the bowl and her plate. Her eyes widened, then her lips curved.

"You are so kidding. Me? Have a man around? Not likely."

"Giving up so easily?"

"The disaster that was my ex-fiancé was many things, but easy wasn't one of them. In the immortal words of my generation—been there, done that."

Jake had been sure there wasn't anyone significant in her life, but he'd wanted to ask just in case he'd missed something. Now that she was getting over Michael and settling in with the idea of a baby, he needed either to come clean with how he was feeling or get over her. Only three things held him back: finding the right words, the concern that he was changing the rules and therefore their relationship, and the realization that the first time he'd started to tell her he was in love with her, she'd announced she was in love with someone else, and the second she'd told him she was pregnant. He wasn't sure he wanted to know what would happen the third time around.

She finished dishing up her fruit. "So we have the house rules in place? I promise not to leave my lingerie hanging in the bathroom and you promise to compliment me on my cooking.''

"You have your own bathroom, but either way I wouldn't mind the lingerie.''

She laughed. "Let me tell you, when a woman gets seriously pregnant, her lacy things take a quick turn for the practical.''

"I might think they were sexy, too.''

"I doubt it.''

She was wrong, but he didn't tell her that. She wouldn't believe him and he didn't want to try to convince her. Not when she had to leave for her shift at the hospital in a few minutes. But soon, he promised himself. Very soon.

Chapter 3

On Saturday, Lily found herself once more in the kitchen. After fixing pancakes for Jake, she started boiling potatoes and chopping up celery.

"Morning," Jake said as he strolled into the room.

He was fresh out of the shower, wearing jeans and little else. Lily's attempt at a greeting got stuck in her throat when she saw his bare, broad chest and tight abs.

"For the, ah, picnic," she said, gesturing to the pot. "I'm making the potato salad."

He crossed to the coffeepot. "So you've arrived in the Stone family. Mom is trusting you with a sacred duty."

"I know. It's pretty exciting. I have her recipe, so I should do okay."

He poured a cup of coffee then moved next to her and lightly kissed her cheek. "Sleep well?"

"Uh-huh. Great."

He smelled of soap and something else. Something male and appealing.

Get a grip, she told herself. This was *Jake.* Her friend. He wasn't a guy she could lust after. Sure, he was good-looking and all that, but she'd known him forever and they just didn't have that kind of a relationship.

But that didn't stop her from wanting to turn and step into his embrace, despite the lack of potential romance when her belly got in the way.

But she didn't move, didn't do anything. Mostly because she didn't want to see pity in Jake's eyes when he explained why they would only ever be friends.

Not that she wanted anything different, she told herself. She didn't. She liked things exactly the way they were.

"Earth to Lily," he said. "You're frowning and holding a very large knife. The combination makes me nervous."

"What? Oh. I'm fine."

"Can I do anything to help?"

Before she could answer—and she wasn't sure whether she wanted him to stick close or move to the other end of the house—there was a knock at the back door. It opened almost immediately and Nadia Stone walked into the utility room.

"I know, I know. I didn't call. I broke the sacred rule. But with Lily in the house, I knew I wouldn't be interrupting my son with one of his girls. And I mean girls."

Jake's mother—petite, rounded and full of life—bustled into the room. She narrowed her gaze at Jake.

"What? It's too much trouble to finish getting dressed? Maybe you should sleep more so you have energy to put on clothes."

But even as she scolded, she reached up and cupped Jake's face. He obediently bent forward so she could kiss his forehead, then his cheeks.

"You look skinny. Are you eating enough? Lily, is he eating?"

"Yes, Mama Nadia. He's eating plenty."

"Good. A strong man like him needs food."

Done with her torture of her son, Nadia turned her attention to Lily. First came the face cupping, then the kisses. Nadia finished by placing both hands on Lily's stomach.

"How's the little one? Are you getting plenty of

rest? Jake, are you making her slave for you? Help out. Get her to put her feet up.''

''I thought she was supposed to be cooking for me. Isn't that what you said?''

''You talk back to your mother? Weren't you raised better than that?'' Nadia glared at him. ''Jake. A shirt!''

He chuckled as he headed out of the room. ''Lily was talking about making changes to the potato salad recipe,'' he called back as he left.

Lily shook her head. ''I didn't say anything of the sort. He's making trouble.''

''He always did.'' Love filled Nadia's voice. ''I love my girls and give thanks every day for them, but my dear departed Frank wanted a boy. We weren't sure God would bless us and then he did. Our Jake. He was always a good boy. In trouble, sure, but with a good heart. So how's the baby? Everything fine?''

As Nadia spoke, she took the knife from Lily and started chopping up the celery.

''I was at the doctor a couple of weeks ago. I'm doing well. Even my weight gain is on track.''

''You're too skinny. In my day a pregnant woman knew it was important to feed the baby. For good health. Now you eat like a bird. I'll bring some pasta by later. For you to have around the house. And don't let Jake bully you into doing too much."

Lily gave into the urge to hug the tiny woman. "You are so special. I love you very much."

Nadia smiled. "I love you, too. You're family. Always remember that."

Lily appreciated the words more than she could say. As an only child she'd always dreamed about brothers and sisters. Her parents had been dead nearly a year when she'd met Jake. Their friendship had been immediate, but meeting his family had cemented the bond between them. Sometimes he complained she didn't care about him at all—that she was just in it for his relatives. While that wasn't true, Lily had to admit that Mama Nadia and her daughters were definitely a bonus.

"Catherine is coming with all four boys, but her husband will be a little late." Nadia lowered her voice. "He's buying her a new car, if you can believe it. That man spoils her so much. So I'm going to keep her busy." The older woman laughed. "Because the four boys don't distract her enough, eh? Check the potatoes, Lily. They look done."

Of course they were. Jake returned to the kitchen, this time wearing a shirt. His mother put him to work draining the potatoes, then cutting them up. Lily was banished to the table where she was told to put up her feet and rest.

"Anne Marie said to tell you she has that baby name book you want to borrow," Nadia said. "She's already at the house. Catherine with four boys and Anne Marie with three girls. Little Teresa with two of each. Every day is a blessing."

Jake glanced at Lily. "A baby name book? I'm wounded."

"Jake thinks I should name the baby Sam," Lily said.

"It's a great name and she doesn't have to worry if it's a boy or a girl," he said proudly.

He mother reached up and slapped the back of his head. He stared at her.

"What was that for?"

"You're not making Lily's life easier. Sam for a girl."

Lily giggled. Jake shot her a wounded glance, which only made her laugh harder.

"I'll get you for this," he promised.

"I can't wait," she said, and meant it.

"So, she lives with you now," Jake's mother said from her place in the shade.

It was nearly four and the picnic was in full swing. Two babies dozed on a blanket, toddlers alternatively walked and sat when they lost their balance, and the older kids raced through the sunny afternoon intent on their game.

Jake leaned against the tree trunk and sipped his beer.

"You already knew that," he said.

"You told me she'd moved in, but that's not the same as knowing. I saw the two of you together this morning. Things are different."

"No, they're not."

His mother's gaze narrowed. "So tell her the truth and change them yourself. You've known her for over ten years, Jake. Creating the universe didn't take this long."

He grinned. "You don't actually know that."

She wasn't amused. "What I know is that you love her. It hurts me to watch you be hurt. There's love inside her, too. There has been for a long time."

"Friendship," he said.

"Maybe more. You can't know until you ask."

"You're right."

His mother raised her gaze to the sky. "May the angels in heaven have a party tonight. My own son said I was right."

He ignored that, instead glancing around until he saw Lily. She sat with Catherine. They were close to the babies and deep in conversation.

"I've been waiting for the right time, but I'm beginning to think there isn't going to be one. As soon as she's back in her own house, I'll come clean."

"Why wait?" his mother asked.

"Because she needs a place to stay while her house is being repaired, and I don't want her to have to go looking for another one because living with me is uncomfortable."

"Good point." She glanced at Lily. "She'll say yes."

"To what?"

"When you propose."

He put down his beer, then held up his hand in the shape of a T. "Not so fast. I don't even know if she's interested in more than friendship."

"She is," his mother said confidently. "And then you'll propose and finally get married. You'll see."

"Maybe." But he had a feeling things weren't going to be that simple.

Lily held Anne Marie's littlest on her lap. The baby girl—Emma after her grandmother—had big brown eyes and a smile that could light up Kansas.

"You're going to be a heartbreaker," Lily murmured as she blew on the baby's tummy and made her laugh. "All the boys are going to think you're amazing and your daddy is going to have a heck of a time chasing them off.''

''He'll have help,'' Jake said as he strolled over and joined her on the blanket. ''I'll be there to keep those guys away. Isn't that right, Emma? Because you'd never love any stupid boy more than your Uncle Jake.''

Little Emma beamed in delight and held out her pudgy arms.

''See,'' Jake said as he took her and held her high above his head. ''Who's my best girl?''

Emma squealed and Lily's heart clenched. Jake was always terrific with the kids. Despite being an unrepentant bachelor, he enjoyed his nieces and nephews at every family gathering. She happened to know he'd done more than his share of babysitting and had an annual weekend of wild fun with all the kids who were old enough to attend.

''So why don't you have any of your own?'' she asked, knowing she wasn't going to get any more information than she already had.

''Haven't met the right woman.''

''You've certainly met enough.''

''But quantity doesn't guarantee a perfect match.''

''Is that what you're looking for? Perfection?''

He set the baby back on the blanket and let her grab his hands. ''It would help.''

"It's not going to happen."

"I'm starting to get that. So I'll settle for someone imperfect."

"Sometimes you are so guy-like," she complained. "Women don't sit around expecting perfection."

He stretched out on the blanket and pulled little Emma up on his chest. The baby balanced there, facing him and grinning with delight.

"What does the phrase *Mr. Right* mean if not perfect?"

"Oh." She really hated it when he had a point. "I guess some women are looking for perfection. You should form a club together."

"I don't know that I'd like the other members. After all, I'm not perfect."

She looked at him as he lay on the blanket. He was barefoot. Worn jeans hugged his long legs and narrow hips, emphasizing his masculine build. His brightly colored T-shirt had grass stains on it from the fast-moving tag game he'd started with the older kids. Little Emma drooled on him and he didn't seem to notice or care. His strong arms held her securely in place with a confidence that came from years of practice. He was good-looking, slightly mussed and smiling. So what exactly was there not to like?

"When is Rob due to arrive?" she asked to change the subject.

Jake glanced at his watched. "Any time now. Think Catherine will be surprised?"

"That he traded in the sports car he'd been restoring to buy her a new minivan? I think she'll be overwhelmed."

"She should be. It's more than I would do."

Lily poked him in the ribs. "You are so lying. That's exactly the sort of thing you would do."

"Give up a sports car for a woman? Not likely."

"What about the time you gave up your trip to Mexico to stay with Anne Marie because Dave was still on active duty and overseas and she'd just had her appendix out?"

"That was different. Mom was in Italy visiting family. I didn't want her to come back early. Catherine and Teresa were busy with their families." He frowned. "I don't want to talk about it."

"See. You're a great guy. You can't help it. In fact, it's kind of like a disease."

Jake blew kisses at the baby. "We're going to ignore Auntie Lily, aren't we, pumpkin? Because she's a big ol' doodoo head."

Lily smiled. "Doodoo head?"

"Hey, I can't swear in front of the kid, right?"

"Absolutely."

Lily stretched out next to Jake and stared up at the sky. This had been a good day, she thought as she placed her hand on her stomach. She felt safe and a part of something. Right now it didn't matter that her house was uninhabitable and that she'd made a mess of the majority of her interpersonal relationships. She had Jake and that was saying something.

"Whatever you're thinking about, stop," he told her, sounding stern. "It's giving me a headache."

"Jenna and Rachel," she admitted. "And Michael. I've messed up a lot in the past year or so."

"Michael is long gone."

"I know. I almost never think about him and the whole anger thing has pretty much faded. Looking back, I wonder why I was fooled."

"Because you're honest and lead with your heart and he was a guy who took advantage of that."

"I like your logic."

She turned toward him and supported her head on one hand. "The Rachel and Jenna problem isn't so easily explained."

He glanced at her. "I'm a little flummoxed by it myself."

Despite the seriousness of the conversation, she couldn't help laughing. "Flummoxed?"

"It's a perfectly good word."

"Sure, if you're from another century."

"I'll have you know, I was born in another century."

"I don't mean the one we just had—I mean the one before that."

The baby relaxed on his chest. He rubbed one hand against her back. "Do you want my advice or not?"

"I haven't stated a problem yet."

"Sure you have. You miss your friends and you want to connect with them."

"Sure, but first I have to figure out what went wrong so I know what I'm apologizing for."

Jake turned his head toward her and touched her cheek with his free hand. "Does it matter?"

"Maybe not." Lily considered the question, then sighed. "Yes. I know I overreacted with Rachel. None of it was her fault."

Jake didn't answer, which was a real clue that he didn't agree.

"Rachel didn't know Michael was the guy I'd been seeing," Lily said. "Remember? They didn't meet until the engagement party."

"She could have said something then."

"I guess." Lily was less and less sure about that. "I don't know what *I* would have done. For the first time in her life, she acts impulsively and gets naked with a guy she barely knows. Two weeks later she finds out that he's not only the mystery boyfriend I've been talking about, but that we're engaged. She made the decision to keep quiet. I'm not sure I would have done anything differently.''

"She knew the guy was a jerk. She should have told you.''

"Oh, sure. That works. Like the time I told you that Amber was dating one of the doctors at the hospital and you didn't believe me? You were furious and we didn't speak for nearly two months.''

He pulled on a strand of hair. "I've apologized for that about four hundred times.''

"And I'm okay with it. My point is, this sort of news isn't easy to tell or hear. Rachel got scared and kept quiet. The real problem came when she told me right after Michael dumped me. I wasn't in the mood to handle it graciously.''

"You know she only told you to make you feel better.''

Lily nodded. "She had the best of intentions and I completely freaked out. Then I wanted Jenna to take my side. Apparently Rachel was also pulling on Jenna, which caused her to disappear rather than handle the tension. What a mess.''

"You're smart,'' he told her. "You know how to fix this.''

"So I should stop worrying about what I'm apologizing for and just say the words?"

"Sounds like a good start."

Lily agreed. The plan made sense. It was time to act because the hospital was big enough that she never ran into her friends. But what she didn't tell Jake is that she was scared. What if she called Rachel or Jenna and they both wanted nothing to do with her? They'd been friends for so long. Living with the hope of a reunion seemed easier than living with certain rejection. Still…

"I think it's time," she murmured.

"I agree."

Smiling, she pushed herself into a sitting position. "Great. So you're going to hold this over me forever, aren't you? That you were right?"

"I wasn't just right. You were…" He paused expectantly. "Come on. You can say the *W* word."

"Wrong," she said with a laugh. "Okay. I was wrong."

"Music to my ears." He handed her the baby and stood. "Come on. Rob should be here any second. I want to see the look on Catherine's face when she sees the car."

Lily held out the baby. When he took Emma back, Lily pushed herself to her feet. As they walked in comfortable silence, she thought about all the years she'd been coming to Jake's mother's house. To the happy celebrations and warm family times. She'd opened presents with them, helped stuff the Thanksgiving turkey and had handed out candy on Halloween so Nadia could go out with her grandchildren. She'd been made welcome and she never wanted to leave. But how much longer would this all go on?

"What happens when you get married?" she asked abruptly.

Jake stopped and stared at her. "What are you going on about?"

"I'm here all the time, but when you get married your wife won't want me hanging around."

"Why would she care? You and I are friends. Marriage isn't going to change that."

"I'm not so sure." Lily couldn't explain the aching feeling she got inside when she thought of Jake marrying.

"Would you have thrown me out of your life if you'd married Michael?" he asked.

"No, but that's different."

"How?"

Jake looked faintly annoyed as he spoke, and she realized she couldn't tell him the truth—that there was no reason, only a faint feeling of dread.

Just then a blue minivan drove into the driveway. As if sensing an impending surprise, children came running from all over the property. Nadia led Catherine out of the kitchen.

"What?" her daughter asked. "Mom, I was in the middle of doing the dishes."

"So, you'll finish them later. I think Rob is here."

"I told you, he had to work today. There was an out-of-town client who..." Her voice trailed off as her husband stepped out of the minivan.

Like all the Stone women, Catherine was petite, dark-haired and lovely. Right now her perfectly shaped mouth hung open. Eddie, her oldest son, raced up and grabbed her hand.

"Look, Mom, it's Dad and he's got a new car. Is it for us?"

Rob, a tall blond man with an easy smile, shrugged sheepishly. "Hey, honey."

Catherine continued to stare at him. "I don't understand. What are you doing with a minivan? You always said you hated them."

Rob ruffled his son's hair, then pulled his wife close. "You always say how you need one. I traded in my sports car for this. For you."

Catherine started to blink very fast, as if holding in tears. "But you love that car."

"No. I love you."

Catherine gave in to tears as she hugged Rob tight. The whole family gathered around the new van and urged her to step inside. Lily felt her own hormones kick in and had to sniff a couple of times.

"That was so cool," she whispered.

"Yeah, it was." Jake shifted the baby to his other arm and looped his arm around Lily. "Rob's a good guy."

"Uh-huh."

Lily watched as Anne Marie cuddled with her husband and Teresa smiled at her spouse. Jake's mother stood surrounded by her grandchildren. It hit Lily that she and Jake were the only two adults here who hadn't experienced a life-changing love. She was thirty-four years old. What if it never happened? What if she lived the rest of her life alone?

She told herself that getting married didn't matter. That she was thrilled about the baby, and delighted to be a mother at last. That given the choice between a child and a husband, she would choose a child. The thing was, she wasn't sure if she believed it, nor did she understand why she had to chose.

Jake came in a little after seven in the evening. He usually worked twenty-four hours at a time, but today he'd worked twelve hours to cover for a buddy at the station. They'd had four runs, one to a serious house fire. He was tired, but content. He liked the days when he made a difference.

As he pulled off his boots and stepped into the kitchen he was surprised to find the room dark. While he didn't really expect Lily to cook for him, she usually had something started for dinner.

"Lily?" he called as he walked toward the hall.

He heard a sound he couldn't recognize. Visions of her having fallen, or doubled up in pain because something was wrong with the baby gave him speed.

"Lily?" he called again, fighting the frantic worry. Dear God, she had to be okay.

"In h-here."

Her voice was muffled, as if she'd been crying. Panic turned to temper. Had that rat bastard been back in touch with her? He wouldn't put it past Michael to dump her publicly, then try to make things right later. As if Lily would ever go back to a man who'd lied about being married then left her at the altar. He walked into the living room and paused. She wouldn't, would she?

Lily sat curled up on the sofa—at least, as curled up as her pregnancy would allow her. She'd been crying, although when she saw him, she swiped her hand across her face.

"Is it seven all ready? I didn't notice the time. How was your day? I'll get started on dinner right away."

He crossed to her and settled on the sofa. "Are you okay? Is everything all right with the baby?"

"What?"

She was still in her scrubs, with her hair pulled back into a braid. Her lashes were spiky from crying and her cheeks flushed. She looked amazing and it was all he could do not to pull her close and kiss her. A real kiss, not one of those brief pecks they often shared.

She cleared her throat. "The baby's fine. I'm okay." A tear spilled out of her right eye. "Well, maybe not completely okay, but there's nothing physically wrong."

Sweet relief flooded him as tension fled his body. If Lily and the baby were all right, then they would deal with whatever the other problem was.

"Then tell me what else is wrong," he said gently.

"Nothing." She shook her head. "It's stupid, really."

"Stupid is one of my favorite things."

She squeezed her eyes shut. "I used to be really together and normal. Lately I feel fragile, like I could snap in two."

"Don't you think that some of that has to do with the hormones?"

"Sure. And carrying the baby. Everything in my body feels weird, but in a good way."

"I'm not sure what good weird is."

She managed a smile. "It's a chick thing." She sniffed again. "Anyway, I'm just going through some stuff."

"Like?"

She stared at him. Her green eyes darkened with pain. "I don't want to be alone for the rest of my life and that's what I keep thinking is going to happen. I've been dating since I was sixteen. What's wrong with me that I can't find someone? There were guys I really liked but who weren't crazy about me, there were guys who wanted to get married who I didn't love enough. There was Michael. Talk about a disaster."

"His being a jerk isn't your responsibility."

"But why couldn't I see the truth? The man was married. I should have known to question him more closely and figure out that his business trips were about a lot more than business."

Jake didn't like the sound of that. "You're sorry it's over," he said, trying not to sound bitter.

"What?" Her eyes widened. "No. Not for a second. I would have been miserable and he never would have changed his ways. Not that his not cheating would have made him less of a rat. This isn't about Michael, it's about me. About the fact that I'm going to be alone for the rest of my life. When my child is grown and gone, I'll be forced to take in cats. Do you know how many cats would fit in my new house?''

''More than I'd want around.''

''Exactly. And eventually the county will come take me away and there I'll be on the news. One of those crazy old cat ladies. And the animal rescue people will give my cats to more sensible people who know only to have one or two pets. And I'll die all alone.''

Tears poured down her cheeks. Jake knew she was really in pain, but he had to fight to keep from smiling. The picture she'd painted was so far from reality. Pregnancy sure wasn't easy.

''Maybe an herbal supplement,'' he began before recognizing the pit he'd just dug for himself.

Lily socked him in the arm. ''Don't you dare go there. I'm not crazy and this isn't just about being pregnant.''

''I know. Sorry. But you're getting all upset about nothing. You're not going to die alone.''

She looked at him. ''You're right, I won't. Not if we get married.''

Chapter 4

Jake was sure he hadn't heard her correctly. "What?"

"Aren't you worried about the same thing?" she asked. "Don't you think about being alone forever?"

He didn't have an answer for that. His problems were more immediate—like how to tell Lily about his feelings for her and make her believe they were real and not about circumstances or pity. And if that didn't work, then how to get over loving her and move on. Only now she was talking as if she didn't want him to move on.

"It's not a bad idea," she said defensively. "We

get along great. We've been friends for years and we rarely get on each other's nerves.'' She touched her stomach. ''You love kids. We could have more.''

Nothing made sense—except Lily looked serious and there was a pleading in her eyes he couldn't resist.

He loved her. Maybe he had for years, even though he'd only figured it out a few months ago. If he married her, he could take care of her. Keep her safe while openly loving her and the baby.

As decisions went, it wasn't a tough one.

''I'll marry you,'' he told her.

''Really?''

''Name the date.''

Lily burst out laughing and threw herself into his arms. ''How about Saturday? We're both off work.''

''Fine by me.''

''You're humming,'' Allison said as Lily checked the supply cabinet.

Lily glanced up from her clipboard and did her best to keep from grinning. It was Friday morning and in about twenty-four hours, she was getting married!

The news still hadn't sunk in, which was okay. She could get floaty just on the possibility.

''I hum all the time,'' she told her co-worker.

"Yeah, but not like this. It's a happy hum."

Lily laughed. "Instead of the funeral dirges I usually entertain you with?"

"No. It's just..." Allison, tall, slender and painfully beautiful, shrugged. "You've been extra cheerful all week. Is it the baby?"

It was really Jake, but Lily didn't want to say that. Her soon-to-be marriage was still a secret.

"I'm just a cheerful kind of girl."

"Uh-huh." Allison didn't look convinced. "Those are some powerful hormones coursing through your body. I may have to get me some."

Allison was all of twenty-three and had the dating attention span of a goldfish.

"You might want to wait a little while," Lily told her with a grin. "Enjoy life, grow up a little more, find the right guy."

"So when I'm old like you I should have a baby?" Allison asked cheekily.

Lily threw a wrapped package of tissue at her. "Exactly."

"I'll make a note of that. I mean, my being old is so far in the future, I'll probably forget."

Lily tried not to smile, but she couldn't help it. "Here, kid. You take care of the inventory and I'll take little Aaron down to X-ray. It's about that time."

"Sure thing. I was raised to respect my elders."

Lily chuckled as she headed for Aaron's room. "Okay, big guy," she said when she entered. "Want to take a first class ride in an elevator?"

The eight year old looked up from his Game Boy. He was pale, bald, but still full of fire. "Hey, Lily. Do I have to?"

"Is anything here an option? I think not. But here's the thing. This one won't hurt. Isn't that cool? And by the time we're done, lunch will be here and I have it on good authority that there's some ice cream on the menu, so hey. What's not to like?"

Aaron put down his video game. "I'm ready. Can we go real fast?"

"We can go at light speed. Of course my big stomach will probably bump some poor patient and send her spiraling down the hall."

Aaron laughed. "Okay. Not light speed."

"You're the boss."

She moved close to the bed to unhook his IVs. He wrapped both his arms around her and she hugged him back. She loved these kids—they were one of the reasons she'd wanted a baby of her own so much. Maybe now that she was marrying Jake she could think about having more children in the future.

Saturday morning Lily found herself waiting outside the judge's private chambers. The past four days had zipped by in a whirlwind of activity. There had been a dress to find—not easy considering she was six months along and working full time—a small reception to arrange and the decision to tell people or not.

Under normal circumstances, Lily would have happily spread the news. Only she'd already planned one big wedding that year and it had ended in disaster. This time she thought it was probably smarter to keep things quiet until she was sure they were going to work out.

In addition to being sensible, she was also dealing with some fairly serious guilt. Excitement and guilt were a unique combination.

"You don't have to do this," she said as she stood next to Jake in the hallway. "You can't really want to marry me. I was freaking out about the whole alone thing."

Jake—tall and handsome in a dark suit—took her hands in his. "Lily, I want to marry you."

There was something in his voice…something rich and amazing that made her insides quiver and her heart thunder in her chest.

"For real?"

He nodded. "In fact, I've been looking for a way to—"

The chamber doors opened and a clerk stepped out. "She's ready for you," the young man said.

Lily was torn between hearing what Jake had to say and getting on with the ceremony. She released one of Jake's hands and picked up the small bouquet of white roses she'd brought with her.

"Ready?" he asked.

She nodded. "You're not feeling to need the bolt, are you?"

He brought her free hand to his mouth and brushed her knuckles with his lips. "I'm not going anywhere, Lily. You've always been able to count on me. Nothing about that is going to change."

His words made her feel all warm inside. Warm and safe—two feelings that had been missing from her life for a long time.

As they walked into the judge's private chambers, she promised herself that she would do her best to make their marriage work. She wasn't sure why Jake had agreed to her proposal, but the second he'd said yes, she'd felt happy. Maybe they didn't have a wild, passionate love to see them through, but sometimes wild passion wasn't enough. She and Jake had friendship and a commitment to each other. They'd weathered storms in the past. They understood the nuances of their individual personalities. She could see herself getting old with Jake. If that was the definition of their friendship, then she knew it was more than enough to see them through.

The ceremony passed quickly and quietly. There was no large congregation, no music. Just a few words in a brightly lit room. When the judge asked about a ring, Jake pulled out a slim gold band inlaid with square-cut diamonds. Lily stared at it. While the ring itself wasn't a surprise—she'd given him her ring size—the expensive and beautiful band was.

"We said just plain gold," she whispered.

He smiled. "*You* said a plain gold band," he reminded her. "I wanted to get you something more special."

Tears burned in her eyes. She blinked them away, afraid that he wouldn't understand that she was crying because he was so incredible and not because she was sad.

She pulled out the diamond-cut band she'd purchased for him and slid it on his finger. As they held hands and faced the judge, Lily's heart swelled with an emotion she couldn't define. Wanting filled her— a need for the man standing next to her. She wanted to hold him and be held. To touch him. She wanted to lie in the dark and talk about their future.

She wanted their marriage to be real.

"I now pronounce you husband and wife." The judge smiled. "You may kiss the bride."

Jake turned toward her and rested one hand on her shoulder. He kissed her lightly. A gentle kiss that left Lily wanting more.

Tonight, she promised herself. Somehow she would convince Jake to see past her swollen belly and seal the promises made this morning. She would explain that she'd meant her vows, that she wanted their marriage to be real. No matter what it took, she would convince him that this was forever.

But first there was the issue of his family.

"Are you sure no one is upset?" she asked as they walked toward her car. "I've been waiting all week for your mom to call and yell at me for making you marry me."

"You didn't make me," he reminded her as he held open the passenger door. "I wanted to do this. Besides, my mother adores you."

Lily knew that things could change very quickly, especially when there was a sudden and unexpected wedding.

"Are you sure she's not mad?"

"I promise." He closed the door and walked around to the driver's side. "Her exact words were that it was about time and thank God I'd picked you."

"You didn't pick me," she reminded him. "I asked you."

He stared at her. The corners of his mouth turned up and something dark, mysterious and very appealing flickered in his eyes.

"Make no mistake, Lily. You were my first and only choice."

Happiness bubbled inside her until she thought she might float. Her baby chose that moment to wake up and start his or her morning exercise program.

"We have approval from this front, too," she said as she put her hand on her stomach.

Jake started the car. "We're married now. I don't want you to worry about anything. No matter what, I'll be here for you. I promise."

She knew exactly what his promises meant. Jake would change the tide if it was necessary to keep his word.

"Thank you. I want you to think the same about me."

"I do."

She sighed in contentment. *I do.* Two very simple words that changed everything.

"Are you sure you don't hate me?" Lily asked anxiously.

Nadia Stone cupped her face and smiled. "I have one thing to say to you. What took you so long? You and Jake have been friends for years. I always thought—where there's so much friendship, there must be love.''

Lily stiffened slightly. Love? She hadn't taken things so far in her mind. Did she love Jake? Was it possible he loved her?

Before she could try to figure it out, Nadia continued.

''People change. They see things differently. For you and my son, this is your time. So be happy. You have always been a part of this family because of your heart. So now you're one of us by marriage. The bonds grow deeper. This is good, right?''

Lily smiled. ''It's wonderful.''

Nadia released her and waved at the groaning buffet that filled her dining room.

''Now we eat.'' She clapped her hands to get the rest of the family's attention. ''Get food. All of you. We eat and then we toast the happy couple.''

The entire family spilled into the room. Lily had been more than a little nervous when she and Jake had arrived, but so far everyone had made them feel welcome.

Catherine came up and hugged Lily. ''You look like you're still in shock.''

''I am. Plus I know this was a big thing to spring on the family.''

Jake's sister shook her head. ''We've been waiting

for it forever. You two have been playing at being friends for a long time while the rest of us have been waiting for one of you to notice the sparks. Thank goodness you came around at last.''

Lily blinked at her. Sparks? She and Jake had sparks?

"Plus now we get to be sisters for real," Catherine said before stepping out of line and chasing after one of her kids. "Danny, you get back here, young man."

Teresa, Jake's youngest sister, moved up next to Lily.

"I made sure we had a bottle of sparkling cider for the toast," she said quietly. "Plus I have an extra bottle of champagne for you to save until after the baby is born. Then you'll have two things to celebrate."

"You didn't have to do that."

"I know, but I wanted to. We're all so grateful that Jake married you. Some of the women he's brought around..." She shook her head. "It was frightening."

One by one the members of the family welcomed Lily. Her sense of belonging grew until it practically spilled over.

"Having a good time?" Jake asked as he joined her at a picnic table.

"The best. Everyone is being terrific."

"They love you."

"And I love them."

"Good." He touched her cheek. "Are you going to tell Rachel and Jenna?"

At the mention of her friends, some of Lily's happiness faded. "I want to. It's just I don't know what they're going to say."

"Won't they be happy for you?"

"Sure." At least she thought they would be. A year ago she wouldn't have even considered the question. The three of them had been friends forever, sharing each other's happiness and sorrows. But then a year ago she would never have thought they would see their friendship unravel.

As always, Jake could read her mind. "So call Rachel. Tell her you miss her. Don't you think she's missing you, too?"

"I hope so."

"I know so."

Lily stared into the dark eyes of the man she'd married. He had been more than her rock—he was her conscience, her voice of reason, truly her better half.

They were married. Really married.

"Thank you for today," she said.

"My pleasure."

Was it? She had big plans for tonight and pleasure was definitely involved. If only she could convince Jake that pregnant and sexy could be the same thing.

After the party began to wind down, Jake walked Lily back to his place. His wedding band felt unfamiliar on his hand, but right. He'd wanted her for a long time and now she was his. So what was he going to do with her?

He'd been asking himself that question ever since she'd suggested they get married and he'd agreed, and he still didn't have an answer.

Telling her the truth was the most obvious response. But he wasn't sure what words to say or if she would believe him. He didn't want her to think that he was saying what she expected to hear. Should he have told her before the wedding?

He shook his head. Getting married should have made things simpler, but instead his relationship with Lily was as complicated as ever.

"My house is going to be ready by the end of next week," she said as they walked up the driveway toward the back door. "We haven't talked about how we're going to handle having two residences."

"I figured we'd move into your place."

She stepped into the kitchen. "Are you sure? I thought you liked your house."

"I do." He followed her and pulled the back door shut behind him. "But this place is small. With the baby coming, a larger home makes more sense."

She paused in the kitchen and looked at him.

She'd worn her hair up for the wedding. A few tendrils had escaped and hung down in seductive curls. Tiny roses and baby's breath decorated the upswept style, their creamy color matching her pearl earrings.

Her sleeveless dress fit her breasts, then hung down to just below her knees. The soft fabric draped over her belly in gentle folds. She was beautiful, elegant and sexy. He'd barely been able to avoid staring at the exposed cleavage during the wedding ceremony. More than once he'd caught himself wanting to move in close and cup those curves. He'd imagined tight nipples straining to escape, his mouth teasing them, her breath catching as he—

He swore silently and forced his mind away from the vision. Lily startled him by moving in front of him and placing her hands on his chest. For a single heartbeat, he thought she'd read his mind and didn't think he was a complete jerk for wanting her.

"I don't want you to lose your house because of me," she said earnestly.

It took him a second to figure out what she was

talking about. Then he remembered they'd been discussing which house to live in.

"You could keep this place as a rental," she said. "You don't have to sell it."

"The place has no sentimental value," he told her. "I'll sell it and put the money away. Maybe start a college fund for the baby."

Her breath caught. "Oh, Jake. I don't deserve you."

Without warning, she raised herself on tiptoe and pressed her mouth against his. The gentle contact caught him unaware and he couldn't help responding.

He tilted his head and wrapped his arms around her, pulling her close. He brushed his lips against hers, learning every millimeter of her. He pressed more firmly, then swept his tongue against her lower lip.

She made a noise low in her throat and parted for him. Telling himself he was playing with fire didn't make a difference. Nor did the voice in his head warning him to be sensible. This was Lily and he'd loved her too long to resist now.

He slipped his tongue inside her mouth and tasted her sweetness. She was hot and tempting and when he kissed her deeply, she squirmed to get closer.

He explored her mouth, circling around her

tongue, stroking her back, dropping his hands to the curve of her hips.

She answered by placing her hands on his shoulder and digging her fingers into his muscles. Heat flared between them. He was already hard with a need that ached and pulsed. He wanted her naked, wet and willing. He wanted her as hungry and desperate as he was. He wanted…

He pulled back far enough to press kisses along her jaw. Her head dropped back as he neared her throat. He nibbled the sensitive skin there, took her earlobe in his mouth and sucked. She gasped and moaned.

Unable to resist the temptation, he drew his hand from her hip to her waist then to her breasts. As he cupped the full curve, he stroked his thumb across her nipple. It was hard and she jumped slightly at the contact.

"Yes," she breathed, clinging to him.

He stroked the nipple again and again. Each time she groaned. He turned slightly to drop his mouth to hers and as he moved, he pushed against her belly.

A sharp kick stunned him.

The baby.

Jake let his hand fall to his side as he did his damnedest to gather up his self-control. He was past hard—he was rigid and aching with need, but he couldn't do this. Not now. Lily was his to protect, not to abuse. What had he been thinking?

"I'm sorry," he said as he stepped back. "I shouldn't have done that. You didn't marry me to get attacked the first second we were alone."

"Attacked?" she repeated, sounding dazed and confused. "I don't..."

He tried not to wince as her voice trailed off. She didn't what? Want this? Expect him to jump her like that?

He struggled to steady his breathing. If she looked at him, she would know what *he* wanted.

"Jake, we're married," she said. "If you want us to be intimate, I don't mind."

He turned away. Sure. Great. Words every guy longed to hear. That the woman he'd just married didn't mind if they made love. There was an endorsement.

She cleared her throat. "That came out wrong. Of course I want us to be together."

He tried to smile. "I can tell."

She grabbed his arm. "No. I mean it. I think you're very sexy and appealing. I'd like us to be, um, well, lovers."

He shook his head. "Don't sweat it, Lily. You're pregnant and fooling around probably isn't a good idea. We'll talk about this later. After the baby's born.''

''But that's three months away. Plus after I give birth I can't, well, you know, for six weeks.''

''I'll wait.''

He didn't have a choice. Besides, he'd already been living in hell. What was another few months of it?

Lily spent her wedding night alone and upset. The feelings of contentment and happiness she'd experienced earlier in the day had faded to little more than memories. There might be a beautiful diamond ring on her finger, but she was still alone in Jake's guest room and confused about her future.

Worse, she couldn't blame anyone but herself for what had happened. Had she really said she didn't mind if they made love? *Didn't mind,* as if it was some giant imposition, but hey she was magnanimous enough to clench her teeth and have at it.

''That's not what I meant,'' she whispered into the darkness as she lay curled up in the bed.

When he'd kissed her and touched her, she'd felt as if she were on fire. His hands had been pure magic. Everything about being near him, touching him, feeling him touch her had made her realize that she'd probably wanted Jake for a really long time. Somehow she'd managed to miss the cues.

She remembered what Jake's mother had said. That where there was such strong friendship there had to be love. Was that true? Did she love Jake? And if she did, was that the reason she'd blurted out her proposal?

Love. The concept was both thrilling and just a little bit scary. She rolled onto her back and felt the baby move.

"Talk about taking on a lot," she murmured. "First a wife and then in three months, a baby." A baby that wasn't even his.

Why had Jake said yes to marriage? Why hadn't he run off in the opposite direction?

She didn't have an answer, nor did she know how to find out. What if he'd done it out of pity? She shivered. That would be too horrible for words.

No, there had to be another reason and she was going to have to figure it out. Which meant there was one more thing on her to-do list.

"I'm a married woman," she told herself as she lay in the dark. "It's time to get things in order and start acting like a grown-up."

She'd let the situation with Rachel and Jenna fester too long. She was going to fix that and figure out what Jake was thinking as well. If he cared about her, even a little, she was going to nurture that feeling into something lasting. While she was busy doing that, she was going to look into her own heart and make sure she was clear on her feelings as well.

"All this, with a full-time job and a baby on the way," she said as she pulled up the covers. "At least my life isn't boring."

Chapter 5

Neither she nor Jake had to work the next morning. Lily hadn't slept much and had been awake since five, so it was easy for her to get up early and start breakfast. She'd just finished whipping eggs for French toast when he walked into the kitchen.

She looked at him and tried to smile, but their last very awkward conversation hung between them. He seemed to feel equally uncomfortable as he shifted his weight from foot to foot. The only sound was the faint ticking of the clock over the stove.

"I made breakfast."

"I'm heading over to my mom's."

They spoke at the same time.

"You first," she told him.

He shoved his hands into his jeans pocket. "I promised my mom I'd change the oil in her car."

"This morning?"

He shrugged.

Lily nodded as if it didn't matter. As if she didn't mind him ducking out on her the first chance he got. If last night had gone the way she'd wanted, right now they would still be lying in bed together. But it hadn't. Somehow everything had gone terribly wrong, and now she didn't know what to say.

"I'm going to go check on the house later," she said. "If you want to come."

"I don't know how long I'll be."

Right. Because changing a car's oil took hours. She drew in a deep breath and tried to be calm.

"Will you be home for dinner?" she asked.

"You don't have to cook for me."

"I was cooking before the wedding," she said as her temper began to slip. "Why would that change?"

"You don't work for me, Lil. You don't have to take care of that kind of thing."

"I want to."

She tried not to sound plaintive or pathetic. They were married—didn't he want to spend time with her at all?

"Why does all this have to be different?" she asked. "Why can't it be like it was?"

"It will be. We need time to adjust."

To what? Nothing had changed. Or was she wrong in that? Had getting married changed the rules so much that neither of them knew what to do or how to act?

"I didn't want to make things bad between us," she said.

"You didn't."

But he spoke the words as he walked out of the kitchen and when the back door slammed behind him, she knew he was wrong.

She'd gained Jake as a husband but lost him as a friend. From her perspective it didn't seem like much of a trade.

Lily showered and straightened up Jake's house, then drove over to her place where she could check out the refinished floor. Various rooms were still roped off so the new finish could dry. Carpeting would come in next, then she was free to move back.

Yesterday Jake had talked about moving in with her. Was that still going to happen?

She put her hand on her stomach. "Whatever is going on with him, I'll still be here for you," she promised her baby. "We're going to be a family."

She crossed to the window in the living room. The sub flooring creaked as she walked. As she stared out at the front yard, she vowed that somehow she would fix all of this. She hadn't come this far only to lose Jake now. She was tired of messing up her life, which meant it was time to get things right—and she knew just how to start.

She drew her cell phone out of her purse and scrolled through the numbers. When she reached the one she wanted, she pushed the talk button and waited. The phone was answered on the second ring.

"Rachel?" she said, her stomach jumping into her throat. "It's Lily."

"Why are you keeping an old woman company when you have a beautiful new wife at home?" Nadia asked as Jake checked the dip stick in her car.

"You asked me to change your oil."

"I see. And you chose this morning to do it? The morning after your wedding night?"

He slid the stick back in place. "It's not like that. She's pregnant."

"Oh, and while a woman is pregnant she doesn't have needs? Or are you saying you don't find her attractive?"

Jake had been on his own since he was twenty. He had a dangerous job, was a responsible citizen and prided himself on knowing his way around the bedroom. But in less than thirty-seven seconds, his mother had him blushing like a fourteen-year-old.

"I'm not talking about this with you, Mom," he said firmly.

"Fine. You don't talk. I'll talk and you listen."

He slammed the hood and busied himself with polishing the already gleaming finish. Escape was only a few steps away, but if he tried to duck out, his mother would follow and possibly want to discuss this outside, in front of the neighbors. Dealing with her in the privacy of the garage seemed much more palatable.

"You and Lily—you're friends for a long time," his mother said. "You have feelings, she has feelings, but no one talks."

"You don't know that she has feelings."

"*I* know."

He risked glancing at his mother and saw affection in her gaze.

"I know, Jake," she repeated. "Trust your heart. Trust her heart. A marriage isn't made in a day. It's not about the ceremony or even sharing a bed. It's about building a life. You have time. So build that life. Be with her. The sex will take care of itself."

He winced. "We're not talking about sex."

"What? You think I have four babies by reading

a book? You think your father wasn't a passionate man?''

Jake dropped the rag into a bucket and held up both hands in a gesture of surrender. ''Gotta go, Mom. Have a nice rest of the day.''

''You should listen to your mother,'' she called after him. ''I give good advice.''

Jake didn't doubt that. What she said made sense. Taking things slow meant starting over—pretending the kiss last night had never happened. If he and Lily could go back to being friends, wouldn't that be better for both of them?

Lily pulled into the driveway of Jake's house shortly after five. After spending some time at her place, she'd gone to the mall, then a movie. Finally, with nowhere else to go, she'd driven back here.

She'd half expected Jake's truck to be gone, but it was parked in the driveway. She frowned as she realized all the windows were open and rock music poured from the house. Was he having a party?

After grabbing her purse, she walked to the back door and entered the kitchen. Here the music was even louder, but that wasn't what got her attention. Instead her gaze was captured by the mess. Every single pot, bowl and dish Jake owned were stacked on the counters or in the sink and the man who had probably done all that damage stood in the middle of the kitchen swearing at the stove.

He looked amazing, she thought wistfully as she took in the stained T-shirt and mussed hair. Strong and tall and safe. He was the kind of man who would always be there in a storm. He didn't judge, didn't demand. Instead he offered shelter.

After banging his fist on the front of the stove, he turned and caught sight of her. His eyes widened slightly, then he pushed a button on the portable stereo and the room fell silent.

''Hi,'' she said as she dropped her purse onto a chair. ''What's up?''

He shrugged. ''I'm making dinner. Lasagna. My mom's recipe. It sounded pretty easy when I read the instructions, but things haven't gone well.'' He motioned to the pile of dirty bowls in the sink. ''I had to start over a couple of times.''

Lily felt the corners of her mouth twitch. ''Mr. I-Can-Only-Make-Chili decided to start cooking with lasagna?''

''Yeah. So?'' He sounded faintly defensive.

''Oh, Jake, the individual directions aren't that tough, but it's a lot of steps and—'' She pointed to the mess on the counter. ''A lot of pots and pans.''

''I'll clean it up.'' He glanced at the stove then back at her. ''I didn't want you to have to be responsible for all the domestic stuff. That's not why I married you.''

She sucked in a breath. ''Why *did* you marry me?''

His dark eyes flashed with an emotion she couldn't read and then it was gone. Silence stretched between them until she was sure he wasn't going to answer. Then he spoke very quietly.

''Because I care about you. I've always cared.''

Caring. It wasn't love, but it was so close. She took a tentative step toward him.

''I care, too,'' she said. ''You're the most important person in my life. I don't want to ruin what we had.''

''You didn't. Last night…'' He pulled his hands out of his pockets and let them dangle at his sides. ''You're pregnant, Lil. I don't want to do anything to hurt you or the baby.''

Pain cut through her. Was that the truth or did he simply find her too cow-like?

Don't go there, she told herself. Stick to the important stuff—like their friendship and what they were going to do now.

''No matter what, I want us to stay friends,'' she said.

''Me, too. So let's start over and go slowly. We have a strong relationship already. We can build on that.''

She liked the sound of that. "Good idea."

He crossed the room and stopped in front of her. "I'm sorry," he murmured as he tucked her hair behind her ears, then kissed her cheek. "About being a jerk."

"You're not a jerk. I was a jerkette."

He smiled. "You're entitled."

"So are you."

"Where did you go?" he asked. "I was getting worried."

"I went by the house. The hardwood is all refinished. I think it's dry but they still have tape up. I'm guessing the carpet will go in Monday or Tuesday, then we can move back in. If you still want to."

"Of course I do. I have a real estate agent coming here next week to look at this place."

She swallowed. "You're really going to sell the house?"

"Isn't that what we talked about?"

"Sure, but after what happened…"

He stared into her eyes. "You think I'm going to disappear from your life after one fight? You should know me better than that."

She knew him better than anyone, but the rules had changed. She flung herself into his arms.

"I don't want to lose you. Not ever."

"You can't, Lil. You're stuck with me."

She hoped that was true. She needed him desperately. She also wanted him and her body reminded her of the fact as he tightened his hold on her. She could feel the heat of his body, the pressure of each finger on her back.

But she'd already been down that path and she wasn't going to risk it again.

"Why were you banging on the stove?" she asked when he'd stepped back.

"It wasn't getting hot very fast. How is the lasagna supposed to cook in an hour if it takes fifteen minutes for the stove to heat up?"

She sighed. "Did you preheat the oven?"

"What?"

"You know—turn it on a few minutes early so it has time to come to temperature."

He turned to the stove and sighed. "Well, hell."

She giggled. "We'll just add a few minutes to the cooking time."

"My mom could have written that on the recipe card."

"She probably figured anyone using it would know."

"She was wrong."

Lily patted his arm. "I won't say a word."

He returned his attention to her and pretended to

frown. "You'd better not. And while we're making up rules, don't you dare tell her that I was cooking. I have a reputation to think of."

"Mr. Macho?"

"Something like that."

Then they were laughing and Lily felt her pain and tension drain away. If they could just stay like this, she thought wistfully, it would be enough.

"I called Rachel," Lily said as she speared a piece of lettuce from her salad.

Talk about a surprise, Jake thought. "What brought that on?"

"I was at the other house and thinking about my life. Rachel and Jenna were my friends for years. Suddenly not talking to them seemed incredibly silly so I called." She smiled at him. "She was happy to hear from me and we talked for a long time. It took her a few more treatments than me, but now she's pregnant, too."

"Are you going to get together?"

"Uh-huh. We're having lunch next week. On Friday. I'm really excited. Once we get things settled between us, we're going to call Jenna together and try and mend that fence."

"I'm happy for you. I know you've missed her."

Lily's expression turned sad. "We haven't talked

in forever. As soon as I heard her voice, I realized I'd been completely stupid avoiding her." She glanced at him from under her lashes. "Something you've been trying to tell me for months."

"I might have mentioned it a time or two."

She sighed. "You were great. As always."

He chewed a mouthful of lasagna and swallowed. "It's tough being perfect, but I do my best."

His teasing was rewarded by a smile. "You're not perfect. Trust me. I know this for a fact."

"I'm close."

"You're okay."

She leaned toward him and rested her hand on his. The light contact was meant to be friendly, to provide connection. It wasn't Lily's fault that it made him instantly want her. Kissing her, touching her, being close to her had only made the problem more intense. Still, as nothing was going to happen for many months, if ever, he had to get his feelings under control.

"So what do you want to do tonight?" she asked.

Sex or a cold shower, he thought grimly. "We could take a walk. Or go bowling." Anything to get out of the house and away from temptation.

She laughed. "I think the bowling ball would be just enough weight to make me topple over. I vote for the walk." She picked up her plate.

"I made the mess. I'll clean it," he said. "Come on. Let's take that walk and I'll deal with this later."

"Okay."

They headed out the back door into the still-light evening. The air was warm, the sky clear. The sun had nearly sunk into the horizon. Tall trees that nearly touched in the center of the street provided an early twilight.

Across the street two boys rode their bikes in their driveway. A young girl threw a ball to her baby sister. Windows were open and the sounds of televisions and conversation drifted out into the night. The scent of flowers and freshly cut grass mingled with the smells of charcoal and grilling burgers.

"This is a nice neighborhood," Lily said as she laced her fingers with his. "Will you miss it?"

"No."

Not when the alternative was being with her. He didn't know what was going to happen with Lily— he couldn't predict the future. All that he knew for sure was that they finally had a chance and he was going to do his damnedest to make it work.

"This feels really familiar," Jake grumbled as he carried a box into the house the following week. "Didn't we just move?"

Lily set down the small suitcase she'd brought and glanced around the newly carpeted living room. "We just moved me. Now we're moving you."

"It feels the same."

"The difference is now I get to have your grand-mother's hutch in my dining room."

He grunted. "That's the entire reason you married me, isn't it?"

She laughed. "It *is* a great hutch."

"Figures."

He set the box against the wall, then left to get the next one. While a couple of guys from the fire station would help him move the big pieces over the week-end, she and Jake were moving his clothes and a few little things before then.

The floors had been pronounced dry on Monday, with the carpet going in that afternoon. Now it was late Tuesday and she and Jake were officially moving into her new house.

Make that *their* house.

In the past couple of days life had returned to nor-mal. She and Jake were once again comfortable to-gether. She loved spending time with him and if looking at him made her body go up in flames, well, they would have to work that through. Once the baby was born and she was back to her fighting weight, she would do whatever she could to seduce her husband into her bed. Until then, she would consider this situation a chance to build character and self-control.

She walked into the kitchen to check out the hot water. The new water heater had been delivered and hooked up the previous week.

She turned on the hot tap and waited a few seconds. Sure enough the water quickly went from warm to too hot to touch.

"Perfect," she murmured and reached for the tap.

It came off in her hand.

Lily stared from the metal piece in her hand to the gushing hot water. This was not happening. It couldn't be! But it was. Water flowed happily, with no signs of stopping.

She heard the front door open, then a string of swear words.

"What happened?" she asked as she hurried to the front of the house.

Jake set down another box and held out his hand. The door knob rested on his palm. She held out the tap. They looked at each other and started to laugh.

By nine that evening, they'd found three more problems and fixed those most pressing. The downstairs bathroom door wouldn't stay closed, the laundry-room sink was clogged and the window in the den wouldn't open.

"Back to buyer's remorse?" Jake asked her as they stretched out in the family room.

"No. All of this stuff is really small."

"I agree. The basic structure is sound and that's what matters."

"And there's new carpeting."

"You also have a new roof," Jake reminded her.

"*We* have a new roof," she said. "And a new water heater and newly refinished hardwood floors."

He grinned. "Oh, so now it's *our* house."

"Absolutely. Did you think I was dealing with all this alone?"

"I guess not, but Lil? Next time let's get a new house."

She chuckled. "Promise."

Trying not to read too much into the phrase "next time," trying not to hope this meant Jake thought they had a chance for a future, she excused herself to go take a shower.

At least their friendship had been restored. That was a big first step. The rest of it could take care of itself.

She entered the master bath and sighed with delight as she took in the new tiles. Jake had done a terrific job with the pattern and had even put a border on the floor by the tub and vanity so it looked as if there was a tile rug in place. She crossed to the shower and turned on the water, then quickly undressed and stepped into the spray.

Ten minutes later she felt relaxed and ready for bed. She grabbed the handle to turn off the shower. Nothing happened. Oh the handle turned easily enough, but the water didn't stop. It didn't even slow.

Lily started to giggle. This could *not* be happening. The giggle got louder and turned into a laugh. Soon she was laughing so hard, she couldn't move. Her breath came in gasps. This was just so typical, she thought, still laughing.

"Lily?" Jake pounded on the bathroom door. "Are you all right?"

"F-fine," she said, trying to catch her breath and get control. "It's the shower."

"What? I can't hear you. What's wrong? I'm coming in."

She weakly gestured that it was all right, then realized two things. First, he couldn't see what she was doing and second, that she was naked.

She grabbed for a towel just as the bathroom door opened. A very worried-looking Jake stepped into the steamy room.

"What's wrong? Are you hurt? Is it the baby?"

She was still laughing and it was too difficult to speak, so she waved at the shower.

As he moved toward her, she pulled the towel up in front of herself and stepped out of the way.

He tried the handle, swore and spun it around in a complete circle.

"Does even one damn thing in this house work?" he demanded.

His outrage made her laugh more. Jake looked at her and began to smile. Then he chuckled.

"I'm glad you're seeing the bright side of things," he told her.

"I love this house," she said with a giggle. "It's a challenge."

"It's more than that."

He crouched by the toilet where there was a small door that opened onto the water pipes. He turned the knobs there and the water in the shower slowed, then stopped.

"I can replace the taps," he said. "I'll get a new set when I buy the ones for the kitchen. In the morning I'll check all the bathrooms."

She tried not to laugh. "There's a sink in the garage."

"That, too."

His expression sharpened slightly and she realized he wasn't laughing anymore. Some of her humor faded.

"Don't be mad," she said quickly. "I know there's a lot going wrong, but it's fixable, right?" She hated the thought of moving, but if he wasn't going to be happy here... "Would you rather live in your house and sell this one?"

"What?"

"You looked really unhappy. I don't want you to hate your home."

"What are you talking about?"

She frowned. "We were laughing two seconds ago. Now you look upset."

He turned away. "It has nothing to do with the damn house, okay?"

He started to leave. Lily didn't like how the conversation was going. She grabbed his arm. "Jake, wait. What's wrong? I feel like we're fighting again and I have no idea why."

His eyes narrowed as he spun toward her. "I know you think of me as your best friend and about as interesting as a neutered dog, but I'm a man. I have wants and needs and standing here talking while you're naked and so damn beautiful that I can hardly breathe is pure torture."

He raised his hands, then dropped them. "You're pregnant. I get that. Even if you were interested we couldn't do anything. It's not right. So I'm just some sick bastard who wants you in his bed. I'll get over it."

He stalked out of the bathroom and seconds later she heard a door slam.

She stared after him. His words sank in and their meaning clicked into place. He wanted her? He didn't think she was a hideous cow? He thought *she* didn't want him?

"Wait," she called as she hurried after him, dripping water as she went. "It's okay. My doctor keeps telling me it's okay for me to make love." She skidded to a stop at the top of the hall. Wait. That didn't sound very romantic. "I mean, I feel the same way."

The door to the guest room opened.

"What?" he demanded, sounding more angry than aroused.

She was still naked and wet and more than a little nervous. She was also cold and shivering.

"I didn't know you wanted me," she admitted. "I thought you stopped the other night because you thought I was gross."

"Not at all," he said carefully. "I felt the baby moving. You're pregnant, Lil."

"I know. But it's still okay..." She shivered again.

"You're freezing."

He wrapped his arm around her and led her back to the steamy bathroom. Once there, he faced her and stared into her eyes.

"Are you saying you *want* to make love with me?" he asked.

She nodded.

"So when I kissed you the other night—"

"I didn't want you to stop," she whispered as happiness and desire fought for possession of her body. "I thought *you* thought I was a cow."

He chuckled. "A cow? Not possible. You're beautiful."

She clutched the towel more tightly to her front. "But I have this big stomach."

"You're beautiful," he repeated and lowered his head to kiss her.

Lily knew there were other things they had to talk about, words they had to say, but none of that seemed to matter right now. There was only this moment and the man in front of her and the way he made her feel when he kissed her.

His mouth was firm and warm and passionate. She parted for him instantly, not caring if he thought she was too brazen. She couldn't help herself. Need filled her, heating her blood, making her body swell in anticipation. His tongue swept inside, brushing against hers, making her quiver with need.

She felt his hands on her bare, damp back. He moved up and down, stroking her skin until she wanted to purr. With a sigh of surrender, she released her towel and let it fall to the ground, then she wrapped her arms around his neck and leaned into him.

"How can you doubt I want you?" he breathed as he kissed her cheek, her jaw, her neck.

He trailed his lips down to her collarbone, then over to her shoulder. He slid his hands from her back to her sides, then toward her breasts.

She stilled in anticipation of his caress, even as she remembered how good it had been the last time.

"Touch me," she whispered.

His hands closed over her breasts. He cupped her, taking the weight of her curves even as his fingers and thumbs teased her nipples.

Fire shot through her. Ribbons of desire wove their way through her body, making her ache with longing. Her legs trembled, her toes curled and she wanted him with a desperation that left her unable to think or breathe or even consider a world without his magic touch.

He bent his head and drew her right nipple into his mouth. The gentle sucking nearly drove her to her knees. She had to hang on to stay upright, which made her think about being in bed, which made her wonder how incredible it was going to feel when he was inside her.

"Jake," she whispered. "Please."

He straightened and stared into her eyes.

"Are you sure?" he asked.

She managed a smile. "More than I've ever been before. Touch me and find out for yourself."

He slipped one hand between her legs. His fingers dipped into her swollen wetness, then rubbed gently. They moaned in unison.

"See?"

He sucked in a breath. "I want you so much."

"Then get naked."

"Good idea."

He released her and tugged at his T-shirt. Within seconds it had sailed over his head to land on the counter. He unfastened his belt, pushed off his athletic shoes then stepped out of his jeans, socks and briefs.

She had a brief glimpse of his arousal before he moved in and drew her hard against him.

"Better?" he asked.

"Much."

She liked the way his skin felt against hers—the warm roughness of his hands, the rock-like muscles in his thighs, the hard-inside velvet-outside of his need against her belly.

He slid one hand under her hair and cupped her head. When his mouth settled on hers, she surrendered to the kiss. Passion grew as her blood heated. Everywhere he touched her, she burned. When he slipped his free hand between her legs, she groaned.

"More," she told him as he searched for then found that single spot of desire.

Her breathing increased as pleasure filled her. She wanted him to keep on with what he was doing, but she didn't know how long she could remain standing.

Her muscles clenched as he continued to touch her. She clung to him.

"I can't..."

"It's okay."

He bent down and grabbed the towel, then set it on the counter. With one quick, graceful movement, he set her on top of the towel.

She instantly saw the possibilities and parted her thighs. He moved between them. His hardness probed and she slipped a hand down to guide him inside.

He filled her slowly, completely, stretching her deliciously until she couldn't control her cries of pleasure. When he'd gone in all the way, he withdrew and did it again. Each slow stroke was better than the one before. The steady movements brought her closer to the edge. Closer and closer until she had to wrap her arms around his neck and cling to him.

He kissed her, keeping time with what his body was doing to hers. Then he moved a hand between them and searched with his fingers until he found that one spot of perfect release. He rubbed it as he continued to push into her. Over and over, deeper and deeper until she had no choice but to fall into her release.

The contractions rippled through her, making her cry out. Her orgasm went on for seconds, then minutes until he joined her, thrusting into her with the force of his need, then stilling as he, too, found paradise.

Chapter 6

Lily woke to an empty bed and some pleasantly sore muscles. A quick glance at the clock told her that she had about five minutes before the alarm would go off and she had to get up and get ready for work.

Jake had already left. She vaguely remembered him getting out of bed earlier that morning to head for the fire station. After they'd made love in the bathroom, they'd moved into her room where they'd repeated the experience only a little more slowly. They'd fallen asleep in each other's arms, which was exactly how she wanted to fall asleep for the rest of her life. With Jake.

She loved him. The how and why, most especially the when of it all eluded her, but she knew it was true. Somehow she'd fallen for him. Maybe she'd always loved him. Maybe their friendship had evolved over the years and changed when neither of them had been looking. Maybe it was something new. Regardless of when it had happened, she knew that her love was real and lasting. There were none of the flashes she'd felt with Michael. No bright lights, no incredible highs or lows. Instead she felt a sureness, a deep inner knowledge of having found what she'd spent her life looking for.

"And passion," she said as she sat up and swung her legs around so her feet touched the floor. "Plenty of passion."

More than she'd ever experienced. Jake had taken her places that probably weren't even legal. She smiled as she remembered how his touch had rocked her. Talk about knowing what he was doing. No wonder the women in his life never wanted to end things.

She walked toward the bathroom, humming as she went. She felt good. Better than good. She felt… content.

Her life was falling into place. First with Jake and later today, with Rachel. She was determined to make things right with her friend. Next she would tackle Jenna. She'd finally learned what was important and she wasn't going to let it get away from her again.

Lily felt a twinge of nostalgia as she walked into the Chinese restaurant where she, Rachel and Jenna had dined a thousand times. Their usual table was in the corner by the window. Whoever faced the hospital always had the job of look-out in case the hunky doctor they'd been talking about happened to stroll by. So many good times, she thought fondly. So many shared confidences, healed broken hearts, so much happiness.

"How many?" the hostess asked.

"Two," said a voice behind her.

Lily turned and saw Rachel. The second she locked gazes with her friend, her throat got all tight and her eyes burned.

What had she been thinking, letting this woman out of her life? Why had she let the silence drag out so long?

"I'm sorry," she said.

"Me, too. I was really dumb."

"No, I was."

They stared at each other another second, then hugged. Rachel laughed when she bumped up against Lily's stomach.

"You've gotten so big!"

"Tell me about it," Lily said.

Rachel sniffed, then wiped her eyes. "You're more than six months along and I've missed everything. I'm so sorry."

"Don't be. There's still plenty to experience. And you—" She glanced at her friend's still flat stomach. "How far along are you?"

"Just three months. Pretty amazing, huh?"

"More than amazing. It's a miracle."

Lily suddenly remembered the hostess and turned toward her. "We didn't mean to keep you waiting."

"Not a problem. I'll show you to your table now."

They followed the petite dark-haired woman to a table in a plant-lined alcove. When they were seated and she had left, Lily leaned forward to study her friend.

Rachel looked as she always had—pretty and full of life. Humor and happiness danced in her brown eyes.

"You look good," Lily said.

"Considering I just spent the past two months heaving my guts out, I look great."

The two women laughed.

"You're okay?" Lily asked. "You're feeling all right?"

"Uh-huh. Except for the morning sickness, I've

been terrific. Trying to keep my weight from bal-
looning, of course. That whole 'eating for two' concept is very tempting.''

''Don't I know it,'' Lily said. ''There are days I
could devour an entire water buffalo. I try to hold
back.''

''The water buffalo of the Portland area will be
delighted to hear that.''

Lily felt an odd combination of happy and sad.
Happy to be with her friend again and sad for all
they'd missed.

''I was an idiot,'' she said quietly. ''I reacted
badly.''

''No, you didn't.'' Rachel sighed. ''I should have
either told you the second I found out the truth about
Michael or kept it to myself.'' She ran her fingers
along the edge of her chopsticks. ''It was almost
funny, really. For the first time in my life, I met what
I thought was a great guy and decided to go for it.
One night of casual sex with no strings.''

Lily nodded as she listened, not sure how to react.
After all Rachel was talking about Lily's former fiancé. It took her a second to realize that she didn't
care. There was nothing Rachel could say about Michael that would upset her at all.

The realization felt good—freeing, really. Her past

was behind her. Now she could focus on her future...and Jake.

"The whole thing was a mistake," Rachel continued. "I was uncomfortable, it all felt wrong. The next morning the only thing I wanted to do was take it all back. That's why I never said anything. I was old enough to know better and still I screwed up."

"You're not the only one who made mistakes," Lily said. "At least you figured out he was a jerk from one night. I showed up to marry the guy."

"You didn't know what he was like."

"Shouldn't I have sensed something?"

Rachel shook her head. "I don't know. He was probably different with you. The thing is, when I saw him again, this time with you, I didn't know what to do. You were already engaged. What was I going to say? 'Hi. You remember me. We slept together a couple of months ago while you were dating my best friend?'"

Lily hadn't really thought about it from her perspective. "You were trapped. If you told me the truth, I might not have believed you. Even if I did, you weren't going to come out as the good guy in all this."

"Exactly. But I never wanted you hurt."

"I know."

The waiter came and they asked for tea. When he

asked if they were ready to order, they glanced at each other and laughed.

"The usual?" Lily asked.

"Absolutely." Rachel listed the dishes they wanted.

When the man had left, Lily smoothed the white tablecloth. "It's too much food for just the two of us."

"Good point. I guess we'll have to take some home with us."

"I'm sorry I took so long to call," Lily said. "I was afraid you didn't want to be friends anymore. I couldn't face that. So I let the silence grow."

"I should have contacted you," Rachel said. "I just felt so horrible about what I'd done."

"You didn't do anything wrong. It was Michael."

"I should have told you sooner."

Lily shrugged. "Maybe. But maybe it wouldn't have made a difference. In your position I'm not sure what I would have done. Can we just put it all behind us?"

"I'd really like that. I've missed you."

"Me, too. And Jenna."

"I almost called her," Rachel said. "To see if she would join us."

"Maybe we should do that for next time."

Rachel smiled. "Good idea. So what's new in your life? Aside from being six months pregnant."

Lily grinned. "Not too much." She held out her left hand. "I bought a house and got married."

Jake sat on a sofa in the firehouse. There was a book open on his lap, but he wasn't reading. He wasn't doing anything but thinking about Lily.

The previous night had been incredible. He'd never felt such connection before. It was as if by loving her, he was able to see into her mind and know what she was thinking. He'd known exactly how to touch her, how to please her. Every second of her delight had been a lifetime of happiness for him. Unfortunately he'd awakened in hell.

He couldn't do this, he thought grimly. He couldn't play the game anymore. He loved her—he wanted her to love him back. The knowledge that she didn't, that he was just a convenient rescue, ate him up inside.

The worst part was the lack of a solution. Did he stay and continue the torture? Did he leave and try to start over?

He considered the latter—life without Lily. How would he survive? How would he breathe without hearing her voice, her laughter. What about her baby? He already loved the child growing inside her.

He wanted to be there, be a father. He wanted them to be a family. But if she didn't love him back…

An alarm bell sounded the second a voice came over the loudspeaker and called out the code and the address. Jake tossed down his book and raced for his gear.

Lily checked the clock for the fourteenth time in the last two minutes and smiled. Okay, so she was a little excited about Jake coming home after his twenty-four hour shift. After her lunch with Rachel, Lily had decided it was time to finish cleaning up her life. She'd left a message for Jenna and had arranged to go in late so she could talk to Jake.

As she fried sausages, she checked the coffee, then the clock, all the while listening for the sound of his truck. The baby stirred, as if sensing her restlessness.

"It's going to be fine," she said as she placed a hand on her belly. "You'll see. We're going to live happily ever after."

At least that was the plan. She crossed her fingers and hoped that Jake didn't mind her organizing their future.

Just when she didn't think she could stand it for another second, she heard a familiar vehicle pull into the driveway. She turned the sausage one more time, flipped off the burner and raced to the back door. She met Jake as he climbed the two steps.

"Morning," she said cheerfully. "How was your…"

Her voice died when she saw him holding his right arm up against his chest. His hand was thickly bandaged and his mouth was tight. Panic swelled inside her.

"You're hurt. What happened? Are you okay?"

"I'm fine."

She stepped back to let him into the kitchen. He headed for the coffeemaker. She got there first and poured him a cup.

"Thanks," he breathed, then took a sip.

"Jake?"

"I'm fine." He waved his injured hand. "Or I will be."

He crossed to the table and she followed.

"How bad is the burn?" she asked.

"Considering how stupid I was, I was damn lucky." He sank into a seat and shook his head. "I've been doing this job for years. I know the rules."

She sat next to him and rubbed her fingers against his sleeve. The fear was still there, but with him walking and talking, it faded. "Tell me. Please."

He sighed heavily. "We were called to a house

fire. Old place with faulty electrical. Everybody got out but the structure was a disaster. They had this little girl.''

He sipped his coffee, then rested his bandaged hand on the table and winced. ''She was three, maybe four. She made me think of you. Big green eyes. Curly brown hair. Pretty and in tears. Her kitten was in her bedroom. He liked to sleep in the closet and she was afraid he wouldn't get out.''

Lily's heart lodged in her throat. ''You didn't…''

''Yeah, I did. I went back in.'' He held up his uninjured hand. ''Don't give me the lecture. I already gave it to myself and heard it from the captain. I found the cat, but it wasn't going to come to me. Not willingly. I was in my gear, probably looked like a feline-eating alien. So I tried to grab it, but I couldn't. Not in my gloves.''

She stared at his hand. ''You took them off?''

''Yup. I've got scratches *and* burns. A beam fell, split into a thousand pieces and a couple went right through my palm. The cat's okay, though.''

She leaned close and wrapped her arms around him. ''Don't do that. Don't you dare get dead.''

He clutched his coffee mug. ''The thing is, Lil, I couldn't stop thinking about you.''

She straightened and stared at him. ''What?''

''I saw you in that little girl. I thought about the

baby you're carrying and how much it all matters. I can't do this anymore.''

She had no idea what he was talking about but it didn't sound good. "Jake?''

He rose and walked to the sink where he stared out the window.

"I can't stay married to you anymore.''

What? She knew she thought the word, but she was too shocked to speak it. "No,'' she whispered. "You can't leave me.'' Not now. Not when she'd just figured out the truth.

Pain sliced through her, cutting her heart into pieces and piercing her soul. She leaned forward and clutched her stomach. No!

"I don't want to be your friend,'' he continued, his voice low and thick. "Not like it was. Night before last…'' He swore. "Last night showed me what it could be. The possibilities. I want it all, Lil. Not this half life we're living. I want you to love me back and we both know that's never going to happen. So a clean break will be better for both of us. You can find someone who matters and I'll…'' His voice trailed off.

"Jake, you can't…'' She straightened and stared at him. Words danced around in her head, forming sentences, disconnecting then forming again.

"What did you say?" she asked. "Why won't you stay with me?"

"I won't play this game anymore. You want us to be friends. I want it all. I know that's unfair. I'm changing the rules and expecting you to live by them. That's why I'm leaving. I don't want you to—"

"I love you," she told him. "Not as a friend, or a brother. As a lover and a husband."

She saw him stiffen. He turned slowly and when he faced her, his expression was unreadable.

"What did you say?"

She stood and faced him. "I love you, Jake. I don't know when my feelings changed from just friendship to something more. I'm beginning to think that I've always loved you but I didn't see it. You were always the one I turned to, the one I wanted to be with. When I thought about a future, you were the man standing next to me."

Jake heard the words, but wasn't sure he could believe them. Not after wanting them to be true for so long.

"I've been feeling different things for a long time," she continued, gazing at him, her eyes wide and bright with love. "Didn't you think it was crazy that I asked you to marry me?"

"No. It's what I wanted."

"Me, too. I could have backed out a thousand

times, but I didn't. You're the one I picture holding the baby. You're the one I want at my side. When we made love, everything fell into place. I knew we belonged together. For always. I love you, Jake, and I want our marriage to be real. Please give us a chance. Please?''

He wasn't sure who moved first. Did he go to her or did she fly to him? Did it matter?

He wrapped his arms around her and drew her hard against him. She melted into his embrace. He could feel the hard roundness of her belly and the fluttering of the baby inside.

''I think she approves,'' Lily said as she clung to him. ''Say yes, Jake. Tell me we have a chance.''

''We have more than a chance.'' He cupped her face and stared into her eyes. ''You're everything to me. You have been for a long time. I realized it was something more about two days before you started dating Michael.''

She winced. ''I wish you'd told me.''

''I wouldn't get in the way.''

''You're such a good man,'' she told him. ''And then I got engaged and you would never have said anything then.''

He nodded. ''I wanted you to be happy.''

''That wasn't going to happen without you.'' She smiled. ''Let me guess. After Michael dumped me, you were waiting for me to recover before saying anything and then I went out and got pregnant.''

"You're never boring.''

Tears filled her eyes. "I'm so sorry I didn't see the truth before. I would have saved us a lot of heartache.'' She pressed her lips together. "Are you sorry? About the baby?''

"Never. I love kids.''

"I know. But this one isn't yours.''

He put his hand on her stomach. "Of course it is.''

Lily gave a half sob, half laugh and kissed him. Jake kissed her back and allowed himself to believe. She loved him and they were together.

Epilogue

"So how are you feeling?" Rachel asked anxiously as she stood by the bed.

Lily looked at her friend and smiled. "I'm great. Have you seen her?"

"Of course. She's beautiful."

"She takes after her mom," Jake said.

Lily squeezed her husband's hand. "I thought we were going to lose you for a while. What happened to the tough hero?"

"It's a little different when it's you, Lil. I didn't like seeing you in pain."

Love filled her heart. She and Jake couldn't be

happier and now they had a daughter. "It was for a good cause."

"The best," he agreed.

The maternity-room door opened and Jenna walked in carrying a baby. She grinned and her blue eyes crinkled with delight. "Look who I found when I went to the nursery. Is she the most precious baby or what?"

Nadia pressed a hand to her chest. "Another granddaughter. Oh, Lily. You've made me so happy. Come here, little one. Come to Grandma Nadia."

Jenna handed over the infant and moved next to the bed. "Tell me that labor wasn't so bad."

"It wasn't," Lily said.

Rachel wrinkled her nose. "We both know you're lying."

"Okay." Lily smiled at Jake. "It was worth it. How's that?"

"Something I can live with," Jenna told her.

"Have you picked out a name?" Nadia asked as she cooed at the baby.

Lily and Jake glanced at each other.

"Samantha," he said. "Sam for short."

Nadia raised her eyebrows. "I thought you hated that name, Lily."

"It grew on me."

Nadia nodded. "Samantha it is." She touched the baby's cheek. "Welcome to your new family, Sam. You're going to like it here."

* * * * *

RACHEL'S BUNDLE OF JOY

Christine Rimmer

For T & E with all my love.

Chapter 1

Rachel Stockham was certain she had to be the only six-months-pregnant woman in the state of Oregon who spent the majority of her non-working hours fantasizing about sex.

Why me? Rachel found herself wondering on a daily basis.

As a medical professional she knew what she needed to know about pregnancy and childbirth. And beyond being a nurse, as a mother-to-be, she'd made it her business to read all the best and most current books on the subject.

She knew very well what her top preoccupations

should be at six months along and none of them were sex. Uh-uh. Leading the list should be heartburn and swelling ankles—those and the bigger questions: Will my baby be healthy? And, in her case, How will I cope with single motherhood, a seriously bi-polar mother of my own *and* my extremely satisfying but also demanding and emotionally draining career?

And, yes, Rachel did know it was perfectly normal for a pregnant woman to still enjoy sex, even *lots* of sex. But if lots of sex is what any given pregnant woman wants, it's helpful to have a man around to have sex *with*.

Rachel had no man. She planned to be a single mother in the truest sense of the word. Her baby's father was donor 1067 at OCS—Oregon Cryogenic Services. She knew his blood type, his ethnic extrac-tion, his height, weight and interests. And that was all she knew. It was all and it was plenty. She did not dream of finding out more, nor did she hope that some gorgeous, perfect hero of a guy would appear in her life out of nowhere and adore her on sight—puffy ankles, bulging belly and all.

Uh-uh. Rachel Stockham was a realist. She didn't expect to be rescued by a man. She wasn't sitting around waiting for some fabulous guy to fall crazy in love with her.

She would like just one wild night of jungle sex,

please. Before she was too huge to manage it, before she got all wrapped up in juggling motherhood, family problems and her career and had neither the time nor the opportunity—not to mention the energy—for a glorious, mad night of sexual abandon.

But was she considering finding a way to act on this burning desire for a single, memorable, all-night, one night stand?

Not a chance. The last—and only—time she had gone out and had a wild, monkey-sex night with a stranger, she'd discovered later that the stranger was her best friend's fiancé. It was a disaster. Never, ever again was she going *there*. And seriously. How many men would go there with her in her condition anyway, even if she *were* out hunting them down?

So. What do you do when you want it bad and you've reconciled yourself to the fact that you're not going to get it?

Maybe you fantasize.

Rachel did. A lot.

About Brad Pitt, shirtless. About Ben Affleck, buck-naked and giving her hungry looks…

But don't get the wrong idea here. Rachel didn't let herself get hot and bothered over just any handsome guy. No, no. She made a point of maintaining certain standards when it came to choosing imaginary partners for starring roles in her forbidden fantasies.

The rules went like this: Movie stars were okay. But no one in her real life. Not the muscular guy who lived down the street and mowed his tiny square of front lawn bare-chested, his baggy cargo shorts riding low on his lean, hard hips. And no one at Portland General—no handsome doctors, no hunky radiation techs. At the Cancer Care Center, she kept her mind firmly on what mattered.

And no innocent bystanders, either. Somehow, it seemed to her just one step beyond awful that she might get caught staring dreamily at some good-looking guy whose only mistake was that he happened to wander into a sex-obsessed pregnant lady's line of sight. Strangers were definitely out.

Or at least, they were until that April day at Becky & Huck's…

It was a Friday, the first day of a three-day weekend for Rachel. When you're in nursing, a three-day weekend is something to savor. A precious, uninterrupted span of time all to herself. Her plans for that Friday included running errands, a little shopping and then a movie…starring Brad or Ben, of course. In the evening, she would sink into a scented bath with a smile on her face and naughty fantasies in her head.

Rachel took care of her errands early and arrived at Portland's biggest mall, Lloyd Center, at a little after ten. By noon, she'd bought herself a couple of new pregnant-lady outfits—on sale at Motherhood Maternity—and wandered through Gymboree, Gap Kids and the Children's Place.

Becky & Huck's was her last stop—before she took a break at the food court and made a decision about which movie to see. The store was brand-new and sold seriously upscale kids' clothes. Out of her price range, really. But no harm in browsing....

Beyond the store entrance, bright banners hung from the ceiling and the cheery décor was in pink, yellow and apple-green. The clerks were right there, asking if they could help her.

"Just looking..." She smiled her most beatific expectant-mother smile and headed for the banner that announced, Baby Girls: Birth to 3 Months.

The clothes were so darling: infant capri sets of organic eyelet cotton; ruffled creations accented in the softest, prettiest lace; tiny dresses with patchwork tops; a downy-soft baby cardigan embroidered with flowers and trimmed in bright ribbons...

And wasn't there just something about baby clothes? Especially baby clothes like these, so sweet and unique and beautifully made. They were the kind of clothes a loving grandmother or doting aunt might

create and they spoke to Rachel of hope—for the
future in general and for her unborn child, specifi-
cally.

Okay, she was doing this solo with no man to lean
on. And true, her mother was not going to be the
kind of grandma who knits darling sweater sets and
begs for a chance to baby-sit. The future didn't look
perfect by any means. But still, Rachel and her little
one were going to do just fine.

Setting her Motherhood Maternity bag between
her feet, she picked up one of the embroidered, be-
ribboned sweaters. It was fluffy as a kitten's belly,
downy as a baby chick. She shook it out and held it
high—and saw that a man was watching her.

He was right across the display stand from her,
directly in her line of sight as she admired the tiny
sweater—and he was gorgeous! A tender mouth,
thick blond hair. He wore a lightweight cobalt-
colored sweater that clung to his broad shoulders and
made his blue eyes look deep enough to drown in.

Before she could remind herself that this was real
life and he qualified as an innocent bystander—
which made him *not* someone she ought to be drool-
ing over—he winked at her.

Seriously. Actually.

That incredible guy winked at her. And she let
herself smile at him.

At that point, she caught herself. She cleared her throat, dropped her gaze and—with slow, exacting care—refolded the sweater and laid it gently back in place on the display table.

Was he still looking at her?

Oh, of course not. She sternly applied herself to the task of admiring a pair of sea-green snap-on pajamas. Really, this was so silly. She must have imagined that wink. Or maybe he had something in his eye.

Since she was studiously looking down, she had a clear view of his pricey-looking, elegantly casual brushed-leather shoes. He hadn't moved.

Well, so what? A man can buy baby clothes, can't he? He was probably a new father, here to pick out something special for his darling baby girl. Yes. That had to be it: a very yummy loving dad.

"I think I need an expert." The hunk—whose voice was as smoothly masculine as the rest of him—had spoken.

Surely not to *her*.

She dared to look up—and right into those waiting laser-blues. He smiled. It was the perfect fantasy-man smile: a sexy hitch at one corner of that achingly sensual mouth.

That did it. She was throwing all her principles to

the wind. Innocent bystander or no, he'd get the leading role in her dreams tonight.

He said, "I think you're it."

What did *that* mean? Her pulse suddenly racing, she made a vague noise in her throat and slid a glance at his ring finger. Bare. And no telltale pale crescent where a ring *should* have been. So. Not a dad, then, after all? Or at least not a *married* dad.

"An expert?" she asked warily.

"That's right. An expert. On baby clothes..."

The faster her heart beat, the slower her mind seemed to be working. It took her a moment to put it together. "Ah..." She brushed a hand over her rounded stomach as a self-conscious laugh escaped her. "Well, I'm not an expert, really. This is my first."

"Your first..." He said it softly, as if the fact that she was having her first child was the most wondrous thing in the world. And it was, to Rachel. What she couldn't figure out was why this heartbreaker-handsome stranger seemed to think so, too.

They stared into each other's eyes, neither speaking. Bizarre. If she didn't know better, she could almost start to think he was coming on to her....

"Congratulations," he said at last.

"Uh, thanks. I'm...excited about it."

"I'll bet. So. Your opinion..." He had a tiny outfit

in each hand. He held them up: a sweet yellow romper and the cutest pair of pink corduroy overalls appliquèd with butterflies. "Which one do you like the best?"

Rachel ordered her heart to slow down and her cheeks to stop flaming and set her mind on applying her supposed expertise. After a moment, she shrugged. "I'm not much help, I'm afraid. They're both so cute. Either one would be just right."

He glanced at the romper and then the overalls—and then at her. "Can't choose, huh?"

"Nope. Better go with your instincts."

"I will," he said, still looking right at her. "I do."

There. That. Definitely.

The man was coming on to her.

And so what? Get a grip, girl, she commanded herself. It's called flirting and he's clearly a master at it. He probably flirts with every woman he meets. "Well. Uh. And how old is your daughter?"

"No daughter. A niece. She's two months old. The most beautiful, brilliant little girl in the universe."

A niece. Not a dad, after all, but a doting uncle. And judging by that bare ring finger, an *unmarried* uncle…

"Mine's a girl, too," she heard herself saying. "The ultrasound was just last week. I watched her suck her thumb…." Rachel cut herself off. Really, was that more information than the poor man needed, or what?

Apparently not, because he said, "You've actually seen her?"

She nodded.

"Is she gorgeous?"

"Of course. And healthy, from all indications. She has all her fingers and toes. And she's active." She felt a tiny flutter of movement beneath her rib cage on the right side. She put her hand to the spot. "Very active."

He shook his head, a musing look on that wonderful face. "Modern medicine. Amazing. And I'll bet your husband is thrilled."

She gulped. "No. No husband."

"Boyfriend, then…"

"Uh, no."

There was another silence—distinctly dreamy—as they gazed at each other some more. And then it came to her: this guy was about to ask for her number.

No, she thought. Better not go there. A blue-eyed hunk like this one could break her heart without even breathing hard. And wasn't it odd, him trying to pick up a pregnant lady? Men in real life never hit on a pregnant lady. And even if her stomach had been flat, she was not at her most alluring. Not by a long shot.

She wore stretch jeans with a preggie-panel and a loose white cotton shirt. Her short mousy brown hair was scraped back with a headband. Her makeup? A smudge of lipstick and a few dabs of mascara. She just knew her nose was shiny…

Uh-uh. There was absolutely no logic to this fabulous-looking man putting a move on her.

She picked up her shopping bag and grabbed a tiny wool hat from the stack near her free hand. "You know. I love this hat." She waved it at him.

"Cute." He gave her a nod.

"And I just realized, I really have to go."

He saluted her with the romper, looking friendly and relaxed—and totally unfazed by the fact that she was suddenly waving a baby bonnet at him and backing away. "Thanks," he said easily. "For the advice."

"Really. No problem…" Clutching the little hat in one hand and her shopping bag in the other, she made her escape by zipping around a floor-to-ceiling divider into the toddlers section.

As soon as she got away from him, she wished she'd stayed. What could it have hurt to have stood and chatted with him for a few minutes more? What had he done *wrong?*

The answer, on both counts, was nothing.

It was being pregnant, she decided. Being obviously pregnant and him *still* seeming attracted. Since she'd started to show, men in general displayed less and less interest. Not that men in general had been beating down her door *before* she got pregnant. But at least they had, on occasion, looked twice.

Nowadays they looked *three* times: first at her face, then at her stomach—and then right past her.

Except for this guy. *He* was different.

Point for him, right?

And the truth was, she did have a shy streak, one she'd battled all her life. So that was part of it, too— why she'd hurried off like that.

Now, looking back, she could see that it was so not a big deal—having a friendly conversation with a handsome man she'd just met. If she had it to do over again, she'd have handled it differently. Been more relaxed, more *natural*...

As she wandered on up the toddler aisle and back down, headed for the check-out counters, she promised herself, grinning a little at the unlikelihood, that the next time some gorgeous hunk flirted with her, he was going to get better treatment.

A moment later, she realized her chance to keep her promise was upon her already. *He* was waiting in the check-out line. She stepped in behind him.

He turned, smiled—this time full-out, both sides of that sexy mouth lifting. "Hey." He held up the romper *and* the overalls. "Decided to get them both."

"Good idea." She stuck the bonnet under her arm and held out her hand. "I'm Rachel. Rachel Stockham."

"Bryce Armstrong." His warm, strong fingers closed over hers. They shook.

She let go reluctantly as the clerk said, "Sir? May I help you?"

He handed over a credit card and his purchases and then he turned back to Rachel. They chatted about the weather—rainy—and the Trailblazers— headed for the finals this year, no doubt about it— as the clerk rang up first his sale and then hers.

It just seemed the most natural thing, to stroll on out into the mall together. They started toward Nordstrom for no particular reason that Rachel could think of—she certainly hadn't planned to go there that day. She glanced at him beside her and knew she had to say goodbye—at the same time as she wished they could just stroll along side-by-side for-ever.

She was so focused on Bryce that she didn't move out of the way fast enough when a woman loaded down with shopping bags came right at her.

"Whoa, careful..." Bryce took her arm to pull her out of the way before she got bopped by one of the bags. A thrill shivered through her at the contact and she beamed him a grateful smile as the woman paused to apologize.

"No harm done," Rachel told her.

The woman lurched on, bags bouncing, and Rachel turned back to Bryce. They stared into each other's eyes. Again. She could smell his aftershave. It was a green kind scent. Fresh. Subtle. She liked it.

Endless seconds passed before she realized she was leaning in close, gripping his strong arm as if it—and he—belonged to her. "Ahem. Well…" She extricated her arm from his and stepped back—gesturing rather wildly over her shoulder, toward the ice rink and the escalators at the center of the mall. "I seem to be going the wrong direction for some reason."

"No problem. We'll just turn around and go back."

"No. Really…"

He shrugged then, looking rueful. "Back to work, huh?"

"Well," she confessed. "It's my day off, actually."

"From…"

"I'm a nurse. Oncology."

"That would be cancer care, right?"

She nodded and volunteered, "Radiation Oncology at Portland General. We have one of the best cancer care centers in the state." Busy shoppers milled around them. Mall music and the tempting aromas from Starbuck's drifted on the air. Maybe, instead of strolling the mall forever, they could just stand right here and chat until the end of time…

He said, "You love your work. I can see it in those big brown eyes."

She smiled a little at his flattering tone, but when she spoke her smile had faded to a somber line. "It's tough sometimes. I'm right there while people are dealing with something that could—and too often does—take their life."

"Sounds very rough."

"Yeah. But there is a certain…reward, I guess, in helping make it better for people going through a hard time, as painful as it can be to watch some of them slip away."

"You're brave," he said quietly.

"No. My patients. *They're* the brave ones." She shook herself. "And I have got to get going."

He just stood there, looking scrumptious. "One more thing…" She knew what it would be. "I wonder…" He looked charmingly hesitant.

She couldn't help prompting, "What?"

"Well, I was thinking, maybe coffee—latte, espresso, your choice. Sometime when you're not so rushed…"

She felt warm all over. A *good* kind of warm. She

dared to tease him, "Coffee and pregnant ladies don't mix. Caffeine's not good for the baby."

He leaned a little closer, bringing with him another faint hint of that tempting aftershave. "Tea, then. Fruit juice. Whatever. I'm flexible when it comes to beverages."

She looked down, innate shyness surging to the fore. "Oh…"

"So…" He waited until she dared to look up at him again. "Will you let me have your number?"

Oh, what was the harm, really? Not only was he perfect fodder for her fantasies, he was so easy to talk to. And she *wanted* to see him again. "Tell you what. Why don't *you* give me *your* number?"

Frowning a little, he studied her face. "I don't know. I think you have a shy side."

She winced. "That obvious, huh?"

"Not obvious at all. It's very…charming, to tell you the truth."

She laughed, her cheeks warming. "Yeah, right."

"No. Seriously. It is. But I'm afraid it just might keep you from picking up the phone and dialing my number. Or maybe you just don't want to see me again—for whatever reason. If that's what's up here, I'd appreciate it if you went ahead and laid it on me right now."

"No. No, really. I *will* call you."

He gave her a sideways look, then agreed, "Fair enough."

The business card he handed her was on thick gray vellum stock. She ran her thumb over the embossed lettering. Armstrong Industries, it read. "Hmm," she said. "Bryce Armstrong, CEO. Very impressive."

He gave her a look—indulgent, good-humored. "What can I tell you? I'm a spoiled only son and also the boss."

Armstrong, she thought as she glanced at the card again. Bryce Armstrong. The name was vaguely familiar....

She almost asked him where she might have heard his name before. But no. She *had* promised she'd call him. If they ended up seeing each other again, she'd learn more about him.

Shifting her purchases to one arm, she stuck the card in a side pocket of her shoulder bag. The purse slid down her arm. She backed away from him, grinning, hands out, dangling her purse and her purchases from either hand. She felt kind of magical, right at that moment—graceful and pretty in spite of her big tummy and scraped-back hair. The world, all of a sudden, seemed chock-full of possibilities.

Truly, just when she'd given up hope that she'd ever meet a really great, handsome, fun and easy-to-be-with guy...there he was.

Across the display counter from her at Becky &
Huck's.

Whatever happened next, he had made her week—
heck. He'd made her *month*.

"Call me," he said again.

"I will," she promised, still backing away. "I
will, I'll call…" She raised her hand to wave, though
her purse was dangling from her arm and it made the
gesture awkward and jerky. She didn't care how
awkward she looked. She didn't *feel* awkward. She
felt like a swan. "You'll be hearing from me."

He gave her a wave in response and turned to go.

And right then, as her purse dangled free from her
arm, someone grabbed it.

"Wha—?" Somehow, she managed to catch the
strap before it slipped past her fingers. "Hey!" She
whirled as the snatcher—a skinny guy in baggy
jeans—gave it a hard yank. She yanked right back,
"Don't!"

The guy didn't listen. He stepped toward her. She
shrank away, sudden terror shivering an icy trail
down her spine. "No…" It came out a whisper of
fear and frustration.

His bony hand came toward her. He shoved her—
square in the chest. The breath flew from her body.
She sucked in air, and somehow managed one sharp,
helpless cry as her feet flew out from under her and
she went down.

Chapter 2

With a yelp of shock and pain, she landed hard on her tailbone.

"Omigod!" someone cried.

"Did you see that?" a man shouted.

"Somebody get that SOB!"

Furious, Rachel scrambled to get up. She was going to catch that skinny little rat if it was the last thing she did. She flailed, groaning a little.

And by then, a ring of people had pressed in close around her. She gaped up at all those concerned faces.

"Is she okay?"

"Oh, God. She's pregnant..."

"Are you all right?" Two women helped her to her feet, one on either arm.

Once upright, she tried to bat their clutching hands away. "I'm fine, really. But my purse—"

"Take it easy," said one of her rescuers, a big woman with hard red hair and kind brown eyes. She patted Rachel on the back. "Breathe deep..."

Her breathing wasn't the problem—it was her aching butt. *And* her missing purse. "That guy...he took my purse. I have to—"

"Honey, it's handled," said the woman on her other side, a shapely platinum blonde with a lived-in face.

"No, I have to—"

"Sweetie, they got him. Look."

She looked where the long flame-red fingernail pointed—at Bryce, about twenty feet away, by the entrance to Starbuck's.

He had caught the bad guy! He held the skinny little creep in a neck lock and he appeared to be handing him over to a couple of husky biker types.

"Hold this guy, will you?" Rachel heard him say. "Don't let the bastard go."

"Wow, man. Sure." One of the bikers—the bigger one, with a bald head, a black T-shirt with the sleeves torn off and an intricate skull-and-barbed-wire tattoo on his beefy right arm—grabbed the purse-snatcher by the scruff of the neck and shook him. Hard. "We ain't havin' no difficulties with you, now, are we?"

The would-be thief hung his head and mumbled something under his breath.

The biker shook him again. "What'd you say, scumbag?"

"Ow, man, you're hurting me!"

"I'll hurt you more," the biker growled. "Unless you plan to behave yourself."

"All right, all right," the snatcher grumbled, "I won't make any trouble."

The helpful redhead suggested, "Somebody better go find Security."

"I will." A tall balding guy in a jogging suit headed off toward the ice rink in search of a mall cop.

The worried shoppers pressing in on her fell back a little as Bryce approached with her purse in hand. "I believe this is yours."

She took it and hooked it in place on her shoulder. Right then, she felt as though she'd known him forever, as though he were a dear old friend who'd shown up just when she needed him most. "Oh, Bryce…" She reached out instinctively.

He gathered her in. "Okay," he whispered, bending his head down a little to breathe the word against her temple. "It's okay..." He stroked her hair, rubbed her back. "Thanks," she heard him say to the people surrounding them. "I'll look after her."

Oh, didn't she just wish...

She pulled away from Bryce's embrace—but only to tell the redhead and the blonde and the others, too, "Thank you. Thank you so much."

"It's okay, sweetie."

The redhead held out Rachel's shopping bags—rescued at some point during the excitement. "You want us to stick with you?"

She took the bags. "No. I'm all right. Honestly."

Another woman handed Bryce his bag of baby clothes. "I think you dropped this."

"Thanks." He touched Rachel's chin, a brush of a touch, so that she would look at him. "How badly are you hurt?"

She didn't know whether she was going to laugh or cry. "Just my tailbone," she confessed in a whisper. "And my pride."

He looked down between them, at the rounded shape of her stomach. "The baby?"

She rested her hand on the firm bulge. "We're fine, really." He still looked worried. She reassured him, "Bryce. Pregnant women and their babies are tougher than people give them credit for."

"Still, just to be on the safe side, I think we should get you to an emergency room."

"No, really. I'm fine. And so's my baby."

"You're shaking."

"Just…after-effects of a major adrenaline surge."

"Come on." He guided her to a nearby bench. "Sit down here…"

She eyed the hard bench. "Ugh. Easier said than done."

He frowned. "You *are* hurt."

"Yeah, a little," she confessed. "But I promise it's nothing permanent…" She lowered herself carefully to the seat, wincing when she got there. "See? I'm sitting on my injury." She held out her hands, palms down. "And the shaking is almost gone. Really, since you caught the guy and got my purse back, this is just not that big a deal."

He sent a hot glance toward the bony purse snatcher, who was flanked by the two helpful bikers and sulkily studying the off-white tiles of the mall floor. "The guy ought to be shot."

She reached up, took his hand and gave a tug. "Sit by me."

Obediently, he dropped to her side, turning his hand in her grip so that he could lace his fingers with hers. She started to lower her head to his broad shoulder—and stopped herself just in time.

She was being altogether too clingy. Gently, she pulled her hand from his. He let go—but with enough reluctance that she found herself wishing she'd gone ahead and held on.

They waited, with the bikers and the skinny thief. It wasn't long before the mall security guy appeared. He took brief statements from them and then put a call in to the city police. They waited some more.

When the police showed up, they gave their statements all over again. Unless her attacker got the bright idea to plead not guilty, the detective told her, she shouldn't even have to go to court to testify against him—given that she didn't want to sue.

She eyed her attacker, who was looking pretty pitiful by then. "As long as he doesn't try to say he didn't do it, I'm fine with letting a judge handle this."

After they led the purse-snatcher away, Rachel thanked the bikers.

"S'all right, no problem," they told her, and moved along.

That left her and Bryce side-by-side on the bench. She dared, again, to touch him, putting her hand over his. A warm little thrill zipped through her at the contact. "Thank you. For catching that guy. For *being* here…"

His other hand closed over hers, capturing it, so

tenderly, between both of his. He gave a squeeze. Her face felt warm and her heart beat faster. Honestly, did a guy have a right to look this good? His skin was smooth and golden-tan. And he had just the faintest manly-looking shadow of beard on that square jaw. And what about those eyelashes? Thick and long and sable-brown. Men shouldn't be allowed to have eyelashes like that. He leaned in closer. She breathed in the tempting scent of him and felt her eyes drifting closed....

Stop. No. Bad idea. She jerked back and pasted on a bright smile. "Really. I am so grateful."

"And why do I get the distinct feeling you're about to say goodbye again?"

She glanced down at their joined hands and then up into his waiting eyes. "Well. I do think it's time that I—"

"Do me one favor."

As if she could refuse him anything now. "Name it."

"There's a halfway decent steakhouse just outside the mall. Have lunch with me."

"Oh, Bryce. I don't think—"

"Humor me. Please. Just stick around for a while, until I can be one-hundred percent certain you're really okay."

"But I *am* okay."

"Just for a while." He was looking very determined—as if he wasn't going to back down easily
on this one.

And in the end, after all he'd done, how could she
refuse him? Plus, there was the fact that she didn't
even *want* to refuse him.

"I'm buying," she warned.

Two hours later they were still sitting in a corner
booth in the cozy, dim restaurant. Their empty plates
had been cleared away. They lingered over coffee—
well, in Rachel's case, a tall glass of ice water in
which the ice had melted long ago.

How had the time gone by so fast? They'd talked
and talked—a lot about her work, a little about his.
He said he was thirty-five, had a business manage-
ment degree from Stanford and described his job as,
"Mostly amounting to delegating effectively." She
figured there had to be a lot more to it than that, but
she didn't press him. She teased him about spending
his workday at the mall. And he tapped the shopping
bag on the seat beside him and said he'd just slipped
out to pick up something for Ariel. And then he'd
met Rachel…

"And then found yourself stepping in to handle a
purse-snatching in progress."

"My pleasure. All the way."

She teased, "And shouldn't you be back at work by now?"

"What's the point in being the boss if I can't give myself an afternoon off now and then?"

"So true," she agreed and they shared another in the by-then endless chain of long, mutually appreciative looks. She broke the lovely silence. "Ariel. It's such a pretty name."

He nodded. "After *The Little Mermaid*. Chelsea, my sister, always loved *The Little Mermaid*..."

And that led to the subject of favorite movies. They discovered that their tastes were astonishingly similar. They shared a fondness for the edgy and off-beat. They both like anything directed by Quentin Tarantino.

"And what about *There's Something About Mary?*" she suggested.

"Just about the funniest movie ever made." He looked at her sideways. *"Two Days in the Valley."*

"Saw it. Loved it." She challenged, *"Suicide Kings."*

"You're kidding. You *saw* that?"

She nodded, feeling inordinately smug. "I'll crawl over ground glass to see anything with Christopher Walken in it." And Brad and Ben, too, of course— at least lately. But she didn't tell him *that*. He might just ask why.

And what about TV shows?

They both enjoyed Sunday night on HBO.

From movies and TV, they went on to music, where their preferences went in different directions. Rachel liked a good country song. Bryce preferred either blues or hard rock.

It was all just surface stuff, just getting-to-know-you casually kind of talk. Rachel thoroughly enjoyed herself. She was ready when the check came and got her hand over it before he could grab it.

"Mine," she said. "And don't say I didn't warn you."

"All right," he conceded. "But next time is my turn."

Next time. He said it as if he meant it—but did she really believe him?

Oh, probably not. He was just so *smooth*…and sexy. And perfect. Too perfect for a harried and hard-working single mom-to-be. He had that look, a look that whispered *money*. From his brushed-leather shoes to his Rolex watch to his fine cashmere sweater. And then there was the subtle, oh-so-expensive scent of him. And that business card he'd given her…

CEO of Armstrong Industries.

She had a sneaking suspicion he was one of *the* Armstrongs.

If so, he was most likely very rich indeed. Even Rachel, who didn't pay a whole lot of attention to the movers and shakers in her community, had heard of the Armstrongs. The family had been around since forever, since the founding fathers flipped a coin and decided to name the city Portland instead of Boston. The Armstrongs were in shipping and land development. There was even an Armstrong High School....

More than once during lunch, she'd started to ask him if he was one of *the* Armstrongs. But he never volunteered the information. And somehow, she couldn't quite figure out how to pose the question without sounding just the wrong side of rude. She did say something about Armstrong being an important name in Portland.

But he only shrugged and they left it at that.

"This was great," she said, as they got up to go.

"*Was.*" He shook his head. "You say that as if the afternoon's over."

A flush of pleasure crept up her cheeks. He didn't seem to want to say goodbye any more than she did. "Well, Bryce…"

"Come on. Let's go over to the theatre complex and see what's playing."

She laughed. He was really so charmingly insistent about this. "I don't know. A wild afternoon at the movies may be too much for this particular pregnant lady. I think I should probably go home and...relax, you know? Rest a little, put my feet up..."

"So how about my place? We can watch a movie there. I offer free popcorn—and a good reclining chair, perfect for propping up a pair of tired feet."

"Oh, I couldn't..."

"Yeah, you could."

"But..." She felt so flustered, suddenly. The thing was, she *wanted* to go with him. But was it wise? "Bryce. I just...well, I have to keep reminding myself that I hardly know you..."

"Come to my place. Get to know me better."

"Well, I...I mean, it seems a little sudden, don't you think?"

"Yeah, it does. But sudden's okay with me. In fact, sudden is just great."

She heard herself asking, "Where do you live?"

"Portland Heights. Ten minutes away, max."

Portland Heights. One of *the* nicest neighborhoods, in West Hills. She wasn't surprised.

But where he lived really wasn't the question. The question was, should she go there with him? Remember Michael Carson, a warning voice whispered somewhere in the wiser part of her mind.

The thing with Michael Carson had happened really fast. She'd asked none of the usual questions, hadn't gotten to know him at all, just thought he was gorgeous and ended up in bed with him. Her one mad indiscretion.

And he'd turned out to be her dear friend Lily's two-timing fiancé. She was never letting anything like that happen again.

They were still standing by their booth. The busboy kept eyeing them, no doubt waiting for them to go so he could clear the table.

She took Bryce's hand. "Come on."

They left the restaurant. Outside, the rain that had been falling for most of the day had turned to a misty drizzle. They rushed across the wet walkway to the mall entrance, Rachel in the lead. Once inside, he slowed. She felt the tug on her hand and turned to him.

"Just wondering." He grinned.

"Wondering what?"

"Where we're going."

"This way." She marched on, dragging him along—to the bench where they'd waited for the mall cop. A pair of elderly ladies had claimed it. The ladies sat with their silver heads close together, shopping bags in a bright spill around their feet. The bench across from them was unoccupied.

Rachel hauled Bryce over to it, commanding, "Sit down." He sat. She perched beside him, sliding her shopping bags between her feet and setting her purse in what was left of her lap. "Are you married?"

His brows drew together. "Rachel, what's—?"

Before he could finish, she demanded, "Well, are you?"

"No."

"Engaged?"

He moved back a little. "No."

"Separated?"

"Rachel. I've never *been* married."

"Is there *anyone?* Some…special woman you're seeing who's not going to be happy when she hears you took a strange pregnant lady home for the afternoon?"

"A *strange* pregnant lady?"

Was he teasing her? She scowled at him. "You know what I mean. A stranger. A woman you don't even know. Forget the fact that I'm pregnant. It wasn't the point."

He was frowning now. "Rachel. What's going on? Why are you so damned angry? What did I do?"

She opened her mouth to tell him…what? She sighed. "It's not you."

"Well. That's *something.*"

"Just answer my question. Do you have a special woman friend? You know what I mean. An exclusive relationship. Are you *committed* to anyone?"

The silver-haired ladies were watching them. Rachel turned her scowl on them and they quickly looked away.

"Rachel."

"What?"

"No."

She forgot about the silver-haired ladies—for the moment, anyway. "No?"

"There's no one…special. There's honestly not."

"Oh." She twisted her purse strap. Now what? "Listen…" She paused to swallow. "I…well, it's not that I think something's going to *happen* between us. I mean, I just, well, I don't want some innocent woman hurt because I didn't have the sense to ask you—"

"Rachel," he said softly.

"What?"

"It's okay. I understand."

"You do?" He nodded. She couldn't help asking again, "You *really* do?"

"Yeah. It's a question you have every right to ask, and, as I said before, the answer is no. There's no one. I am one-hundred-percent unequivocally single. And while we're on this subject, what about you?"

Her throat kept clutching. She swallowed some more. "Me?"

Now he looked very patient. "Yes, Rachel. You."

"Well, but I told you, back there in Becky & Huck's. I'm single. Completely, totally, utterly single."

"And what about your baby's father?"

Her baby's father…

Oh, she could not explain that one, especially not here in the mall, with shoppers strolling by and the silver-haired ladies very likely listening in. "He's… not involved. I promise you."

"How 'not involved?'"

"Bryce."

"Yeah?"

She leaned close and whispered, so that only he would hear. "For now, you're just going to have to trust me on that one. The father of my baby is not a factor. That's all I can say, at this point." She hitched her purse back over her shoulder and reached for her shopping bags. "And you know, maybe we should just—"

He caught her arm before she could stand, warm strong fingers digging in just a little. "Don't run away."

She sank back to the bench. "Oh, I don't know…"

He let go of her arm and he shrugged. That shrug told her everything. She should come to a decision. He was through pushing her.

"All right," she said, feeling just a little bit foolish that she'd made such a big deal about all this—but then again, not *that* foolish. She really had needed the answer to the question she'd asked him. "Yes, let's go to your house."

He started to smile.

"But I get to pick the movie," she teased.

"Your choice. All the way."

Chapter 3

Rachel agreed to follow him to his place in her own car. But first she got his home address and phone number and took a minute to call a friend, so someone would know where she was going. Michael Carson had not only almost cost her her two best friends, he'd also made her more than a little careful when it came to hooking up with a new guy.

She'd learned the sad truth that a dream man can very easily turn into a girl's worst nightmare.

"I think someone should know where I am," she explained to Bryce, "since I did only just meet you…"

He seemed to have no problem with her emphasis on caution. "Makes sense to me."

She got out her phone and auto-dialed Lily Tyler—correction: Lily Stone. Lily had been married for months now, to Jake Stone, a longtime friend who had turned out to be the hero—and the husband—Michael Carson could never be.

"Rachel." She could hear the smile in her friend's voice.

There was whimpering in the background. "Is that Samantha I hear?" Lily's baby was three weeks old.

"We are very fussy today."

"Give her a big kiss for me."

"Will do. So what's up?"

Bryce had wandered over to the Nordstrom entrance and appeared to be studying a display of camping gear—giving her space to make her call. He seemed to sense she was looking his way. He met her eyes. Warmth flooded through her.

"Rachel?" Lily prompted.

"I'm right here." Rachel ordered her mind back on the business at hand—at which point it occurred to her that she hardly knew where to start. "You're not going to believe this…I, well, I met someone. I mean, it's nothing serious. I only *just* met him. But I like him. A lot. He invited me to his house. And I want to go."

"Where are you now?"

"Lloyd Center."

"You met him at the *mall?*"

Rachel stiffened. "Something wrong with that?"

"Don't get cranky. Please. I've got Sam if I'm looking for someone to fuss at me. I'm just trying to understand what's going on."

Rachel muttered a contrite, "Sorry—and it's a long story. I'll fill you in later. The deal is, I like him and I'm going to his house for the afternoon and I want you to have his phone number and address— you know, just so somebody knows where I am."

The fussing baby on the other end whimpered more insistently. "Rachel…" Lily sounded doubtful. And distracted.

"Look. Got a pen and paper?"

"Hold on…" Rachel waited. She could hear Sam whining and her friend making those cooing, soothing noises a mother will make to a crying baby. Lily came back on the line. "Okay. I'm ready."

"His name's Bryce Armstrong." She repeated the information Bryce had given her. "Got it?"

"Just a minute…yeah." About then, Sam let out a long, unhappy wail.

"I'll let you go," said Rachel.

"Just a sec. This guy…" Lily's voice trailed off. Rachel could hear her talking to Sam. "Just a minute, honey. Give mommy just a minute…Rachel, can you hear me?''

"I'm here."

"This guy. Bryce Armstrong, you said his name was?" Rachel made a noise in the affirmative. "The name's familiar…"

"I know. I kind of thought so, too. But it's probably just the last name. You can't live in Portland and not have heard the name Armstrong."

"No, I mean his whole name. *Bryce* Armstrong. I'm sure I've heard of…" Sam's wail turned to something very much like an angry scream. "Rachel. Sorry. I have to go. We still on for Monday?" They were meeting for lunch.

"Wouldn't miss it."

"Great. Jenna?"

"Oh, yeah. I'll call her."

"Good." Sam wailed all the louder. "Jake volunteered to watch Sam."

"The man is a saint."

"He does have his uses—and plus, he adores her. Rachel…"

"I'm here."

"Please take care."

"I will. Promise." Sam wailed again, louder than ever, and Rachel heard the click as her friend hung

up. She put away her phone and started toward
Bryce.

He turned when she was almost to him and when
her eyes met his, her breath got all tangled up in her
chest. What a truly gorgeous guy...

He arched a brow. "Ready?"

Rachel nodded and held out her hand.

Bryce's house—on one of the highest hills in Portland Heights—was huge, Tudor in style and surrounded by trees. A long, curving drive led up to it.

"All I have to do is stay on the yard guys to keep
the greenery trimmed," Bryce told her as they waited
for the corn to pop, "and I've got views all around.
Mountains in the daytime. Both St. Helens and
Mount Hood..."

She stared out the kitchen's rain-jeweled bay window. Through the gaps in the lush maples and stately
oaks, she could see the wide white cap of Mount
Hood. "I *am* impressed."

"...and city views at night."

"What more could a bachelor ask for?"

"If I answered that honestly, you'd only say I was
putting a move on you."

"Are you?"

"Absolutely—but hey. No pressure." The microwave beeped. He took out the bag of popcorn, tore

it open and tumbled the fat, fragrant kernels into the bowl that waited on the black marble counter. "Soda?"

"Do you have something without caffeine?"

"Sure." He went to the stainless steel refrigerator—along with the Viking stove, it made the kitchen look like something straight out of a spread in *Gourmet* magazine—and got two cans of soda. "Grab the bowl and follow me."

He led her past a living room the size of a baseball diamond and down a wide hallway to a room with eight padded lounge chairs, all facing the biggest television she'd ever seen.

"This wouldn't be the media room, now would it?" In her mind's eye she could see her own cozy living room, complete with her trusty 27-inch Panasonic.

He sent her a grin and gestured at a chair, taking the one next to it, so they could share the popcorn on the table between them.

"The lever on the left side of the chair will put your feet up for you."

She pulled the lever and she was in lounge mode. "I think I'm in heaven."

The technical aspects of the setup amazed her. He explained, "As a normal, red-blooded American male, I have a weakness for electronic toys." He picked up a silver remote, pushed a button and the lights went down. Then he pointed the device at the screen. "I have over five hundred movies stored in the system." Titles began scrolling down the screen. "Here." He handed her the remote.

"I don't believe this. No man lets a woman hold the remote—at least not on the first date."

"Enjoy the feeling. It probably won't last—push that button to move down the list." It took several minutes to scroll through the choices and make a decision. "Hit Enter," he instructed approvingly when she chose the Coen brothers' latest release. "Good. Then hit Enter again."

The movie began and two hours flew by.

When Bryce brought the lights up, she started to tell him she had to be on her way.

"Just stay a little longer...."

She didn't need a whole lot of convincing. She was having a great time. Somehow, the drive home alone through the rain, a long, hot bath and naughty dreams of Brad or Ben didn't stack up to staying right there with Bryce.

Just for a little while...

Bryce led her back to the living room and lit the gas fire beneath the wide stone mantel. They shared the long sofa facing the cheery blaze.

And they talked. About the movie, at first.

He was just so easy to talk to. After just this one day with him, she felt as if she'd known him forever. And it was nothing short of a fantasy-come-true to have this incredible guy treating her like a queen, hanging on her every word.

She found herself telling him the most private things. About how her mother's emotional problems really got to her sometimes, though bipolar disorder *was* an illness. "It's not my mom's fault," Rachel said. "If only she would just be consistent about her meds…"

"You resent her." He said it frankly, and she knew he saw nothing wrong with her feeling that way.

She admitted that sometimes she did. "She wasn't the most attentive mother. I guess, deep down, I still have issues about that. I know now that she was battling her illness even back then, when I was a kid and nobody knew what bipolar was. They called her 'moody' and 'overly sensitive.' Until the condition became acute, ten years ago, she never would get professional help. My father couldn't deal with her. He left when I was five. And then, really quickly, he married again, had another family. I haven't seen him in years. It's as if…I don't even have a dad." She slanted him an ironic look. "Stop me when you're so depressed you'll slit your wrists if I go on."

He didn't stop her. And she just kept talking. Eventually they went into the kitchen to raid the refrigerator. He had Ben & Jerry's Rum Raisin.

They sat at the table by the bay window and enjoyed the cold, delicious treat. The rain had intensified. It drummed against the window and cascaded down in rivulets, glittering as it went.

By the time they settled near the fire again, she was into the stuff about Lily and Jenna and their three-way pact to try artificial insemination if they got to the age of thirty-four without husbands—or at least serious relationships. "And we did it. Lily's had her baby. Jenna's about four months along…"

"And *you* meant what you said about your baby's father not being an issue."

She nodded. "He's twenty-eight, five feet eleven inches tall, has brown hair and blue eyes and no health problems. Oh, and he loves mountain biking and has a degree in biology. And that's the sum total of what I know about him, which is plenty as far as I'm concerned."

He listened as she talked, his gaze on her face. He seemed so *interested*. So she went on.

Into the whole fiasco with Michael Carson.

"I was a fool," she told him. "I didn't ask the right questions. I didn't ask *any* questions. I met him in a club. My mom had been driving me up the wall.

I needed a break, decided to treat myself, to do something crazy and fun. To have my very own wild night on the town. There he was, sitting down the bar from me. He was incredibly charming. We had a few drinks. The truth is, I pretty much fell into bed with him, you know? A one-night stand is what it was. And then he never called and, well, what do you do?''

''Forget him.''

''Yeah. After I got over the whole thing not going anywhere, I told myself I'd had a good time, kind of busted out a little for once and there was nothing wrong with that. Then he turns up with Lily on his arm. And I put it together. He was *her* Michael, the one she'd been talking about for months. He was *her* Michael and he'd spent the night with *me* while he was supposed to be her guy…and by the time I met him with her, he was a lot more than her boyfriend. By then, he'd asked her to marry him. He was her fiancé, can you believe it?''

His eyes shone with a knowing light. ''So that's why the third degree before you'd come to my house with me.''

''That's right. I learned my lesson. If you want to hang with me, I need to know upfront if there's a woman out there who trusts you and is waiting for you to come home.''

He looked at her levelly. "There's not."

"I believe you."

"And back to your friend Lily and her slimeball fiancé. What did she say when you told her what had happened?"

Rachel shook her head. "That's the problem. I couldn't figure out how, exactly, to tell her. When I saw them together, I felt like something you scrape off the bottom of your shoe. I kept my mouth shut."

"Bad decision."

She couldn't have agreed more. "Very bad."

"But when you spent the night with him, you didn't have a clue he was your friend's guy, right?"

"Of course I didn't."

"So you really did nothing wrong."

"I kept trying to tell myself that. But somehow, I still felt like a creep. And then, when I didn't tell her right away, it got worse. I felt all the time that I *should* tell her, but the longer I didn't tell her, somehow, the harder it got to get the words out. And then, the day of their wedding, the lowlife dumped her. She was devastated. I did what a friend does. I comforted her. And while I was agreeing what an SOB the guy was, it just kind of…slipped out."

Bryce was shaking his head. "That's what I call bad timing."

"Yeah. You're right on both counts. It was a bad

decision to start with, to keep my mouth shut—and then, when I did finally tell her…could I have chosen a worse time to do it? Doubtful. She was so hurt. I was *so* guilty. It drove a major wedge between us. And we put our other friend, Jenna, in the middle of it, until Jenna decided she couldn't deal with either of us.

"For a while there, I thought I'd lost the two best friends I'd ever had. And the real irony was, one of the lottery tickets we were always buying together paid off for five-hundred-thousand dollars a few days after everything went so wrong. The three of us were hardly speaking, but we split the money as we'd agreed. And we each went ahead—on our own— with our plans to have babies without the benefit of husbands." It caused a sharp ache in the vicinity of her heart to remember it. "We'd always talked about how, if the guy thing never worked out for us, we'd at least have each other when we became single moms…"

"But I take it that now things are improving, between you?"

"Yeah. Lily made the first move a few months ago, to repair the breach. And Jenna and I were both there the day Lily's baby was born."

"So…a rotten mess. But it ends well."

"Mmm, hmm…" She fell silent, looking at him.

She'd kicked her shoes off long before and turned toward him on the couch, drawing her legs up to the side. She looked down at her white shirt where it curved over the growing bulge of her tummy and then back up at him. And she couldn't help laughing.

He wore a musing smile. "What?"

She rested her elbow on the back of the couch and braced her head in her hand. "Oh, I don't know. You're clearly the most eligible of bachelors. And yet here you are, by the fire on Friday night, listening for hours on end to an incessantly chattering pregnant person. Tell me. Do you know more about me than you ever wanted to know, or what?"

He lifted his hand and ran his index finger, a touch like a breath, down her cheek. The caress shimmered through her, leaving a trail of tender heat. "A woman who talks about what really matters to her is a fascinating woman. And then there's also the fact that vulnerability and honesty make a woman damn near irresistible."

"What a kind thing to say." She was whispering, a very husky whisper, though there was no one but him to hear. She had that fluttery, heated feeling down inside—a yearning feeling, frankly sexual.

"This is not about kindness..." His voice was husky, too. He touched her again, cupping his warm hand around her neck, his fingers brushing up into her hair.

She made a small sound in her throat—of surprise, of longing. He answered that wordless question by covering her mouth with his.

They were kissing! Oh, boy, were they kissing. She sighed and let her lips part a little and his teasing tongue came inside. She moaned low and arched toward him. He pulled her in.

And her stomach touched him!

She let out a small, embarrassed cry and jerked back. "Oh, God. Sorry..."

"What for?" His lips were soft from kissing her, his eyes low-lidded, dreamy...

She glanced at her watch. "Uh, well. You know, I should probably—"

He was shaking his head. "Don't go."

"But it's after eleven. I really have to—"

"Just stay. You can have your choice of guest rooms. I have too many of them."

"Bryce..."

He gestured toward the French doors several feet away. The rain was still coming down hard. "It's pouring out there. You don't need to be out in that at this time of night."

She put her hand on her stomach, smoothed the wrinkled shirt a little, and then, slanting him a self-conscious glance, she dared to say what was on her mind. "It really doesn't...bother you? Kissing a seriously pregnant woman, having my stomach get in the way?"

Her face was flaming. He touched her cheek again, as if to cool the burning heat of it. The caress was so tender, it just about broke her heart.

"No, it doesn't bother me. I like kissing you. A lot. And I've only known you pregnant, so that's kind of part of the package, isn't it?"

"You've only known me pregnant—and that's been for less than a day."

"I thought I told you, sudden is okay with me."

"But I just...well, I'm not sure it's okay with me."

"I noticed." His eyes had rueful gleam in them. "And from all you've told me tonight, I can understand why you feel that way."

"You've just been so...terrific."

"And this is a problem?"

She reached out and touched his face, felt the warmth of his skin, the slight roughness of beard-stubble...

Oh, he was so perfect. *Too* perfect. She looked in his eyes and she felt beautiful. Beautiful and more than a little bit drunk, even though she'd had nothing with alcohol in it.

But still, she definitely felt high. High on this great guy who hung on her every word and seemed to love kissing her, who touched her with tenderness, who said that she was honest and vulnerable and that he found her fascinating and that her big stomach was part of the package.

Could this be real?

Oh, probably not. It wasn't something that was likely to last. It was just…one of those things that happens. A little bit of magic in her otherwise strictly ordinary, way too demanding life.

There was Brad and there was Ben.

And now…Bryce.

Oh, yes. It fit. It definitely fit.

She said, her voice gone husky again, "If I stayed, could I sleep in your room?" The words were out almost before she realized she would say them. She made a sound halfway between a bark of laughter and a sob and she put her hand over her mouth. "I can't believe I just asked you that."

He didn't look the least bit fazed. "But the real question is, did you mean it?"

She couldn't quite meet his eyes. "I, um…" Oh, how to explain herself. "It's just that lately my libido seems to be way out of control. I have a lot of…fantasies. I would just really like, one time before I get big as a house, for my fantasies to come true.''

Oh, beautiful, she thought, staring bleakly down at her growing waistline. Way to go, Rachel. Was she going to tell him every last embarrassing secret she'd ever had?

She could hear the rain spattering the windows, and also the friendly hiss of the fire in the grate. He wasn't saying anything. Not that she blamed him. What was he thinking? She just could not look at him…

He whispered, so softly, "Rachel…" She made herself raise her head. What she saw in his eyes sent heat in a flash fire blazing all through her. "Spend the night in my bed," he said. "Please."

She blinked. "Tell me you didn't just say what I thought you said…"

"But I did say it."

"You're serious?"

He was nodding.

"You and me…tonight…right now?"

"Yeah."

"Oh. Oh, well…"

"You're so charming when you're blushing."

"So, you mean, you *would?* With me?"

"In a heartbeat."

"Oh." She put her hand against her throat where

she could feel her pulse frantically beating. "This is so unreal. And I am incredibly nervous."

"That's okay."

"Oh, I don't know. In my fantasies…" She didn't quite know how to finish that thought.

He whispered, "Go on. Tell me. Say it."

"Well, I mean, in my fantasies, I'm not six months pregnant, you know? But now… Well, in reality, I'm thinking it could be kind of…awkward."

"Awkward is fine with me."

"Oh, Bryce…"

He took her hand and pried open her suddenly-stiff fingers and brushed a kiss right there in the heart of her palm. Her senses were humming, she felt warm and shaky—but in a good way.

A very, very good way.

He guided her hand to his shoulder, a coaxing gesture. It was all the encouragement she needed. She went for it, sliding her hand up, wrapping her fingers around his nape, leaning in as he leaned toward her.

Their lips met for the second time. His strong arms came around her and he gathered her close. And that time, when her stomach pushed against him, she had no urge to pull away.

Chapter 4

They went up the wide staircase hand-in-hand. The door to his room stood open. He led her through, into the shadows, toward the wide shape of the bed.

When he reached for the lamp, she caught his hand. "Could we...leave it off?"

"Sure."

She sought his eyes through the dimness—and then she laughed.

"What?" His white teeth flashed with his questioning smile.

"Oh, just...all my wild fantasies. I was so brave and so bold in them. And in the end, now it's really happening, here I am, asking you to leave the light off.''

He touched her cheek, so lightly. ''I already told you I think you're brave. But bold...? You know, maybe you'd better describe these fantasies of yours.''

''I'll tell you this much....'' And she lost her nerve. She slanted him a look. ''On second thought, not tonight.''

If he was disappointed that she wouldn't tell him all the naughty details, he wasn't showing it. ''It's your call—and don't knock the dark. The dark has plenty to offer. A sense of mystery, of secrets that you have to find the answer to by feel.''

''If you say so.''

He studied her. ''Nervous?''

''Extremely.''

''Come here.'' He pulled her close for another long, bone-melting kiss and when he lifted his head, he slid the band from her hair. ''There.'' He dropped the headband to the nightstand and ran his fingers through her short, dark curls. ''Pretty. Soft...'' He kissed her again, easing her nervousness, soothing her fears.

He began to undress her—and himself—pausing for tender kisses between each undone button, each loosened sleeve. He unwrapped her like a precious gift—with such reverent care, his eyes gleaming through the darkness, his hands brushing so lightly against her skin as he whisked away the barriers between them.

The rain drummed in a hollow, haunting rhythm against the windows and the wind made faint, sweet crying sounds. Rachel cried, too—small, hungry little cries. Of yearning. And wonder.

He laid her back on the bed and kissed his way down her body, pausing for a number of erotic detours: to take each nipple in his mouth, to lay his golden head against the swell of her belly, as if listening for whispered secrets from the little one inside. He pressed his palms against the roundness, long fingers spread, on either side of her navel. And then he waited...

"There," he whispered. "Did she just kick me?"

"A kick or a punch. Pretty hard to tell the difference most of the time."

His hands moved. She sighed. He caressed his way downward, over the slopes and the hollows. He stroked her thighs, following the long caresses with brushing kisses.

When he found her, when his fingers gently parted her, she whimpered, in need...in hunger. In stunned delight. He lifted his head and he looked at her, as she writhed and moaned at the touch of his hand.

An Important Message from the Editors

Dear Nora Roberts Fan,

Because you've chosen to read one of our wonderful romance novels, we'd like to say "thank you!" And as a special way to thank you, we've selected two books to send you from a series that is similar to the book that you are currently enjoying. Plus, we'll also send an exciting Mystery Gift, absolutely FREE!

Please enjoy them with our compliments.

Pam Powers

Peel off seal and place inside...

EDITOR'S
FREE GIFT
SEAL
THANK YOU

How to validate your Editor's
FREE GIFT
"Thank You"

1. Peel off gift seal from front cover. Place it in space provided at right. This automatically entitles you to receive 2 FREE BOOKS and a fabulous mystery gift.

2. Send back this card and you'll get 2 brand new novels from Silhouette Romance®, the series that brings you traditional stories of love, marriage and family. These books have a cover price of $3.99 each in the U.S. and $4.50 each in Canada, but they are yours to keep absolutely free.

3. There's no catch. You're under no obligation to buy anything. We charge nothing—ZERO— for your first shipment. And you don't have to make any minimum number of purchases— not even one!

4. The fact is, thousands of readers enjoy receiving their books by mail from the Silhouette Reader Service™. They enjoy the convenience of home delivery...they like getting the best new novels at discount prices BEFORE they're available in stores...and they love their *Heart to Heart* subscriber newsletter featuring author news, horoscopes, recipes, book reviews and much more!

5. We hope that after receiving your free books you'll want to remain a subscriber. But the choice is yours—to continue or cancel, any time at all! So why not take us up on our invitation, with no risk of any kind. You'll be glad you did!

6. And remember...just for validating your Editor's Free Gift Offer, we'll send you THREE gifts, *ABSOLUTELY FREE!*

The Editor's " Thank You" Free Gifts Include:

- Two Silhouette Romance® novels!
- An exciting mystery gift!

YES! I have placed my Editor's "Thank You" seal in the space provided above. Please send me 2 free books and a fabulous mystery gift. I understand I am under no obligation to purchase any books, as explained on the back and on the opposite page.

310 SDL DZ3T   **210 SDL DZ3S**

FIRST NAME   LAST NAME

ADDRESS

APT.#   CITY

STATE/PROV.   ZIP/POSTAL CODE   (N-SR-1-04)

Thank You!

The Silhouette Reader Service™—Here's How It Works:

Accepting your 2 free books and mystery gift places you under no obligation to buy anything. You may keep the books and gift and return the shipping statement marked "cancel." If you do not cancel, about a month later we'll send you 4 additional books and bill you just $3.34 each in the U.S., or $3.80 each in Canada, plus 25¢ shipping and handling per book and applicable taxes if any.* That's the complete price and — compared to cover prices of $3.99 in the U.S. and $4.50 in Canada — it's quite a bargain! You may cancel at any time, but if you choose to continue, every month we'll send you 4 more books, which you may either purchase at the discount price or return to us and cancel your subscription.

*Terms and prices subject to change without notice. Sales tax applicable in N.Y. Canadian residents will be charged applicable provincial taxes and GST. Credit or debit balances in a customer's account(s) may be offset by any other outstanding balance owed by or to the customer.

If offer card is missing write to: The Silhouette Reader Service, 3010 Walden Ave., P.O. Box 1867, Buffalo, NY 14240-1867

BUSINESS REPLY MAIL
FIRST-CLASS MAIL   PERMIT NO. 717-003   BUFFALO, NY

POSTAGE WILL BE PAID BY ADDRESSEE

SILHOUETTE READER SERVICE
3010 WALDEN AVE
PO BOX 1867
BUFFALO NY 14240-9952

NO POSTAGE
NECESSARY
IF MAILED
IN THE
UNITED STATES

"Rachel," he said, as if the mere sound of her name excited him. "Rachel…" He slid up beside her as his hand continued its shattering play below. He kissed her as he stroked her. She pushed herself hungrily against his pleasuring hand and gave him her lips and her tongue to do with as he pleased.

When she hit the crest, his kiss only deepened. She cried her delight against his mouth as she went over the brink and into that floating state of pleasure on the other side.

"I can feel you," he whispered, his hand still cupping her. "Feel the pulsing. Feel you coming…"

She moaned. He kissed her again, with such slow, delicious care.

And when the pulsing finally stopped, he rolled away from her and pulled open a drawer in the little table by the side of the bed.

"Bryce…?"

He came back to her. He had a condom in his hand. She watched him through the shadows as he rolled it down over himself. He did it smoothly, expertly. She lay there, dazed with delight, and wondered at him. At all she didn't know about him…

But then he was sliding a hard knee between her thighs, raising up over her, lowering his mouth to take her lips.

He kissed her—teasingly this time—his lean, hard

body braced on his arms, holding himself above the swell of her stomach. And then he whispered, "I'm afraid to put my weight on you."

"It should be all right..." Though the truth was that, in the past few weeks, pressure on her swelling midsection felt odd and uncomfortable.

He must have heard the doubt in her voice. "I think maybe we're going to have to slide you over to the side of the bed."

It was a fairly high bed, with a thick, firm mattress. If he stood at the edge of it...

She reached up, ran her fingers lightly through the silky hair at his temple. "That would work better."

He was watching her probingly. "You're sure about this?"

She nodded, gave another low laugh. "But are you?"

He lowered his head and glanced down between them at the proof that he was still very interested in continuing this activity. He looked up at her again. And he winked. A smile trembled across her mouth as she remembered that first moment she'd become aware of him—was it really only hours ago?—across the display counter at Becky & Huck's.

Never in a hundred thousand years would she have guessed she would get here, from there—and in such a short time, too.

Oh, my, she thought, I am such a wild, wicked mother-to-be.

"Come on, scoot this way…" He guided her hips to the edge of the bed and slid off to stand before her, with her thighs on either side of his.

In a slow, smooth stroke, he was inside.

Inside, and careful—at first. He moved cautiously in and slowly out—or almost out. But not quite.

She moaned and he came back to her. And that time, when she felt him go deep, she rested back on her elbows and let her eyelids droop shut.

He bent closer, slid his hands under her hips and lifted her.

"Oh!" she cried.

"Wrap your legs around me."

She did as he instructed. And then he stood taller. Her hips were off the bed and he supported her lower body in his arms. He began to move more swiftly.

And it was…

Just heavenly. She moaned and rolled her head from side to side as they found a mutually pleasing rhythm, as he held her tight and she pushed her hips against him, as he filled her and retreated and then filled her again.

In the end, he held so still, gripping her hips, pressing deep into her. She could feel his release, feel him pulsing within her. And, oh, that did thrill her. It was just so…erotic, so beautiful and right.

Her own release began. She felt the tightening, the gathering deep inside…

They were so still, locked together hard at the point of joining. So still on the outside, while within there was that rising magic flowing out along every nerve.

He held her hard against him, supporting most of her weight, until the pulsing faded down to a glorious, soft glow. Then, at last, he bent his legs—they were shaking, she could feel them—until her hips met the bed. And then he slipped from her. She let out a long sigh at the loss. ''Come back…''

He sent her a tender look over his shoulder. ''I will.'' He got rid of the condom and returned to her. Together, they scooted fully onto the bed again.

As if they'd always slept together, she turned on her side and he wrapped himself around her, pulling the covers over them. His thighs were a cradle for hers, his breath stirred her hair. She reached back for his hand, guided that muscular arm to rest on the cove of her thickened waist. His chest was warm and solid against her back.

Strange, she thought drowsily, how natural it felt to be here with him. How perfectly right.

He cuddled her closer. She sighed. For a while,

they whispered together in the darkness. He stroked her hair, brushed a kiss now and then against her shoulder. Finally, with a small, contented smile curving her lips, she dropped off to sleep.

Chapter 5

In the morning Rachel discovered that Bryce had a live-in housekeeper and a cook. The housekeeper greeted them when they came down the stairs. Now, *that* was an interesting experience. Bryce said, "Rachel, this is Mrs. Davenbrook. Mrs. D. takes excellent care of me."

Rachel murmured "Nice to meet you," and Mrs. Davenbrook nodded crisply in response, a bland smile on her pleasant face. Rachel didn't even let herself wonder what the housekeeper was thinking. She did, however, kind of wish she'd taken a moment to comb her hair.

The cook served them breakfast at the table by the bay window. Outside, the day was bright and clear, the snow cap on Mount Hood seeming to twinkle at them through the lush branches of the trees.

"Stay," Bryce said as they inhaled their eggs Benedict. "We'll watch another movie. Or drive over to the Pearl District, if you'd like that. We can wander through the galleries, do some serious window-shopping, have lunch at a great new place I know…"

She was just about to say yes when her purse, on the chair in the corner where she'd abandoned it the night before, began playing the theme from "The Addams Family." "My phone…" She got up and answered it.

"Rachel. Rachel, where *are* you? I've been calling all night…" The frantic edge to her mother's voice sent a quiver of alarm racing through her. The gorgeous, sunny day seemed suddenly not quite so bright.

She spoke gently. "I'm sorry, Mom, I wasn't near my—"

Ellen Stockham was beyond the point of letting Rachel get out a whole sentence. "I can't…I can't *do* this. And don't you accuse me."

"Mom, I'm not—"

"Those pills…I just, well, I thought I would try it for a while, you know? Without them? And I…I felt fine. I really did. Well, a little bit down, you know? And then, last night, well, I was thinking about washing the curtains. You know how I am, I do like things *clean.* And then, I couldn't seem to get the rod loose from the wall-hook thingy and then I... Oh, Rachel...I..."

"Mom. Listen."

"Oh, what? What *is* it?"

"Did you call Doctor—?"

"The *curtains,* Rachel. They are impossible. I had to *cut* them off. And now, this morning, the sun came out. It's too bright in here. I just can't...I can't..."

As her mother rambled on, Rachel accepted the fact that this was not something she could handle over the phone. "Mom. Just sit tight."

"Oh, I don't...I just...I...Rachel..."

"I'll be right over."

"But Rachel—"

"Mom. Just wait. I won't be long."

"Let me take you," Bryce said, when she told him her mother was seriously down-cycling and she had to go, *now.*

"Thanks, but I'll handle it." She spoke as calmly as she could while racing for the door.

He followed her out and held the door for her as

she got in the car. "I'll call you later, make sure you're all right."

"Yeah, okay. Thanks." She started up the car.

"Rachel."

"I have to go, Bryce."

"Your number?" She must have looked as frantic to get moving as she felt, because he added, "Just tell me. I'll remember."

So she rattled off her home number and he shut the door and she tore off down the drive.

Somehow, Rachel managed to make it to her mother's across the river a few blocks from her own place without getting a ticket or causing a wreck. She ran up the flight of steps to the second-floor apartment, noting as she got there that the curtains that usually hung on the window by the door weren't there anymore.

Just as she was collecting herself to knock, the door opened.

Her mother stood on the other side, wearing a pink chenille robe and a pair of black sneakers, the frayed laces untied. Blood oozed from a cut on her right cheek and dripped from another shallow gash on her hand. Behind her, on the living-room rug, what looked like every curtain in the apartment lay in a tangled mound.

Rachel whispered despairingly, "Mom…"

"Oh, Rachel," her mother cried. "Oh, Rachel, what will I do?" The dark eyes, sunken and haunted, but otherwise the same eyes Rachel saw when she looked in the mirror, pleaded for answers that Rachel didn't have. Yesterday's mascara ran in tracks down her too-thin face.

Rachel stepped over the threshold and carefully pried the bloody scissors from her mother's shaking hand. "It's all right, Mom. I'm here, now. I'm here…"

Chapter 6

Four hours later, Rachel sat in the main waiting room in Portland General's psychiatric wing. She wasn't really *waiting* for anything—except maybe for the moment when she'd find the energy to get up and leave. Everything that needed doing for the day had been done. She could go home, draw a hot bath, pour in the scented bath salts...

Double doors to the main hall swung open—and there was Jenna Cooper, four months along now, her stomach gently rounded under her scrubs. Frowning, she scanned the waiting area.

Rachel dragged her tired body upright. ''Jenna...''

Jenna spotted her and smiled. She hurried over and they shared a quick hug. "I heard a rumor you were here," she whispered in Rachel's ear. They stepped back from each other and Jenna took her by the shoulders to look in her eyes. "How are you holding up?"

"I've been better."

"Your mom?"

"They're keeping her here for a few days, until the crisis is past."

"How bad is it?"

"Bad enough. But she'll be okay once they get the meds back on track—are you on duty?"

Jenna nodded. "How can I help? What can I do?"

"Nothing. Honest. It's done. But thanks for checking on me…"

"You look beat."

"Yeah. I'm wrung out."

"You need someone to take you home. I can—"

"No. Really. I have my car. I'll manage. I'll just drive *really* slowly."

"You're sure?"

Rachel nodded, firmly—and then she remembered about Monday. "Wait. There is one thing…"

"Name it."

"Lunch. One o'clock Monday, the usual place.

You, me and Lily. Jake's watching Sam, so it'll be just like old times.''

Jenna's comforting hands dropped away. ''Oh, I don't know. You should see my schedule…''

Sometimes Rachel wondered if Jenna was still a little wary, if she hadn't completely put the Michael Carson fiasco behind her. She patted her friend's arm. ''No pressure. Just, you know, if you can…''

''I'll try…''

The phone was ringing as Rachel let herself in the door. It was Lily. ''At last. I called your cell, but it was only taking messages.''

''Sorry. I turned it off while I was at the hospital.''

''Jenna called me and told me about your mom. She said things were…well, handled, anyway.''

''Yeah. She'll be okay. Till the next time…''

''Listen. Jake's here.'' A firefighter, Jake would work round-the-clock and then get several days off in a row. ''I can leave Sam with him and be right over.''

''Thanks, but no. I just want to sink into a hot bath…for about a year.'' Rachel knew what her friend's next question would be. She was right.

''So…how was last night?''

From the perspective of a day spent having her

mother temporarily committed, the magic of last night seemed so long ago…

"Rachel?"

"Sorry. Last night was wonderful. I…I do really like him."

"Ah."

Rachel knew when her friend had something on her mind. "When you say 'Ah' like that, I know there's more coming."

"Well, I told Jake you'd met a guy named Bryce Armstrong. We both felt sure we'd heard the name before. And then Jake remembered that a Bryce Armstrong showed up at the last Logan Burn Center fundraising drive. He delivered a huge check courtesy of Armstrong Industries. You think maybe this could be the same guy?"

"He's the CEO, actually."

"Ah."

"Lily. Say it. My bathtub is calling me."

"He's one of *the* Armstrongs."

"Figured that one out."

"Rich as they come."

"You only have to look at him to know that. But if I had any doubts, well, I followed him in his Mercedes to his mansion in Portland Heights. That he's got money is just not news."

"You sound defensive. I'm not telling you this so

you'll get your guard up. This is only…information, you know?''

"I know. So go ahead. Tell me the rest.''

"Okay. The guy's not only *an* Armstrong, he's the major heir. I think there's a sister, but you don't hear a lot about her.''

"There is a sister. Her name's Chelsea. She has a baby named Ariel that Bryce adores. So what else?''

"Well, don't you remember him? He even made *People* magazine once. That issue on sexy CEOs. He got a whole quarter page. They wrote about how he had a different gorgeous woman on his arm every night…''

"Oh.'' Rachel sank to a chair. "Well. That's news…I mean, I kind of remember that article now you mention it.'' She'd read the brief piece and mused a little over how the other half lives. Oh, and she'd thought he was gorgeous, too. Unbelievable. Really, how *could* she have forgotten that article until now? She pulled at a loose thread on the chair seat. "Well, I guess that's me. Just another in an endless chain of stunning, willing women.''

"Oh, come on. I only told you because we had an agreement, remember? No more secrets when it comes to men.''

"I know. And I'm glad you told me.''

"And it's not a huge issue that he's dated a lot of women, is it?"

"Well, no. No, of course not."

"Rachel. Wait a minute. You didn't happen to…?"

"Oh, you're just so tactful this afternoon."

"Well. *Did* you?"

"Yes. I slept with him." She stopped tugging on that thread and sat up a little taller. "And it was great. Believe it or not, lovely, passionate sex *is* possible even when you're six months along."

"Don't I know it."

Rachel actually giggled as she realized that Lily had been there, too. "And before I would go home with him, I at least made sure there was no special woman in his life."

"Good for you. And you know, if *he's* unattached and *you're* unattached and you treated each other with understanding and mutual respect, well then, is there really a problem?"

She let out a long sigh. "Oh, probably not. Other than the fact that's he's way out of my league."

"Stop that. There is no one—*no one*—who is out of your league."

"You are the very best friend a girl could have—and I have to stop falling into bed with every charming, handsome guy I meet."

"Oh, puh-lease. Two guys. It's hardly a pattern."

"Maybe not. It's just that, after this morning, it's a challenge to have a positive attitude about anything."

Lily made an understanding noise low in her throat. "Sure you don't want me to come over?"

Rachel demurred again, with many thanks, and told her friend she had to go. Once she hung up, she headed straight for the tub, shedding her clothes as she went. She took the phone in there with her, just in case the hospital called. It rang as she was settling back in the fragrant, soothing hot water.

"I'm guessing you just got home and don't want to deal with some guy who won't let you have a minute to yourself."

The world was suddenly a better place. "Bryce. Hello."

"How's your mother?"

She hesitated over what to say, then settled on a bare-bones version of the facts. "Not good. I took her to the hospital. Just got home a few minutes ago."

"Want some company?" Her first reaction was a delighted, *yes*. But she hesitated a fraction too long before she said it and he gently suggested, "Tired?"

She sank deeper into the lovely warm water. "Mmm, hmm."

"Then maybe later..."

She smiled at the thought. "Yeah. I'll hold you to it." She said the words and then wondered if she really meant them.

After all, he was Bryce Armstrong, sexy CEO— just ask anyone who read *People* magazine. With him, there was a different glamorous woman for every day of the week. Their brief time together had been perfect. But she didn't really fit the profile, now did she?

They talked about nothing in particular for a few minutes more and then he said goodbye.

On Monday, one of her favorite patients lost the fight for his life. He was only a kid, just twelve years old, as sweet and gutsy as they come. He'd been battling leukemia for over a year.

While the boy's father made the necessary arrangements, Rachel sat with the mother for a while. They whispered together of the twelve-year-old's goodness and bravery, how he greeted each day with a smile, how even at the end, he saw life as a great adventure. Rachel reassured his mother that he would never be forgotten, that years from now, people would remember him and speak of him with fondness and admiration.

But no matter what uplifting things she said—and

meant—he was still gone. She looked in his mother's eyes and saw that awful, gaping hole of loss and felt her own inability to make things any better as a blow straight to the heart.

Yes, she was trained to help cope with the death of a patient. But coping seemed a paltry thing, so pitiful and small and useless when stacked against the agony in a grieving mother's eyes.

She met Lily for lunch at their favorite place. Jenna didn't show.

Rachel told her friend about the loss of her patient and for a while they sat there, looking at all the food they'd ordered, neither of them really feeling much like eating.

Eventually, they started talking about Jenna. Jenna worked in the E.R. She saw death close-up and far too often, and somehow she'd kept her plucky, ready-for-anything attitude intact.

At one point, Rachel dared to suggest, "Do you think, maybe, she's still kind of…I don't know… *guarded* with us?"

Lily was shaking her head. "She just works too hard." And then they started talking baby showers. Rachel had had hers the month before.

"But Jenna hasn't." Lily was looking very pleased with herself.

Rachel asked, "Should we go for it, you think?"

It was a purely rhetorical question. Of course, they would go for it.

Before they left the restaurant, they had Jenna's shower halfway planned and Rachel's spirits had lifted, at least a little.

After her shift, she stopped in to see her mother. Ellen Stockham turned her face to the wall and whispered, "Go away."

The bright spark of optimism kindled during Rachel's lunch with Lily seemed to wink and go out.

When she got home, the guy down the street was mowing his postage-stamp of lawn—bare-chested in baggy cargos as always. He had an impressive six pack and shoulders for days. And she didn't even have to remind herself that he was out of bounds as an object for her fantasies.

Really, how could she lose herself in fantasy when her mother was in the hospital suffering from acute depression and a fine, bright young boy had just died?

She dragged herself inside, where the message light was blinking on her answering machine. It was Bryce. The sound of his voice, of the simple words, "How are you? Call me," sent a shiver of pleasure running under her skin.

So. The sight of the half-naked guy down the street

didn't tempt her anymore, but she had shivers to spare if Bryce Armstrong was calling.

Was this good news?

She couldn't decide. She didn't *want* to decide. She didn't want to do anything much. Maybe brew a pot of tea and watch the news, broil a lamb chop, turn in early…

Somehow, she never got around to calling Bryce back.

The week dragged by. She went to her patient's funeral on Thursday. The little chapel was packed. She listened to the minister talking about fearing no evil and the hope of the righteous and the innocent in death and didn't feel particularly comforted.

That night, she lay in her bed with her hand on the firm mound of her stomach and cried.

Friday, her mother didn't turn away when Rachel entered the room. Ellen Stockham even managed a quivery smile. Rachel sat with her for a while, holding her thin hand.

Before she left, she spoke with her mother's doctor. She learned that if her mother continued to improve, she would be discharged in a week or so. The doctor said what her mother's doctors always said. ''You're a nurse, Rachel. You have to know that, with proper medication, almost all bipolar patients can lead normal, productive lives. But then, the patient must be willing to stick with the course of treatment.''

Rachel nodded and promised—as she always promised—that she would encourage her mother to take her meds.

Bryce called again that night. She was there when the phone rang. She listened in as he left his message. ''Rachel. Just trying again. Call me back when you get a moment.'' His voice was flat. She almost picked up before he disconnected.

But she didn't.

Okay, she felt a little like a jerk. But her life was too complicated as it was. She just didn't have it in her to add a man to the mix. Especially not a guy like Bryce, who would probably get tired of her in no time flat. She just couldn't deal with it, with anything casual—or with letting herself start to feel too much for him and then having him walk away.

She wasn't regretting their one night or anything. She could never regret something so beautiful.

But if there was going to be more than one night, well, she wanted it all: a guy who would love her *and* her baby. A guy who could put up with her mother's scary, often overwhelming emotional disorder. A guy who was going to *be* there, just like in the marriage vows: For better or for worse.

It was a lot to ask of a man. And especially of a

man like Bryce, who had money to burn and a high-powered job and status and good looks and women falling all over him.

Really, that was the biggest fantasy, now wasn't it? That of all the gorgeous, willing, glamorous women he might have had, Bryce Armstrong had somehow decided he wanted *her.*

Only in her dreams.

So she didn't pick up—and she never called him back.

Lily asked about him three days later, on Monday night, during a phone conversation when they were *supposed* to be talking about Jenna's upcoming shower.

"So, what happened with the sexy CEO?" Lily asked—way too casually, Rachel thought. "You haven't mentioned him in days."

Rachel tried to be casual right back. "Oh, he called a couple of times," she said airily. "But you know how it is. I don't really think he's the guy for me."

"Why not?"

So okay. The airy approach wasn't working. Rachel moved on to huffing a little. "Well. Isn't it obvious?"

"No, not particularly."

So she let out a big sigh and ran down the list: the money, the Armstrong name, all the women…

Lily said, "Give a rich, powerful, hunk of a guy a chance, why don't you? And hey, so what if there have been lots of women, as long as he's ready to settle down now?"

"Lily, I only spent that one night with him. There was absolutely no talk of settling down."

"So maybe you should bring it up to him."

"Oh, I don't even imagine Bryce Armstrong is going to be interested in settling down."

"See. There. That's a conclusion and you're totally jumping to it. You don't know what the man's interested in. You don't know what he's willing to do. Because you haven't asked him."

"Well, but, I mean, he's not going to appreciate—"

"How do you know what he'll appreciate? Have you asked?"

Rachel huffed out another exasperated breath. "Why is it married people suddenly think they know it all when it comes to how to relate to a guy?" Lily, not only a true friend, but a smart one, knew when to say nothing. And that's what she did. Finally, Rachel grumbled, "Well, okay. Fine. Just what do you want me to do?"

"Oh, something simple. Maybe give the guy a chance?"

"What do you mean, give him a chance? We weren't...well, you know. It wasn't anything... serious, between us."

"Maybe it wasn't. And just maybe that's because you wouldn't let it be."

"Why does this all have to be my fault? You're my friend. Why can't you just do the usual and be blindly loyal?"

"This isn't about whose fault it is. And I *am* loyal. But sorry, I'm not blind."

There was a smudge on the counter. Rachel got the sponge and scrubbed at it—hard. "Well. He probably won't even call again."

"So call *him.*"

Rachel tossed the sponge into the sink. "I think we should get back to the subject of Jenna's baby shower."

But Rachel did take her friend's urgings to heart. She called him—or at least, she *started* to call him. Repeatedly. She would pick up the phone and begin dialing. Sometimes she'd even dial his whole number. But she could never bring herself to stay on the line until it actually rang.

On Thursday night, six days since the last time

he'd called and she hadn't answered, she *started* to call him again. But—surprise, surprise—she lost her nerve.

Thoroughly disgusted with herself, she went ahead and called Sears to order the curtains that she and her mother had picked out from the catalog that day. She disconnected the call—and the phone instantly rang again.

Without stopping to think that it might be the very man she didn't have the courage to call, she hit the talk button. "Hello?"

"Rachel," Bryce said. "At last."

Chapter 7

Rachel clutched the phone in a death grip. It was the only way she could keep herself from hanging up out of sheer nervous tension.

"Rachel. Are you there?"

"I...uh..."

"Rachel, please don't hang up."

She cleared her throat. "No. No, I won't. I'm here. I really am."

"You sound so strange. What's the matter? Is it the baby?"

"No. She's fine."

"Your mother, then?"

Her pulse was slowing a little, the feeling of blind panic passing. "She's better. She's, um, going home in a few days. I was just ordering her some curtains, as a matter of fact."

"Curtains…" He sounded puzzled.

Rachel told him the part she'd left out before. "She took a pair of scissors and really went after every curtain in her apartment. Sliced them to shreds. They were unsalvageable, so we're getting some new ones."

For a moment, there was silence. Then he asked hopefully, "But she *is* better?"

"Yeah. She is. And whether she stays better is a lot about the choices she makes. I can go on and on to her about sticking with her medication, taking care of herself, but if she won't do it…"

"Rachel."

"Yeah?"

"There are just some things you can't control."

"Tell me about it. And the good news is she does have decent insurance, which these days, is a miracle in itself. When she needs the care, she *can* get it."

There was a pause. Then he asked, "And what about you?" His voice was so soft. Can you wrap the sound of a man's voice around yourself?

Rachel longed to do just that. "Oh, I'm…" The words trailed off. She swallowed convulsively and forced herself to say what needed saying. "I'm so sorry I never called. It's just been…a bad time. And I don't really…well, I just didn't expect…''

''What? Tell me. You didn't expect…''

''You. I didn't expect *you*. You're just so…'' Words failed her. They seemed to keep doing that. But he waited so patiently until she finally said, ''I told myself it was just that one beautiful night. I was…ready for that. I could…deal with that…''

''Rachel?''

''Umm?''

''That one night?''

''Yeah?''

''It *was* beautiful.''

''Oh. Oh, yes. But…'' Again, he waited until she found the words. ''I, well, I told myself you couldn't possibly want more than that and at the same time, deep down I've been thinking that maybe you do. And, well, I don't seem to know how to handle that…how to just…let it happen.''

''I know,'' he said. And she realized she believed him, believed that he accepted her just as she was— imperfect and confused at times, and way too much on her guard. ''And Rachel?'' She made a small, questioning noise. It was the best she could do with her throat closing up and tears pushing behind her eyes. He said, ''I do want more. A lot more.''

''Oh,'' she whispered, clutching the phone so hard

she was vaguely surprised it didn't shatter in her hands. "Oh, God…"

"Rachel, let me come over. I won't stay long. I just need to see you."

She glanced from her aging refrigerator to the cracked tile on the counter by the coffeepot—and then up at that faint watermark on the ceiling where the roof had leaked last spring. She'd gotten the leak patched, but never quite found the time to repaint the kitchen.

A small, tight laugh escaped her. "Bryce. I have to warn you. It's hardly Portland Heights around here. No gourmet stove, you know? And the furniture in my living room cries out for reupholstering."

"I'm not coming to see the furniture. I want to see *you*."

"You…sound so sure."

"I *am* sure."

"But…well, you've been in *People* magazine. You're one of *the* Armstrongs. Gorgeous women fall all over you."

"There's only one gorgeous woman who interests me. I mean it, Rachel. Only one woman. And that woman is you. Give me your address."

She did—really fast, before her nerve got a chance to desert her again.

"I'm on my way."

* * *

They sat on her slightly threadbare sofa and kicked off their shoes and she told him about her twelve-year-old patient, the one who hadn't made it, about how death was hardest to take when they were so young, when there should be a future shining out in front of them—middle school and football and science projects and that first special girl…

Bryce listened as she poured it all out. When her voice trailed off, he held out his arms. She went into them eagerly, with a long, grateful sigh.

He brushed a kiss against her hair and didn't say anything—not that he was sorry, not what she should do, not how he was going to somehow make everything right.

She hugged him close and listened to the steady beat of his heart and then whispered, "Thanks."

He kissed her hair again. "For what?"

"For just listening and holding me. For not offering one single word of advice."

He chuckled, the sound a low, lovely rumble against her ear. "I see you've noticed I'm a man."

She grinned against his chest. "Hard to miss."

He hugged her closer. "And men give advice." He tipped her chin up with a finger. "I think I read somewhere that it's genetically programmed."

She stared into those wonderful, warm blue eyes. "But you didn't give me any advice just now."

"I didn't think you needed any. Your patient died. It's a hard thing to deal with, but you're doing it. I can't see any quick fix. If I could, I promise you, I'd be laying it on you." She sat up straight again. He let her go with obvious reluctance.

"As usual, I've been yammering on and on."

"Fine with me."

"So nice of you to say that. And obviously, I could yammer away at you all night—but if I did, I wouldn't learn anything I didn't already know. And there's so much you haven't told me…"

"Such as?"

"Well, your life story, for starters."

"Oh, that." His expression was deadpan, but there was no mistaking the smile in his voice.

"Please. I want to hear it all."

He chuckled. "You say that now."

"Honestly. I do want to know about you. You can start with your childhood…"

"Got a week?"

"Quit stalling."

"Okay, okay. My childhood was…" He thought for a moment, then finished, "Busy."

It seemed an odd word to choose. "You were a busy little kid?"

''I was an Armstrong. I was brought up to excel. There was always pressure to do well—at sports and especially in my studies. I look back on being a kid and what I remember is that I never really felt like one. There was too much I had to do and not enough time to do it in. It was understood from the first that I'd take over the business from my grandfather some-day.''

''But what about your dad? Wasn't he the next in line?''

''My dad had no interest in working. Didn't have the drive for it, he'd always say. It was one of the few things he and my grandfather were in complete agreement on. My grandfather didn't believe my dad had it in him to run a major corporation and my dad was perfectly willing to live off the income from his massive trust and support my grandfather in his dream to make *me* the next head of the company.''

''And where was your mother in all this?''

''Good question. One I'm still not sure I have the answer to. I remember my mother as beautiful and unavailable. Like some rare bird or an exotic butter-fly. She seemed to be always flitting into rooms and then flitting out again. If I tried to get near her, she'd just…fly away.''

''You didn't feel close to her?''

''*Close* is not a word I would use in conjunction

with either of my parents. They weren't close to their children. And they never seemed particularly close to each other. They made their perpetual mutual estrangement official when I was fifteen.''

''Meaning they divorced?''

He nodded. ''My mother promptly moved to Tuscany to be with some Italian guy she'd met at a wine-tasting. My father moved to L.A. She's been married twice since and he's been married three times.''

''What about you? And Chelsea? Did you go with one of them?''

''No. We stayed here—under the care of our grandparents. I lived with them when I wasn't at school. Chelsea had special needs. She was at school most of the time.''

''Special needs...''

''My sister's developmentally disabled.'' He grinned when he saw her surprise. ''Your mouth's hanging open, Rachel—and yes, as ideal as the life of an Armstrong might seem to the casual observer, there has been a challenge or two.''

''Chelsea...'' She said the name and then didn't know what to say next.

But Bryce did. ''She's a fighter, my sister. She's as brave and strong as they come. She's fortunate that she's what they call 'high-functioning.' She does have the capacity to live on her own, after painstaking training in the basic stuff: personal care, cooking and all the other daily living skills. Thanks to the family money, she's always had the best care and the best teachers, people who not only knew how to help her become more self-sufficient, but also gave her the love, support and encouragement our parents never provided.''

''And…now she's married?''

''That's right. His name is Thad Grover. He's also DD and high-functioning. They both went to the same special-needs school. Their marriage caused a major uproar in the family—at least with the grandparents. Our parents weren't here and didn't care.''

''Oh, Bryce…''

But he wasn't looking the least upset. ''And when I say uproar, I mean *strictly* within the family, of course. Nothing was allowed to leak to the press. My grandmother likes to think of herself as open-minded, but she's way old-school. She saw Chelsea as someone to be hidden away. God forbid my little sister should want a real life.''

''That's terrible.''

Bryce didn't seem to think so. ''You don't know Chelsea. She never gives up. She finally broke even our grandmother down. And now, since Ariel was born…''

Rachel saw his point. "A great-grandchild. What grandmother could resist?"

"Exactly. Especially a great-grandchild like Ariel. I swear to you Rachel, she is so special."

"Spoken like a doting uncle."

"I don't deny it," he said and she turned to lean back against him, hoisting her feet up onto the couch in front of her. He wrapped his arms around her and kissed the top of her head. "Anyway, so now, both the grandparents are busy rewriting history. To hear them tell it these days, it was their idea that Chelsea and Thad should get married in the first place."

"So. It all...worked out, then?"

"Yeah. Well, as long as you don't count my parents. They're both still more or less wandering in the wilderness. Last I heard, my dad checked himself into rehab. Again. And my mother's got a new boyfriend, though there's no rumor of a wedding. Yet."

He felt so warm and solid at her back. Really, he was a great guy for leaning on. He'd laid one arm along the top of the couch. The other he rested, lightly, on the swell of her stomach. "There," he said and felt for her hand so he could press it against the right spot. "Feel that..."

She smiled her secret mother's smile and didn't remind him that the movements were happening inside her and of course she felt them—whether she had her hand at the spot or not. "Umm…"

He brushed his lips over her ear. "It's getting late…and I said I wouldn't stay too long."

With a happy sigh, she snuggled in closer. "Let's sit right here, forever."

He smoothed her hair aside and kissed the pulse at her temple. "Don't you have to work tomorrow?"

"Yeah, so?"

"You need your sleep."

She sighed again. "You may have a point."

He nuzzled her hair. "But how about tomorrow evening?"

"Hmm. I could be available…to the right guy."

"It's only fair to warn you, I'm talking about a big step here. A major step. A very scary step…"

Her mouth felt dry enough that she had to swallow. And then she elbowed him in the ribs.

"Hey! Watch it." He chuckled in her ear.

"Stop teasing. What are you getting at?"

"Dinner with the family…and relax. I only mean Chelsea and Thad and Ariel. My grandparents are out of town until next week. You can meet them then."

"Dinner with the family?" she gulped again. "Already?"

He whispered in her ear, "Please don't start talking about how we should take things slow…"

"But I...well, isn't this all just happening really fast?"

"And didn't I tell you that first day that fast was fine with me?"

"Yeah, but—"

"And we can stop by for a quick visit with your mom on the way."

"My mom? But—"

"Come on." He guided her to sit up and reached for his shoes. "Walk me to the door."

She went out on her tiny square of porch with him and he pulled her close for one last kiss. She concentrated on the strength in his arms around her, on the sweetness of his mouth playing over hers.

"Tomorrow," he said, as he turned to go. "Six o'clock. Be ready."

Chapter 8

Rachel slept poorly. Second thoughts kept her awake.

Bryce said he was just fine with things happening fast. Good for him.

She wasn't fine with it. She simply didn't have his guts, his go-for-it attitude—at least not when it came to giving her heart.

Her heart was a tender thing, thank you. And she just wasn't up for having it broken again.

Oh, and what about the baby? Could he really be ready for that?

As she lay there, curled around her burgeoning

stomach, staring at the shadowed wall a few feet from the bed, she found herself thinking of her father, remembering the times he was supposed to come for her and didn't show up. How she'd sit on the creaky front porch step and wait.

And wait some more…

Until the door behind her would open and her mother, standing inside the screen, would coax, "Come in now, Rachel. Just come on inside."

And Rachel would argue, "But I can't. I have to be here when he gets here."

The screen door would screech open and her mother would step outside. Arms wrapped tight around her middle, she'd loom over Rachel, scowling down. "If he was coming, he'd be here by now." Her mother's lips were always a thin, pressed-together line at those times, as if she was barely holding in a lot of very mean words.

"Mommy, I can't go in. What if he comes and sees I'm not here and thinks I didn't wait?"

"Rachel. For crying out loud. If he was coming, he'd have been here three hours ago. He's *not* coming for you. Get that through your thick little head…"

Rachel squirmed in the bed, flipped to her other side, then flopped right back to where she'd started.

Oh, she was just a classic case, wasn't she? A

manic-depressive mother and an absentee father had made her into someone who was really bad at giving her trust.

And now she was a grown-up. Thirty-four years old. Wasn't it about time she stopped living by the emotional limitations so painfully acquired in her childhood?

She thought back on the two serious relationships she'd had—one with a guy she'd met at a party while she was still in nursing school, the other, more recently, with a pharmaceuticals salesman. Both men had broken up with her in the end. But if she were honest, she'd have to admit that she'd never let either of those guys get too close. Danny Davison, the salesman, had even bought her a ring and asked her to marry him. She'd put him off, said she needed more time….

Danny had grown tired of waiting. And so had Tate Connor, the guy she'd dated while she was in nursing school. In both cases, she'd blamed the men for leaving her.

But now, lying here wide awake in the middle of the night, terrified to go ahead and take a chance on Bryce, she was seeing things in a different light.

She'd made Danny and Tate *wait*, hadn't she? Just like her dad had made *her* wait all those years before.

And now, here she was, three months away from

having a daughter of her own. What lessons—consciously or otherwise—would she teach her child? Would her little girl grow up as afraid of trusting a man as she seemed to be?

Rachel pressed a hand protectively over her belly and the new life inside her. "I'm going to do better," she whispered to her little one. "I'm going to...put myself out there, put my heart on the line. Sweetheart, I want to be able to show you what love really is. I want to be ready, to be the best mom I can be."

At five-thirty the next afternoon, Rachel was all dressed up in a heather-gray twinset and black A-line skirt, ready to go to dinner at Chelsea and Thad's—following a delightful detour to the psychiatric ward, of course. She paced back and forth in the living room for a few minutes, ordering those old demons to get out of her head when they kept trying to whisper in her ear, *He's not coming.*

After ten minutes or so of walking back and forth and fighting off her ingrained fears, she decided she couldn't stay in that room one minute longer. She grabbed her purse and went out the door.

She sat on the step, just as she had done so long ago, when she waited for her father, who never came. It seemed appropriate, somehow, to defy all her own inner terrors so boldly.

Appropriate, and awful. Her heart pounded as if she'd run a long race. And her palms were sweating. And those old demons in her head?

They seemed to be chanting in glee: *He's not coming, not coming, not coming...*

She wanted to leap up and run back inside, lock the door, shut the curtains, turn off all the lights. She wanted, above all, *not* to be waiting if he didn't show up. But somehow she made herself sit there, made herself take slow, even breaths.

And silently, she talked back to those demons in her head: He *is* coming. I can trust him. He *wants* to be with me...and with my baby.

By the time Bryce's Mercedes eased up to the curb—two minutes early—she was sweating up her twinset and trembling a little, but she was still sitting right there on the step.

She rose on shaky legs and started down the walk as he got out and came around the front of the car.

They met on the sidewalk.

Frowning, he scanned her face. "You're white as a sheet. What's happened?"

She let out a tight laugh. "Oh, nothing. I was just sitting on the step. I was just...waiting..."

He touched her face. "You're sweating."

"Yeah..." She swayed against him and his strong arms were waiting to pull her close.

"You're shaking. Are you sick?" He held her so gently, so cherishingly, stroking her hair, rubbing her back.

She laid her head against his shoulder, breathed in the heavenly scent of him. "I'm okay. I'll be okay…"

He lifted her chin and made her look at him. "You're sure?"

She nodded. "Really. I'm okay." She stepped out of the shelter of his arms and pulled her shoulders back. "I have…some things to tell you. Later. But for now, let's go. Let's get this done."

His silky brows were still drawn together. "You're nervous? About my meeting your mom? About dinner at Chelsea's?"

"Right on both counts. Now, let's go."

Chapter 9

Her mother was sitting in the chair by one of the room's two narrow windows when Rachel led Bryce in. It was a double room, a drawn curtain down the center of it, masking off a second window and the other bed on the far side.

"Rachel." Her mother's smile was genuine. Then the big dark eyes found the man who filled up the doorway. Her thin hand went to her uncombed hair and fluttered quickly down to her lap. "I...wasn't expecting company..."

Rachel reached behind her, felt for Bryce's hand. It was right there, his fingers automatically slipping between hers, sending a message of warmth and support. He moved forward to stand beside her. "Mom. It's okay. We won't stay long. I just…I want you to meet Bryce Armstrong."

Her mother stared at him for a moment, her expression unsure. And then her smile returned. "Well. Hello, Bryce. I'm Ellen. So nice to meet a friend of my daughter's."

"Hello, Ellen."

So, okay. They'd gotten through the introductions. Bryce was smiling. Her mother was smiling.

What next?

Sit, she thought. They should sit down for a minute or two. She pulled her hand from Bryce's—well, yanked it free, really. "Uh. Chairs. We need—"

"Right here." He'd already picked up the one by the door. He carried it over and set it down next to her mother.

There wasn't another one. "I'll ask the orderly." Rachel started for the hallway.

"Wait," said her mother. "Linda?" she called. "May we use your chair?"

"Oh, all right," a voice from behind the curtain grumbled.

At Rachel's questioning glance, her mother mouthed, "Suicide attempt" with a philosophical shrug. Then, in a whisper, "They put her in here this morning.'' And finally, at full volume, ''Thanks, Linda!''

''Yeah, whatever,'' Linda called back grudgingly.

Bryce went behind the curtain. She heard his words of polite greeting.

Linda mumbled something and Bryce emerged with another chair. They sat. Her mother looked from Rachel to Bryce and back again. Rachel slid a glance at Bryce. He looked so at ease, so completely relaxed. How did he do it?

Her mom cleared her throat. ''So, this is something…special going on here?''

As Rachel agonized over her answer, Bryce said, ''Yes, it is.'' He said it so simply, without the slightest hesitation. Rachel wanted to grab him and hug him—and never let go.

Her mother's smile widened. ''Well.'' Ellen shot a pointed glance at Rachel's round stomach. ''How nice…'' She'd made no secret of the fact that she thought Rachel should have found a husband first and *then* started thinking about having a baby. It was an attitude that Rachel had found supremely irritating. After all, when you got right down to it, a fat lot of good it had done her mother to find a husband first.

Bryce asked how her mother was doing and Ellen launched into a blow-by-blow of her most recent stay

at Portland General's psychiatric ward: which nurses
were angels, which ones she couldn't stand. How the
food here was pretty good. She especially enjoyed
the rice pudding, which she could get on Tuesdays
and Fridays. And she was making a point to take *all*
her medications. And she *was* doing better. She sent
Rachel a defiant look.

Oh, yes.

Better every day...

Every time Rachel dared to hope she might be
winding down, Bryce would ask another question
and off she'd go again.

Rachel almost interrupted more than once to say
they ought to get going. But clearly, Bryce could take
care of himself. If he'd had enough of her mother's
never-ending answers, he could stop asking questions.

She watched her mother chattering away about the
minutia of her days and a certain tenderness welled
up inside her. Tenderness and gratitude.

Ellen Stockham might not have been the best
mother in the world, but she *had* always been there,
she'd stuck with it. As poorly suited as her illness
had made her for mothering, she'd never walked
away from the job.

There was much Rachel would have to learn for

herself about raising a child. But when it came to loyalty and commitment and sticking around…

Thanks to her mother, she had those qualities.

When they got up to go, Bryce bent to kiss her mother's dry cheek. "I'll see you again, Ellen. Soon."

Her mother beamed up at him. "That would be so nice…"

Chelsea and Thad and Ariel lived in a three-bedroom cottage nestled in the oaks on Bryce's property.

"This way they have their privacy," he explained. "And I'm right here if they need me. There's a driver to take them wherever they need to go. And Mrs. Davenbrook, who's worked for our family for over thirty years, is devoted to Chelsea. She looks in on her several times a day."

Bryce rang the bell. When the door flew back, a tall, stunning blonde in a sweet-looking floral-print dress stood on the other side. Childlike pleasure flooded her angel's face. "Bryce! You're here!"

He held out his arms and his sister, long, silky hair flying, flung herself into them. She clasped her slim hands around his waist, squeezing hard. "Hug, hug," she crowed and laughed in delight.

Behind her, a man stood holding a wooden bowl

full of pretzels. He was six or seven inches shorter than Chelsea, with brown hair and dark eyes and a slightly befuddled expression. "Hello, Bryce," he said shyly and then he looked at Rachel. "Hello," he said carefully, as if not quite sure of the word.

"Hello," Rachel replied.

Bryce managed to pry his sister's hugging hands away and made the introductions.

"Rachel!" Chelsea repeated when Bryce said her name. "Hello!" She reached right out and patted Rachel's tummy. "A baby. How nice."

"Sleeping," Chelsea announced when Bryce asked about his niece. "But you can see her..."

So they all tiptoed into the nursery and stood over the crib and Chelsea pantomimed "Shh..." with great enthusiasm as they admired the dreaming darling in the pink fleece footie pajamas.

They trooped back out into the living room. "Please have a pretzel," offered Thad solemnly.

So they sat and munched a few pretzels and chatted for a while. Rachel explained that she was a nurse and Thad spoke of his own job. He worked full-time at a local Burger King.

"He is the best worker there," Chelsea piped up proudly and patted her husband's leg. "And sometimes he brings me home a Whopper."

Eventually they moved into the kitchen for the meat loaf and mashed potatoes Chelsea had prepared.

"But Charles helped," Thad announced. Charles, Rachel remembered, was Bryce's cook.

Chelsea took that extra few seconds both she and her husband seemed to require to digest whatever was said to them and then nodded. "Charles is always helping. I *like* Charles."

Thad considered. "Me, too," he said.

Chelsea turned to Rachel. "And I like *you.*" She beamed and Rachel's heart just went to mush. "You can come see us any time. You and your baby, too, when your baby comes. Ariel will like that. She will want to have friends."

Rachel promised she would come again and a little later, when Thad and Chelsea walked them to the door, Chelsea made the offer a second time. "Please come back. Come back soon."

"I will. I promise…"

Rachel and Bryce walked out into the brisk early-May evening, Thad and Chelsea moving into the open doorway behind them. Bryce took Rachel's hand and they started down the walk to the garages behind the main house.

"Goodbye, come again!" Chelsea called from behind them. Rachel glanced back and saw Bryce's sister and her husband standing in the doorway, the flood of light from inside pouring out around them.

"I will!" Rachel called back.

At Rachel's house, Bryce came around and opened the car door for her. He took her hand to help her out. The cracked concrete walkway was too narrow for them to approach the house side-by-side, but she held tightly to his hand anyway, leading him along.

Inside, she turned on the lamps and they sat on the sofa, shucking out of their shoes, shifting around so they were facing each other.

"You were so great with my mother," she said. "Thank you. And your sister and Thad...they're really happy together, aren't they?"

He nodded. "They have what matters most. In fact, I'd say the two of them showed me what life—and love—could be."

"I can see how they could do that."

He looked so solemn suddenly, as solemn as Thad. "I've...been with a lot of women, Rachel."

She felt her mouth twisting wryly. "So I've heard."

Now he looked earnest. He leaned in a little closer. "But in the last couple of years, I *have* been seriously looking for the *right* woman. The one who'd not only have me wanting to make passionate, wild love to her—but the one I'd want to talk with for hours, the one I'd want to hold so close while we're sleeping. The one who, when the day's over, I wouldn't be able to wait to come home to.''

''Tall order,'' she whispered.

''That day,'' he said. ''That first day, that first moment I saw you, all dewy-eyed over that little sweater with the ribbons all over it, a voice in my head said, There. That's the one. Too damn bad she's already taken…I almost turned and walked away. Fast. But then I couldn't stop myself from getting you talking, couldn't fight the need to hear your voice. And when you looked up at me with those big brown eyes…*pow*. I was done for. I was gone for good. And then you told me that you *weren't* taken. From that moment on, my fate was sealed…''

Rachel knew she should say something. But what do you say when a guy you almost didn't dare dream of tells you he knew the moment he saw you that you were the woman for him? There were no words, just a warm pressure at the back of her throat, a lifting feeling in her chest.

He asked, so gently, ''What happened to you, tonight, before I picked you up? Can you tell me now?''

She nodded.

He waited, then gave her his crooked grin.
"Well?"

Oh, where to start? She didn't know how to explain. But then she just opened her mouth and said, "When I was little..." and it was okay. She was talking about it, all of it, from the father who abandoned her to the men she had kept waiting who'd finally given up and left her, too. She said, "So I was making myself sit on the porch and wait for you. I was...proving to myself that I could trust you, that you would come through, you wouldn't let me down."

"I won't let you down, Rachel. I swear to you. I'll be here, for you and the baby. If you'll have me."

"Oh," she said, her heart light as air. "Oh, yes. I'll have you. I..." Her nerve kind of wavered. She cleared her throat. "But what about your grandparents? How are they going to react when you tell them you're marrying an ordinary, everyday woman who's six months pregnant by a man she's never met?"

"They'll be shocked. At first. And then they'll get to know you and everything will work out fine."

"I don't know..."

"Rachel. They *will* accept you. And if they were really stupid and didn't, well, it would be their loss— but it's not going to happen that way. Don't forget, in the end, they accepted Thad."

She was shaking her head. "You're a brave, brave man."

"I'm a smart man. I know what I want. And Rachel, what I want is you. And your daughter. I want her to be *my* daughter, too. And I want to be your husband for the rest of our lives." He leaned closer, whispered, "I love you…and do not start telling me how this is so sudden."

"Well, but it—"

He put a finger to her lips. "There you go again."

"Oh, Bryce…"

"Sudden," he whispered, "is fine with me. Sudden is just great."

"Oh, Bryce…"

"I love you," he said again, the words so simple, direct. Honest.

With a glad cry, she reached for him. His arms were there to take her in. "Oh, Bryce…"

"I love you," he said one more time.

And she bravely whispered, "I…love you, too," just as his lips met hers.

* * * * *

JENNA'S HAVING A BABY

Laurie Paige

To the Wanderers, for whom no mountain is too high.

Chapter 1

Jenna Cooper glanced at the clock. Time for her dinner break. Actually it was two hours past time, but who noticed the little things when one was having fun? Fun, as in a wreck on the freeway during rush hour, a shoot-out between neighbors over a cat using a flower bed as a litter box—a flesh wound, but it could have been much worse—and a fist fight between two teenage brothers that had resulted in their mother getting a black eye and a scratch on her cornea when she stepped in to break it up.

The boys were contrite and shaken by the incident. As they should be.

What was with people this weekend? It was only the second Friday of May. The Oregon weather was balmy; it wasn't like July, when tempers frayed due to the heat.

The facetious streak evaporated as she thought of the victims of the car accident. Luckily only two vehicles and three people were involved in the mishap. The drivers had escaped with minor injuries, but the two-year-old girl who had been in one of the cars was now in critical care in the pediatrics wing of Portland General.

Jenna hated for children to be hurt. Adults were supposed to protect the little ones, not tailgate each other on the interstate highway at seventy miles per hour.

Frowning with disapproval, she closed up the Emergency Room report on the toddler, placed it in the stack to be filed, then stood, yawned and stretched. Using the tips of her fingers, she massaged her lower spine.

Had anyone mentioned that pregnancy was hard on the back in those baby books she'd been ardently reading of late? Now in her fifth month, she was beginning to burst out all over, one might say.

"I'm going to eat," she told the E.R. receptionist.

"Got your pager on?" the woman asked.

Jenna checked to be sure. "Sure have."

Last night the E.R. doctor had been irked with her when she couldn't be reached because she'd accidentally hit the off button. However, she hadn't been goofing off.

As the senior nurse on her shift, it was part of her job to make sure the emergency medical supplies had been replenished from the main stockroom, and that's what she'd been doing when the next case, a heart attack patient, had come in. Dr. Thompson had been coldly, but politely, furious when she'd returned, innocently unaware of a problem.

There were other nurses in the E.R. besides her, she'd felt like telling him. Instead she'd checked the pager, apologized and continued her duties as if her feelings weren't smarting at the reprimand, the first she'd ever gotten from him.

Oh, well. She shrugged philosophically and stopped in the bathroom to freshen up before going to the cafeteria.

Frowning at herself in the mirror, she noted the fact that she'd forgotten mascara so that her eyes looked like two chips of lapis lazuli surrounded by barely discernible light-brown fringes. Her string-straight hair hung like limp curtains at each side of her face when she removed the band that held it out of the way.

At least the hair was naturally blond. That was the

only good thing she could find to say about it at present.

After combing, then refastening the fine strands into a ponytail, she splashed water on her face, dried off, put on lipstick so she didn't quite look as if she should be laid out on a gurney bound for the morgue and hurried out.

She retrieved her food from the refrigerator in the E.R. supply room and walked briskly along the corridor. It seemed to be a slow night in the rest of the hospital.

Dr. Thompson, head of E.R., was at the table reserved for medical personnel in the cafeteria. A surprise, that. He was sort of gruff, taciturn and aloof from the rest of the staff. But very handsome.

He was thirty-eight to her thirty-four, four or five inches taller than her five-eight height and had black hair and brown eyes. While he was invariably civil, his thoughts and emotions were as inviolate as a sphinx.

Since there wasn't another soul in the staff area, she plunked her home-prepared food down at the round table where he was reading the paper. A muffin and a cup of coffee were in front of him.

"Is that your dinner?" she asked, setting a pint of milk on the table, then opening the containers that held her own nutritious meal.

He glanced at her, at the plastic dishes filled with good things, then the muffin. "It's enough," he said.

"Huh," she said in disagreement.

He glanced her way again. She expected a frown, but he smiled slightly.

"Wow," she said softly, "you're incredibly good-looking when you do that."

The thick eyebrows rose fractionally. His eyebrows and lashes were jet black like his hair. She envied him that.

"When I do what?" he asked.

"Smile." She wrinkled her nose at him, then grinned.

He was technically her boss, so she probably shouldn't be teasing him. Her smart mouth was her besetting sin…well, the main one, at any rate.

"I'll share if you will," she told him.

Before he could object, she went to the counter and grabbed a paper plate, along with a plastic fork and knife. She returned to the table and divided her bowl of chicken salad, which was crammed with almonds, apples and raisins as well as white chicken cubes, into two even portions. She did the same with the fruit salad, baby carrots and whole wheat, low-fat, low-sodium crackers.

"Here," she said and pushed the plate toward him with one hand while she confiscated the unwrapped

muffin with the other. She opened it, cut it in half
and kept one for herself. "There," she said in sat-
isfaction, giving his part back to him. "There's non-
fat milk in the fridge."

"Aren't you going to bring it to me?" His tone
was dry, but it did contain a shred of amusement.

"Why? You got a broken leg?" She silently
groaned after the wisecrack slipped out. She waited
for him to put her in her place. Politely, of course.

His smile broadened a tiny bit as he went to fetch
his own drink. He wasn't given to throwing pleas-
antries around, she'd noticed in the years they'd
worked together.

Two months ago, he'd assumed total charge of the
Emergency Room after the old doctor who'd been
there about a hundred years finally retired. She wondered if she should mention her plan for when the
baby came. She was going to take six months off,
thanks to her split of the $500,000 lottery she and
Lily and Rachel had won last year.

The other two were her best friends from high
school days. The three had gone through nurses'
training together at the University of Oregon. They
had also agreed to have babies via artificial insemination when they reached thirty-four, assuming three
Mr. Rights hadn't come along by then.

The ideal man hadn't materialized for any of them,

so they'd put their plan in action after winning the money, which they'd taken as a good omen.

They'd needed the change in fortune, Jenna mused. Lily had been left at the altar on her wedding day a year ago last June. The three had won the lottery that same day.

That's when they'd decided to heck with men, they would have children without 'em!

Well, not exactly. They'd gone to a clinic for a little help in that department. Later, tired of Lily pining over her lost love, Rachel had admitted she'd had a one-night stand with the former fiancé, not knowing at the time that he was Lily's mysterious Mr. X, the man she'd been dating in secret while his divorce came through.

Mr. Louse was a better description, Jenna mentally corrected. He'd caused a terrible breach in the women's friendship, and Jenna had been caught in the middle between the other two. They'd only recently started speaking to each other again. It had been a difficult year—

"What is it?" her companion asked.

Jenna was shaken out of her introspection. "What?"

"You're frowning," he told her.

"Oh." She opened her mouth, then closed it. The three pregnancies had already caused the gossip mill to grind overtime in their community. She wasn't going to add to it by airing her feelings.

"Are you doing okay?" He gestured vaguely toward her.

"Yes. I've had no problems since I got past that dreadful first three months."

He nodded solemnly.

She felt heat creep into her face. Everyone in the E.R. had been aware of her distress. She had never had trouble with nausea in her life, but during those early days she'd dashed to the rest room frequently while her body adjusted to the pregnancy. The other nurses had thought the situation was hilarious.

Right. Ha-ha.

Glancing his way, she saw his eyes locked on her, his gaze starkly intense as he studied the portion of her body visible above the table. She was sure his mind wasn't on her, but on the past.

His wife and unborn child had died in an accident two years ago when her car had been struck by a drunken driver. For months afterward, looking into his eyes had been like looking into twin pits of hell. Everyone knew he blamed himself. The couple had quarreled and his wife had driven off in a fury.

Since Jenna had become noticeably pregnant, she'd found his gaze on her at odd moments in this same manner, as if all were dark and hurting inside him, as if she reminded him of that painful time in his life.

She lowered her gaze and concentrated on finishing every bite of her dinner. She needed the energy to make it until ten o'clock. She'd opted to work four ten-hour shifts, Wednesday through Saturday, since the pregnancy, thinking she'd get more done on refinishing the baby furniture her father had brought up after she'd told him the news.

"Now you're smiling," the doctor said. "Your moods are as changeable as the weather."

"I'm refinishing my old baby furniture. I've never tried anything like that, so it's been an interesting learning experience."

"I've found most learning experiences result from some disaster or another," he said wryly.

She had to laugh. "Yes. I've discovered you can't mix water-based paint with oil-based. Actually, I knew that, but I was so excited to be doing something for the baby, I forgot to check the labels when I poured the new paint into the roller tray over the remains of the first can." She sighed loudly. "One can recover, though. It's a matter of patience and persistence."

His eyes seemed fathoms deep as he observed her over the edge of the milk carton. When he set the empty carton aside, he murmured, "There are some things beyond recovery."

Her heart went out to him. He hadn't forgiven himself for his part in his family's tragedy. Just as her pregnancy signaled a new turn in her life, she thought the competent, workaholic doctor needed a new turn in his.

He also needed something to focus on besides the hospital and the trauma cases he treated. There had to be more to life than other people's tragedies. Thank goodness she had something special to look forward to.

She laid a hand on her side where the baby was kicking as if practicing for a soccer game. She was aware of her own blessings and grateful that she'd decided to have this child, that she had a dependable career and could afford to take care of it.

"Maybe," she said gently in answer to his statement. "But most are, I think."

His expression hardened and his gaze became cynical. "Not all."

There didn't seem to be much to add to that. After polishing off her half of the banana-nut muffin, she rose. "I think I'll get back."

At that moment, the pager on her belt vibrated. She jerked, startled.

Eric Thompson looked at his pager. ''Emergency,'' he said. ''Let's go.''

Together they hurried down the hall to meet the new crisis.

Chapter 2

Two hours later, Eric threw the wrinkled E.R. scrubs into the laundry bin, then washed his hands and face. After drying off on paper towels, he used an alcohol gel on his hands as a final precaution.

Heading for the parking lot, he wondered why he was so careful. Habit, he supposed. He'd tried not to bring germs home to his family. Now, he no longer had anyone at home to be careful for.

Pushing the dark thoughts into the back corner of his mind, he hurried across the parking lot. After unlocking his car, he paused before climbing in and frowned as a boy on a skateboard, who looked around thirteen or fourteen years old, hurtled down the slope of the E.R. driveway. If the kid couldn't stop in time and shot across the sidewalk into the street, there could be a serious accident.

He glanced toward the hedge that divided the parking area from the street. No vehicles in sight, thank God.

Every nerve in his body jerked when he spotted someone on the other side of the hedge, a person with smooth blond hair. Jenna! She'd left the hospital by the side door and was on the sidewalk, heading that way.

The kid, making no attempt to slow down, whizzed toward the spot where the hospital driveway and the sidewalk crossed. Jenna, looking down, hurried on her way toward the same spot. Eric shouted and sprinted toward the pair.

He saw the surprise on her face as she paused by a car parked at the curb, and glanced toward the E.R. entrance to make sure no ambulance was about to pull out.

The boy, looking equally startled, was headed directly at her. She leaped back.

Eric's heart gave a painful lurch as he witnessed the kid's shoulder swipe Jenna. The boy swept past her at full tilt and disappeared down the street, obviously wanting to get away from the scene and the possible repercussions.

The pregnant E.R. nurse careened off the fender of the parked car, then hit the sidewalk. Fear crawled over his skin like a thousand millipedes leaping onto his back. He muttered a curse as he finally reached Jenna, who struggled to a sitting position.

"Don't move," he advised, kneeling beside her and visually examining her for injury. At least she wasn't bleeding anywhere that he could see.

"Can't," she gasped.

He realized she'd had the breath knocked out of her. "Arms over your head," he said and helped her lift them. "Now compress."

He gently coaxed her to bend forward to push air out of her lungs until her diaphragm began working once more. He heard her breath catch, then she inhaled fully. Supporting her as she leaned into him, he let her get her breath back before slipping his hands around her and palpating her abdomen to assess any possible damage.

"I'm okay," she said. "A bit bruised but not broken. Help me up."

He did so, but kept an arm around her waist as she stood. He could feel tremors running through her body.

"Let's go inside. You'll need to stay overnight—"

"I want to go home."

He frowned as she pushed away from him and, hand shaking badly, tried to fit the key into the lock of her car she'd crashed into.

"You could have been seriously injured," he scolded. "You need to pay attention to what's going on around you. Surely you heard the noise from the skateboard and realized it was close."

"I'll listen more carefully next time."

Spunky, he thought, a tug of admiration surprising him. But foolish. "You live alone, don't you?"

"Yes, in a condo on Burney." She opened the door.

"You're in no shape to drive."

Her hair band was gone, and the wind blew the long gossamer fine strands around her face. Without thinking, he tucked it behind her ears when she tried to get it out of her eyes with a toss of her head.

For a second, he let his fingers linger in the silky warmth. The fragrance of flowers came to him from her body, heated from the accident.

"I think I'm going to be sick," she said in a low voice, as if she didn't want anyone to overhear her admit to weakness.

As she turned and bent forward, he moved with her, cupping his body behind hers and putting his hands on her abdomen and forehead as her body reacted to the trauma with dry heaves. After a few seconds, she brought the spasms under control and leaned against the car, her forehead resting on her arm, hiding her face from him.

"Jenna?"

"I'm all right," she assured him.

Eric didn't move away or release his hold around her waist. With his free hand, he rubbed her shoulders until he felt her relax. Now that the emergency was over, other sensations came to the forefront of his mind.

He noticed her breasts brushed his arm with each long, shuddering breath she took. He sternly curbed an urge to turn his hand just enough to cup the alluring weight, and tease her nipple into attention.

Next, he became aware that his feet were planted on each side of hers so that her hips fit snugly against his groin. When she shifted her weight, he felt the movement in an intimate manner. To his shock and more than a little consternation, his body reacted with a strong surge of blood in the nether regions. Hunger pulsed through him, causing a wave of need so strong he almost groaned aloud.

He cursed silently and tried to imagine diving into a snowbank in the middle of winter. His libido reminded him it was spring and hot...damned hot...

She moved again, and he stepped back a few

inches. She indicated her purse, clasped to her side. "When I heard you shout, I thought it was a mugger." She laughed. "At least I still have my dowry."

Her words didn't make any sense. He gazed deeply into her eyes when she glanced at him over her shoulder. Was she hallucinating?

"A line from a play," she explained. "*Sweet Charity*. Neil Simon. Her boyfriend ran off with her savings—"

"Come on," he said, "let's get you home."

He locked her car door, then led her to his vehicle. After fastening her into the passenger seat, he got in the driver's side and started the engine.

"My car—"

"Will be fine for the night," he told her. "I'll call the security chief at the hospital and tell him what happened. He'll keep an eye on it."

She nodded, sighed and leaned her head on the seat without further argument. He kept an eye on her after she closed her eyes and seemingly went to sleep.

"Which one's yours?" he asked when they arrived at the residential complex. He'd recalled the place after she'd mentioned the street.

"Park in the next section," she directed. "Slot 2A."

He eased into the parking space and turned off the engine. "Stay put," he ordered.

Going around the four-wheel-drive SUV, he helped her out and, holding her elbow, ushered her to the condo she pointed out. She kept stealing glances at him.

"What?" he finally asked, wondering if she'd caught the vibes of desire he was probably giving off with every step.

"I didn't realize you were so chivalrous, doctor."

"Eric," he corrected.

"Eric," she said softly.

The wind blew across the back of his neck just then, making the word feel like a verbal caress. Another wave of hunger washed over him. He set his jaw and helped her up the three steps to her front porch.

The outside light gleamed on her hair, turning it into a pale halo around her face. He'd never really noticed how pretty she was, not in any personal way, at any rate. Now he couldn't seem to stop.

Her lips were full and well-defined as if they'd been chiseled by a master sculptor. Her eyes were deep, pure blue. Her hair was Nordic blond.

Viking blood. The image fit with the fantasy that was growing in his imagination.

Inhaling deeply, he managed to direct his mind to

the practicalities of taking her key and opening the door, then flicking on the wall switch and seating her on the sofa before taking her purse, which she gave up without a struggle, and placing it on the coffee table.

"Lie down," he said.

Her glance was plainly startled. "What for?"

"I, uh, need to examine you for bleeding or amniotic fluid seepage."

"Oh." She looked past him. "I can check," she said.

He started to protest, then he realized she was embarrassed. That surprised him. After all, he was a doctor and quite used to looking at the human body.

But not hers. A strong surge of heat rioted through his blood at the thought. It had been a long time since he'd reacted this way to a woman. It was damned annoying.

Sitting beside her, he laid his hands on her abdomen. He watched her for signs of discomfort as he pressed along her sides. "Do you have pain anywhere? Any cramps in the lower back or abdomen? Does your head hurt? Your shoulder?"

She shook her head to each question.

"Follow my finger," he ordered, unwilling to give up until he was sure she was okay.

She rolled her eyes in exasperation, then smiled in

her usual sunny fashion and did as she was told. Her eyes stayed focused. She'd walked from the car to the condo without wobbling. She didn't seem to be in pain.

"Where's the bathroom?" he asked.

She nodded down the hallway. He helped her to her feet.

"I'll walk you to the door," he said in no uncertain terms when she tried to step away from him.

"Yes, sir, doctor, sir," she said meekly.

He grinned. She was back to normal. Her insouciance was one of the things he liked about her. That, and her way with panicky patients, not to mention their relatives, in the Emergency Room. She was an excellent E.R. nurse.

Propped against the wall, he waited for her return. His stomach growled. He was hungry in more ways than one.

"How about a cup of hot chocolate?" he asked when she reappeared. "I'm expert at making it."

She considered, then nodded. "The kitchen is that way." She pointed down the short hallway.

A fact he'd already ascertained. A set of stairs led to the second floor, where he assumed the bedrooms were. "Let's get you to bed, then I'll bring it up to you."

Again a quick glance from her before she started

up the steps. There were three rooms upstairs, he found. Two were bedrooms and the other a home office with a nice desk and computer. He wondered what she used them for.

"In here." She pointed to one of the bedrooms.

The room was painted with one of those faux finishes that looked like real plaster with a blue wash on it. The bed was made up with a blue and yellow floral coverlet and striped sheets that matched the drapes. Like her, it was pretty and compelling in its femininity.

He left her to get into her pajamas while he raided the kitchen and put in the call to hospital security. In less than ten minutes, he'd completed his task and was carrying a tray with two cups and a plate of cookies up the stairs.

Jenna was just pulling the sheet back when he entered the bedroom. Her nightgown was ankle length, but that didn't stop him from seeing the shape of her legs, the sweet curve of her hips and rounded tummy or the thrust of her breasts against the cotton. The bedside lamp was behind her and displayed her charms in a mind-boggling silhouette.

He stopped at the foot of the bed as if his feet were suddenly glued to the floor. His mouth went dry. A pulse hammered in his temples, sending a deep bass *kaboom-kaboom-kaboom* throughout his whole body with each beat.

She glanced at him with a smile as she slipped into bed and pulled the top sheet over her legs. "That smells delicious," she said. "You found the cookies. Good. I'm hungry. I'm always hungry," she added on a lament.

He managed a smile although his face felt as if it was made from stiff plastic. After placing the tray across her lap, he took his cup and stepped back. Hooking a toe on a side chair next to the lamp table, he pulled it closer to the bed and took a seat.

She ate a cookie and was on the second one when she narrowed her eyes at him, apparently becoming aware that he wasn't eating. She offered the plate to him.

He accepted one. While he ate, he noticed the roominess of the queen-size bed and dragged his gaze away with an effort. "Nice room," he complimented her. "Very pleasant. I like the colors."

"Men do. Blue is their universal favorite color."

He wondered about the men who'd seen the room. Mmm, the rumor was that Jenna and her friends, also nurses, had all been artificially inseminated. Now why would a beautiful woman like her need to go to a clinic to get a baby?

Some part of him wondered if he would have volunteered for the job if she'd asked. The idea sent the blood whirling through his veins at warp speed.

She yawned when she'd finished the snack. "Now I've got to brush my teeth again," she complained, but with a smile.

While he finished off the last two cookies, she went to the master bathroom. He heard the water come on and the sounds of her brushing and rinsing.

Memories interrupted the hard pound of hunger. His wife had been six months pregnant the last time he'd taken a shower with her, a few days before the stupid quarrel that had sent her from the house in a fury...and to her death.

He pressed the bridge of his nose as pain and guilt washed through him, then carefully forced the useless emotion at bay. Guilt would never bring her and their child back. They'd been expecting a girl—

"All done," Jenna announced and returned to bed. "You must be exhausted. I'm fine, so you can go home."

He shook his head. "I'll stick around for a while."

She studied him for a moment, then shrugged and slipped down in the bed and tucked the sheet under her arms. When he carried the tray and used dishes out, she flicked off the light. He heard her sigh as if weariness had overtaken her.

In the kitchen, he rinsed the dishes and put them

in the dishwasher while he considered what to do. He couldn't leave, not yet. Jenna might go into labor or something during the night. The kid must have hit her pretty hard in the stomach to cause her to lose her breath.

Going into the living room, he made a decision. The sofa looked comfortable enough. He could sleep there as well as at the empty house where he lived.

Hmm, there was a guest bedroom upstairs. He'd be closer to Jenna… He thought of her and the queen-size bed. On second thought, it was better to stay down here, farther from temptation but close enough to hear if she needed help.

He kicked off his shoes and stretched out. The sofa was about two inches too short. He turned onto his side and let his feet hang off the edge. The bed upstairs would be long enough for him and a companion, too.

His body hardened again at the thought. He frowned and wondered what the hell was the matter with him tonight. The situation called for the skills of a doctor, not those of a lover. He sighed wearily.

He hadn't expected the passion.

Chapter 3

Jenna woke shortly after six. A groan escaped her when she tried to move. She'd never been so sore and stiff in her life. Carefully assessing her aches and pains, she rose from the bed and toddled into the bathroom.

All parts present and accounted for. Including the baby. She patted her tummy and smiled, then decided to get dressed and have breakfast. This morning she would have her five-month sonogram and maybe find out if her child was to be a girl or a boy.

After a quick shower, she blow-dried her hair, put it up in a ponytail and pulled on her first pair of maternity slacks and the matching top, both in perky blue with flowers embroidered across the front. She'd bought three outfits on sale two days ago.

She checked herself in the mirror on the bathroom door. Really, she didn't look preggie at all. She smoothed the top over her tummy. Well, maybe in the side view she did.

Grinning, she slipped on her favorite sandals and gingerly went down the steps, holding the railing and trying not to groan each time she shifted her weight.

At the bottom of the steps, she halted as a shock of recognition sped through her. On her sofa, sound asleep, lay her Good Samaritan.

Crossing the carpet soundlessly, she tiptoed to the kitchen and put on a pot of coffee. Getting bacon from the freezer, she cooked several slices in the microwave oven.

Thank goodness the aroma no longer sent her rushing to the bathroom, a hand clutched over her mouth. She scrambled eggs and put bread in the toaster.

"Good morning," a deep masculine voice spoke behind her.

She gasped and whirled, then grabbed the counter as the room spun ominously. Hands clasped her upper arms and steadied her.

"Sorry," he said. "I didn't mean to scare you."

Laying her palms on his chest, she said, "That's

okay. I'm not used to having another person around, especially first thing in the morning."

His dark gaze went to her stomach. Several unexpected flutters went through her.

"When the little one comes, I guess I'd better get used to it, huh?" she quipped. "Breakfast is almost ready. Coffee cups are, oh, but you know where they are."

"Yes."

When he moved away from her, she breathed in relief. His nearness did things to her…like frazzling her nerves and making her act stupidly.

She'd always thought he was an attractive man, but he'd also been married. She'd met his wife at parties and hospital fund-raisers and dedications to those who contributed generously. He'd had eyes for no one but her.

Just the way it should be, Jenna acknowledged, feeling a tiny bit of envy for women who had such good fortune.

Her own luck in the happily-ever-after department hadn't been so great. During high school and college, she'd thought herself in love two or three times, but the longer she'd known the guys, the less she'd found to like about them.

Deciding she was too quick to take the other person at face value, she'd become more critical of her own feelings and attraction toward the opposite sex. She'd learned to deal with men on a logical, unemotional level and be wary of instant attractions.

Mmm, what was she to make of the tug she felt toward this man? It certainly wasn't instant...well, she had instinctively liked him from the first. They worked together like two halves of a whole, hardly needing to speak. The more she knew of him, the more she liked and admired him.

And he was undeniably good-looking.

She kept her smile to herself at this last thought. Physically, she found him quite compelling. The stray thought had once crossed her mind to ask him if he would father a child with her—

No! That was just too ridiculous, not to mention the complications that would arise, given that they worked together and also that he wasn't the type to sire a child and not take part in its raising.

While he poured a cup of coffee, she took up the eggs on two plates, buttered the toast and set the food on the table in the breakfast nook. She adjusted the blinds so they could see the duck pond and tennis courts without the sun glaring in their eyes.

"Nice," he said, taking his seat. "How do you feel this morning?"

"Fine. As long as I don't move."

He studied her for a long minute. "You should

take tonight off. Better yet, a week. Stay off your feet while you work the kinks out."

"Is that an order, doctor?"

"A mere suggestion. I've noticed you do whatever suits you in most cases."

She couldn't decide if she'd been insulted or not. "Are you implying I'm willful?"

He laid a hand over his heart. "Never," he vowed in the dry tone that passed for humor with him.

Their eyes met and they both smiled at the same instant. Her nerves went all fluttery again. "Better not smile too often around me," she told him. "It does weird things to my insides."

His gaze zeroed in on her like a hunter sighting prey. "Don't get any ideas," he warned, then added grimly, "I've got enough of those for both of us."

She was so startled and intrigued by his confession, she couldn't think of a comeback. "Well," she finally murmured and concentrated on scooping a bite of egg on her fork. "Well."

"Yeah, a deep subject."

He sounded so dismal and looked so forbidding, she thought better of pursuing the conversation, no matter how intriguing it might be. They finished the meal in silence.

She heard a thump outside. "The newspaper has arrived. I'll get it—oh!" She couldn't help the exclamation as she started to rise. Pain laced through muscles she didn't know she'd had before this morning.

"Sit still," he ordered. "I'll get it."

He took over and soon she was reading the headlines of the paper and enjoying a fresh cup of coffee while her guest put the dishes away and straightened the kitchen.

"This is nice," she told him when he joined her again.

Glancing up from the sports section, he asked, "What are your plans for the day?"

"I go for a sonogram at nine. I'm so excited. I hope we can see whether the baby is a boy or girl."

"You prefer to know which it is?"

"Yes. Did you and your wife know—" She broke off, but it was too late to take back the words. "I'm sorry. I didn't mean…it's none of my…I didn't mean to bring up painful memories."

"It doesn't matter."

But it did. She'd seen the flash of agony in his eyes and felt dreadful about it. Her and her smart mouth. It was time she learned to think before she spoke.

"I need to go home for a change of clothes," he continued. "I'll swing back by here at eight-thirty and pick you up."

She tried to figure this out. "Why?"

"To take you to your appointment."

"Oh, you don't have to do that. I can drive. Really," she added at his skeptical snort. "As soon as I get my car—"

"It's too dangerous. Your reaction time will be slower while you recover. Take next week off," he ordered. "Keep your feet elevated. Your ankles looked swollen last night."

He'd noticed her ankles? She tried to figure out when. One thing for sure—things were getting very interesting.

Cool it, she advised her overactive libido. Since becoming pregnant, her whole body seemed to be much more sensitive to fine nuances.

Or—were the funny sensations caused by proximity to the man across the table, who resembled a wooden totem at the moment? His confession to having ideas about them wasn't the type of thing a woman could easily forget.

Sympathy stirred in her breast. He still felt guilty over his wife's death. He needed to get past that. After all, it took two to have a fight, and his wife had made the decision to rush out in a huff and drive off...

Mmm, maybe that was the reason he was worried

about *her* driving. He didn't want anything bad to happen to her and the baby. Put in that light, she couldn't refuse.

"That's very kind of you," she said sweetly.

He cocked one sardonic eyebrow while studying her as if she were a new bacterium he'd just discovered. "Don't go mushy on me," he advised. "It isn't your way."

Annoyed, she ignored him until he got up to leave. "Lock the door on your way out," she said and kept her nose buried in the paper. She barely nodded at his grunt of assent as he left.

She wondered if he would return and tried to decide if she wanted him to. Well, she did, but for what purpose?

Pressing a hand to her chest, she went very still. Hunger pinged through her, making her aware of her body in ways she hadn't even thought of in ages. She'd liked the brush of his body against hers as he came to her aid. She'd liked the way he'd been concerned for her and the baby. The man was attractive in many ways....

She tried to think logically about all this. Should a woman, a five-months-pregnant woman, be feeling this way?

Thirty minutes later, she heard a sharp rap on the

door knocker. Dr. Eric Thompson was indeed a man of his word.

With a groan, she picked up her purse and went to answer the door.

Eric's mind buzzed with half-formed thoughts and impressions as he drove Jenna to the clinic. Her doctor was the same one he and his wife had used.

So?

The appointment had nothing to do with him. Jenna was a friend he was helping out. That was the extent of his involvement. He didn't have to worry about her or take responsibility for her health or that of the baby.

He continued in this logical defense of his actions during the short trip to the medical building. After parking, he got out and went around to help her to her feet. Although she didn't complain, he noticed the slight grimace each time she moved.

She was also a bit distant and introspective. She was probably irritated with him for insisting on driving her to the clinic. Tough.

Her moods were changeable, a thing that was common for pregnant women, he reminded himself when she tried to pull her arm away from his clasp. He held on and she acceded to his determined help.

After she signed in, they sat on a small sofa and

each looked through a magazine. Her name was called ten minutes later. He escorted her to the examining room where a medical technician was setting up the equipment.

"Hi," the man said cheerfully. "Ready for a picture of the papoose?"

Eric felt like socking the guy for reasons he couldn't define.

"You don't have to stay," Jenna said.

"I want to make sure the baby is okay." He wasn't leaving the room until he was positive of it.

The technician looked from one to the other. "Did something happen? Did she fall?"

"She was knocked down by a kid on a skateboard," Eric explained.

"You okay?" the man asked Jenna.

She nodded.

Eric stared out the window while she was hooked up to the machine. The doctor came in, glanced at him in surprise, then at Jenna. "How are you feeling?" he asked.

"Fine," she said.

When she didn't elaborate, Eric filled the obstetrician in on the details of the accident.

"Kids," the doctor said. "A woman in Texas was killed not too long ago. Same thing. Three kids were racing down a hill on their skateboards and hit her."

Jenna looked stricken. "That's terrible."

Eric wanted to strangle the doctor for mentioning the case. Jenna didn't need to be upset over some unfortunate woman a thousand miles away.

"Well, what have we here?" the doctor said, peering at the monitor and moving the sonogram wand over her tummy.

"Oh," Jenna said, her face filled with wonder and delight as she glanced at Eric.

She held her hand out. He had no choice but to let her grasp his hand while they stared at the image on the screen.

"Eric, a boy," she said, her eyes bright with tears. "A darling little boy."

He held on to her hand as the floor shifted under his feet. He felt as if he was standing in quicksand and sinking fast. He looked from the baby to her, then back to the baby. He could see the beat of the infant's heart, the cord that gave it life and nourishment from its mother's body and the tiny penis that proclaimed it a male child.

A giant, invisible hand squeezed his heart into a tight ball. He was sinking…sinking… Unable to stop, he bent forward and kissed Jenna on her soft, trembling lips.

Passionately. Tenderly. Endlessly.

He had no idea what made him do it.

Chapter 4

The telephone was ringing when Jenna opened the door to the condo. She tossed her purse on the sofa and groaned, then lifted the portable phone and groaned, and settled into her favorite chair and groaned.

"Jenna? Is that you?"

"Yes," she replied to Rachel. Rachel was a couple of months farther along in her pregnancy than Jenna. "You sound excited. What's up?"

"That's what I want to know. What's going on with you and Eric Thompson?"

Jenna was instantly wary of the question. She'd

known word would get out about them going to the clinic together, but this was unusually fast. "Not a thing that I know of."

"The new girl in the lab is dating a guy in Security. She said that he said that Dr. Thompson called in last night and said you'd been hurt and that he was taking you home and for them to keep an eye on your car. Are you okay?"

While the city might be large, the medical community was rather small, Jenna reflected. She should have known word of her mishap would soon be the latest news.

"Yes, I'm fine. In fact, I just got back from my sonogram and guess what? It's a boy!"

"A boy? Oh my gosh!" she exclaimed. "That's wonderful!"

"I think so, too. Poor Eric, I just couldn't stop talking about it the whole way home, or rather, to the hospital so I could get my car—"

"Wait a minute," Rachel interrupted. "Are we talking about the same person? Are we speaking of silent-as-the-grave Dr. Eric Thompson, trauma specialist and head of E.R. at our own dear Portland General? *That* is the Eric to whom you so intimately refer and who accompanied you to the clinic for the sonogram?"

Jenna had to laugh at her friend's disbelief. She

laid a hand on her abdomen. "Don't make me laugh," she pleaded. "It makes me hurt." She explained about the skateboard accident and Eric insisting on driving her home and then staying in case she had a problem.

"He what?" Rachel broke in.

"Spent the night. On the sofa," Jenna added. "Then he went home to shower and change clothes and came back to drive me to the clinic. I nearly had to throw a tantrum to get him to let me drive my car home. Even then, he followed to make sure I arrived safely. I walked in the door just as you called."

"Wow, wait until I tell Lily."

"Really, there's nothing to tell. The incident is over and all can go back to normal. I did agree to take tonight off, though, when he insisted. He said I might endanger a patient if I couldn't function normally. Since I'm sore all over, I decided to take his advice."

"Good thinking," Rachel told her. "So Eric spent the night at your place and took care of you. Interesting."

Jenna could hear the speculation in her friend's voice at this piece of news. She was glad to be back on friendly terms with her two oldest and dearest friends, but she was still a bit wary in her dealings with them. Being trapped in the middle of their quarrel had been awkward, so she'd withdrawn from both of them.

Although they had apparently found their soul mates, Lily with Jake Stone and Rachel with Bryce Armstrong, Jenna was leery of speaking of men and relationships in case the specter of the ex-fiancé returned to haunt them.

"Poor man," Jenna said again. "He was so anxious to be rid of me, he practically threatened to send me home in chains if I showed up in the E.R. this afternoon."

"He's probably afraid you'll have the baby during an emergency," Rachel said, laughing with her, "and he'll have to deliver it."

After they dissected and laughed over the incident once more, Rachel had to go. Jenna bade her goodbye and hung up.

The smile disappeared as she propped her feet on a hassock and mulled over the strange events of the past twelve or so hours. Everything was explainable until she came to the part about going to the clinic, having the sonogram and then, the kiss.

She thought of it in capital letters—THE KISS— like the title on a theater marquee. Running a finger over her lips, she wondered what had prompted his action.

Thinking of it caused her lips to tingle and burn as if an electric switch had been turned on. She put both hands over her face and groaned in dismay as she thought of her response. She'd returned the kiss with a passion that had matched his.

Had it been an impulse of the moment? Simply a reflection of her excitement and need to share the precious moment with someone? Or had it been the memory of his wife and a happier time between them?

Whatever had prompted the kiss on his part, she couldn't deny that she had responded with whole-hearted, unrestrained, wild and wanton passion.

He'd known it, too.

Who didn't? The air in the examining room had sizzled as the kiss had deepened unbearably. Her heartbeat on the monitor had nearly gone off the scale while her blood pressure had zoomed twenty points on the high side.

The sonogram doctor and the technician had both laughed out loud, and that was the only thing that had brought her out of the whirling enchantment of his kiss.

She moaned in wretched humiliation. She didn't want to return to her job. How could she ever face him in the E.R. and pretend nothing had happened?

* * *

Eric was aware of the sly glances cast his way by the staff in the E.R. He ignored them and signed off on the multitude of forms that accompanied any admission to the hospital.

Insurance. Medicare. City Services questionnaires in triplicate for those on welfare. As a newly fledged physician, he'd been impatient with the red tape, but after thirteen years, he'd gotten used to whipping through the forms and getting the job done without wasting energy on resentment and impatience.

Finished, he put the last piece of paper in the outgoing mail stack and the copies in the to-be-filed box on his desk.

Leaning back in the comfortable executive chair, he closed his eyes. Things were slow for a Saturday night. He'd rather be busy. The time went faster.

And he wouldn't have to keep thinking about Jenna Cooper. Or how insane he'd been that morning.

Heat flushed through him like hot water from a tap. What had he been thinking? Where had his brain gone? Why had he given in to that crazy impulse?

He'd tried for hours to explain it, excuse it or at least make some sense of it. He couldn't. It wasn't like him. He wasn't an impulsive sort. Yet it had happened.

He muttered a curse. ''Go back to sleep,'' he told his raging libido.

It ignored the command. His body was hard and demanding. He could taste her lips and feel their softness under his. She'd opened to him, and he had delved inside, taking the honey of her mouth in a kiss that went deeper with her than with any woman that he could recall.

He'd tried dating a couple of friends he'd known for years, one widowed like him, the other divorced. It hadn't worked. He'd spent the night with the widow, but his heart hadn't been in it. The morning after had been awkward. They both had admitted they weren't ready for a new relationship at present.

He still wasn't. He didn't want the responsibility of another person's happiness. He was preoccupied with his work. His steady in medical school had broken off with him because of inattention. His wife had accused him of forgetting she existed. That's what their final quarrel had been about. He didn't know how to please women—

The pager vibrated against his side. E.R. was calling. He'd planned to go home at four that afternoon, but here it was, after six, and he was still there. As usual.

He had to tell one of the nurses to help him with the scrub jacket and gloves before he could assist the duty doctor with the patient. Jenna would have had them ready when he walked into the E.R. cubicle.

"O.R.," he said after checking the accident victim. "Who's on duty in there? We need a neurosurgeon for this one," he told the floor nurse while she checked the on-call roster. "Tell them to alert the resident, then call Dr. Morgan. He's the best. This case is going to need it."

For the next six hours, he assisted the specialist in the operation to save the sixteen-year-old. The boy hadn't been wearing a seat belt and had been thrown from the pickup truck onto the pavement.

"Okay, that's all we can do for now," the neurosurgeon said. "We'll have to treat the symptoms from here on and pray we can keep ahead of them. Are the parents here?"

"In the first waiting room," one of the O.R. nurses said.

Eric and the surgeon exchanged glances. Dealing with relatives was one of the most difficult tasks for a doctor.

"I'll go talk to them," the surgeon said, his face drawn with fatigue.

Eric stripped the surgical garb off and washed up. Heading down the corridor, he saw it was midnight. He'd meant to go by Jenna's one more time to be sure she was still feeling okay. She was an independent type and might not decide to call for help until it was too late if she had cramps or something.

Again the sensation of a giant hand squeezing his heart assailed him. He would never forget her face or her smile as they'd looked at the child growing inside her.

The glow…that's what had made him kiss her. Her joy had been contagious. For a second, it seemed as if the child had been theirs. His and hers.

It wasn't, and he'd better get his head screwed on straight before he saw her again. He drove home, the residential streets nearly deserted at this hour. His neighbors were safe in bed.

He parked in the garage and went into the silent house, remembering to punch in the burglar alarm code before it went off and summoned the police to his door. He'd done that once last year. The cops hadn't appreciated it.

The house had been under construction two years ago when his wife and child had died. It was a home for a family, one with a big yard and lots of trees to climb and a creek running through the back edge of the property.

He'd moved into it because their smaller house had been sold, so he'd had to get out. Besides, there were no memories of either quarrels or laughter here.

After kicking off his shoes and leaving them in the laundry room between the garage and kitchen, he went to the refrigerator and reached for a beer. He hesitated, thought better of it and decided on a glass of milk instead.

Jenna would be proud of him, he thought wryly as he went into the den and flicked on the TV. He was still wound up after the grueling surgery. He'd catch one of the late-night shows or a movie. Those always put him to sleep.

An hour later, he strode out the patio doors to the pool, threw off his clothes and dove in. He swam twenty-five laps, climbed out, showered off in cold water and headed for bed. Thirty minutes later, he was still awake.

He swore, but that didn't help, either. He hadn't had this problem since he'd been a teenager and hot for the lead cheerleader in the senior class.

The lack of control over his wayward body annoyed him. He believed in mind over matter, or whatever. Tonight nothing seemed to be listening to his mental orders.

At last he headed back for the shower. He was off tomorrow, but if he was called in on an emergency, he had to be alert and able to function at his best. He turned the cold water on full blast closed his eyes and reviewed his day. Slowly, thoughts of Jenna began to subside.

When he returned to the empty bed, he fell asleep in less than a minute.

Chapter 5

Jenna was watering the flower pots on the porch when she spotted a familiar vehicle pulling into a guest parking space. It was her rescuer. Or keeper, however one wanted to view the situation. He was coming to check on her, no doubt.

She put a curb on her tongue and smiled brightly at him when he came up the walkway and stopped at the bottom of the steps, his eyes checking her out. In the medical sense.

"Good morning," she said.

He nodded. "How are you feeling?"

"Fine, actually. You were right. Staying off my

feet yesterday helped a lot. Other than my shoulder, which I must have fallen on, I'm not achy this morning.''

"Did you sleep okay?"

"Yes. Did you?"

A wry smile flitted over his lips. "Yeah," he said.

She set the empty watering can in its usual place behind the fig tree. "Uh, would you like a cup of coffee? Or breakfast? I can fix—"

"I've eaten. Coffee would be fine."

"Have a seat," she invited, gesturing to one of the two chairs on the porch.

"I'll get it. You sit down."

To her surprise, she did as ordered. It was rather nice to be taken care of. "I'm used to being the caregiver," she told him when he brought out two steaming mugs, handed one to her and took the other patio chair.

His dark eyes went to her tummy. "You need to take care of yourself now. The baby will need a healthy mother."

"I know. Usually I'm very careful. I was thinking of the sonogram and wondering about the baby's gender. That's why the boy on the skateboard took me by surprise."

"I see," he said.

He smiled again, and her heart thumped really

hard. She tried not to stare at him. This morning, he wore tennis togs and looked good enough for an ad in *GQ*. His hair gleamed like finely polished ebony. He was tanned and muscular and incredibly handsome in white shorts and a yellow knit shirt.

The hum of sexual interest buzzed through her. She turned her gaze from him to the sweep of lawn that ran down to the duck pond. "Are you playing tennis this morning?"

"Yes. One of the surgeons and I try to get in a game once or twice a week."

"That's good," she told him. "Most people don't keep up an exercise program, then all of a sudden, they're forty and overweight, their blood sugar is high and they're in danger of diabetes and/or a heart attack. Then they wonder what happened to their youthful energy and health."

He started laughing.

Jenna smiled self-consciously at her sermonizing—after all, he was a doctor—then she forgot it and was simply enchanted with the sound coming from him. He had the most wonderful laugh, low-toned and coming from deep in his chest, like the bass notes of an organ underscoring the higher notes of a melody, adding drama and a certain masculine beauty to the musical theme.

Their eyes met.

They were both silent as a thousand messages flashed between them. She saw hunger in those dark depths, hunger that matched her own. It was the oddest thing…and yet the most natural one in the world.

Her breasts beaded, and she had trouble breathing regularly. She saw him open his mouth and inhale slowly, fully. It was both comforting and exciting to know he was having the same problem that she was.

His gaze left her eyes and meandered down her throat, then lingered at her nipples, wantonly outlined against the soft blue knit top she wore. His eyes came back to hers.

"I have to go," he said, standing. He put the nearly full coffee cup on the small table between their chairs. "I'll be back around noon."

"What for?" she asked, her eyes going wide as her imagination ran riot.

Again that sexy sweep of his eyes. "Lunch. What do you want me to bring for you?"

"Fried chicken, potato salad and baked beans," she promptly answered. When he looked surprised, she added, "That's my favorite meal. My mom used to fix it almost every Sunday for me and my dad."

"Do your parents live around here?"

She shook her head. "My mother died of cancer a few years ago. My father retired last year and moved to Arizona where he can golf all year. He was a medical pathologist.''

"You're an only child?''

She nodded. "I had a brother, two years younger, but he died when he was six. He was trying to ride my bike, but he lost control and went into the street in front of a car.''

He looked away from her and stared into the far distance as if seeing the tragedy unfold. She wished she hadn't mentioned the accident.

"I felt terribly guilty about letting him try my bike, but my parents told me it wasn't my fault. They said it was human nature to want to try new things, or else we would still be in the stone age.''

"Your parents were wise,'' he said after a beat of silence. "Guilt for something like that would have been too great a burden for a child to carry through life.''

She observed the shadows that gathered in his eyes and hid his emotions. "Life happens,'' she said softly, "to all of us.''

"Yeah,'' he said on a harsh note and strode down the walk and to his car.

She stayed there for a long time after he left, thinking of life and guilt and grief. Eric needed a friend, she decided. He needed to open up and let his feelings out, or maybe put them behind him.

His unexpected laughter had been wonderful. She wanted to hear it again. After all, wasn't it supposed to be the best medicine?

Eric parked in the guest slot he'd used earlier. He lifted the plastic bag from the seat and headed up the sidewalk to Jenna's place. The front door was open when he stepped onto the porch.

"Come on in," she called before he could knock.

His eyes slid over her in a visual caress he couldn't suppress. Like him, she wore shorts and a knit top. Her legs were long and slender and shapely. Her ankles weren't puffy as they had been Friday night, but then she'd been on her feet for ten straight hours at the hospital that day. Today, she was both refreshed and a refreshing sight.

"How did the game go?" she asked with a sunny smile.

"Beat the socks off me the first set, but I got him back on the next two," he said, placing the bag on the kitchen counter. He'd stopped by his place to shower and change to fresh clothing after the hard-fought game.

One good thing—the exercise had cooled his libido somewhat. His glance went to her legs again. But not much, he amended as a surge of heat whipped through him.

He removed two containers of the requested food while she prepared tall icy glasses of tea.

"Lemon?" She held one up.

"Please."

"I made a veggie platter. It's in the refrigerator. Plates are in the cabinet to the right of the cups."

He set the platter and plates on the table, then got forks, spoons and knives from the drawer where they were stored. She brought the iced-tea glasses.

She eyed the meal. "This looks delicious."

After holding a chair for her, he took his place across the table. For some reason, sharing a meal was beginning to feel familiar. That, he warned himself, was not a good thing.

"Have you gained much weight during your pregnancy?" he asked, unable to come up with another topic.

She shook her head. "About seven pounds so far. I don't want to put on too much. It may be too hard to take off."

"I don't think you have to worry." He paused. "I find it amazing that you and your friends resorted to…"

"Artificial insemination," she supplied when he didn't continue the thought.

"Yes. Didn't you know any men who would be happy to do the, uh, the…"

"Dastardly deed?" she suggested.

He was a doctor, for Pete's sake. He didn't know why he was having problems discussing the situation. It didn't seem to bother *her*. Those sky-blue eyes were alight with merriment, he observed. At his expense.

"Well, I thought of asking you since you were the only unattached male I knew who fit my requirements."

An invisible hand stuck a sizzling hot poker right into his chest. He couldn't breathe. Or think.

Images sprang full-blown into his mind. Him and her wrapped in a passionate embrace on that nice big bed upstairs, right over their heads. Kisses that burned clear down to the soles of his feet.

"What requirements?" he heard himself ask.

"Under forty, for one. Intelligent, for another." She tilted her head slightly, her smile charming and sort of dreamy as she counted out the prerequisites. "Good looks, but not necessarily movie-star handsome."

Her eyes roamed his face in a teasing, but sincere manner.

"I'm flattered," he said, putting a wry twist to the words. "Why didn't you ask?"

"I was afraid you'd refuse. You don't indulge in the party circuit, at least not that I know of. Also, you, uh, tend to take charge. I didn't want you telling me every little thing I was doing wrong in raising the child."

He had to smile. "So that's what you think of me?" he demanded. "You think I'm bossy?"

"Well, if the surgical booties fit…"

"I get the picture." He found himself relaxing as the conversation veered to the hospital and the staff. The sexual tension still hummed through his veins, but he no longer felt it was something he had to guard against every second while he was around her.

She covered a yawn at one point. He realized they had been sitting chatting for almost two hours.

"You need to rest," he said, rising and clearing the table before she could do it.

"You're very helpful around the house," she told him, putting the remaining veggies in a plastic bag and storing them in the refrigerator. "Your wife must have trained you well."

The mellow feelings disappeared. "She was a

gourmet cook. She didn't like anyone messing in the kitchen while she was in it. It distracted her, she said.''

''I can understand that. If I were an expert, I probably wouldn't want someone in my way, either. Since I'm not, I'll take all the help I can get.''

The tension slipped from him. ''You're easy to be around,'' he told her. ''I missed you yesterday at the hospital. The other nurses—''

He stopped, realizing it wasn't good form for the head of the department to talk about the staff to one of them.

''None of them has worked with you as long as I have,'' she continued his thought, ''so it isn't as easy for the others to anticipate what you need.''

''Sometimes you seem to read my mind.''

Her smile bloomed. ''I know the routine.''

For a second, the ambiance between them was the same as yesterday when they'd kissed. He felt a compelling urge to do it again. He wasn't sure he would stop this time. They were alone in her home and he knew exactly where the bedroom was located.

''I have to go,'' he said and headed for the door.

''Thank you for the lunch. And for helping me after the accident. And for driving me to the clinic yesterday.''

He paused and glanced back at her. The window over the sink backlighted her golden hair, turning it into a shimmering halo around her perfect face. She looked like an angel come to life.

He strode out and down the sidewalk, putting distance between them. One thing he knew—angels weren't for mortals like him.

Chapter 6

On Wednesday evening, after a slow four hours in E.R., Jenna retrieved her dinner from the fridge and headed for one of the little-used waiting rooms. She and another nurse had decided to eat in there where it was quieter and more comfortable. And Jenna could prop her feet up.

She heard a "Shhh" as she approached the door and was disappointed. Someone was using the room. Well, maybe they wouldn't stay long—

"Surprise!" a chorus of voices rang out when she entered the room.

Every nerve in Jenna's body jerked as adrenaline

flooded her system, ready to send her into "fight or flight" mode. She grinned and pressed a hand to her breast in exaggerated relief. "Definitely a surprise," she told her friends as they crowded around her.

The room was decorated in blue crepe-paper streamers and balloons proclaiming It's a Boy! A cake held pride of place on the nearest table along with gaily colored plates and napkins. Presents were stacked on another table.

"A baby shower? For me?"

"Yes, for you," her long-time friend, Lily, assured her, stepping forward and tugging her to a seat at the cake table. "We also brought healthy food so you could have a piece of cake without suffering a guilty conscience."

Jenna laughed. She was rather strict on herself about eating well-balanced meals. For the baby's sake. "Rachel, hi," she greeted her other best friend. "Did you two plan this?" she demanded, gesturing toward the decorations.

"Yep," Lily said.

"With the help of the E.R. staff," Rachel added.

Jenna glanced at the crowd. There were at least twenty people in the room, many of them co-workers on other shifts in E.R. and several from the pediatrics wing where she had often volunteered to feed babies or just hold the fretful ones if their parents weren't available.

Looking past the smiling faces, she spotted Eric at the back of the room. He was putting on a pot of coffee. He looked around at that moment and winked at her.

It was so surprising, she was almost shocked again.

"Your boss said it was okay," Rachel told her. "He even said you could take longer for your break."

"Eric was in on this?" Jenna did have trouble believing that. He was so…so solemn, as a rule.

"He was. He thought it was just the thing to cheer you up after your mishap last Friday."

"He did?"

While the people around her chuckled at her amazement, Jenna realized she'd probably made her boss sound like a curmudgeon or something. "He's been really wonderful this past week, helping me and all."

"Right, he must have been taking 'nice' pills," the other E.R. nurse who'd tricked her into coming here said and laughed delightedly when several glances went from her to Eric and back, speculation definitely in their depths.

"Dr. Thompson is always nice," Jenna said, feeling compelled to defend him.

"Huh," the nurse said, but under her breath as the doctor came forward at that moment.

"Dinner is served, madam," he intoned.

Everyone seemed to know what he or she was supposed to do. Soon Jenna was seated in front of a feast of dishes prepared by her friends. Eric had supplied a honey-cured ham from a local deli that was already cut and ready to eat, along with their delicious home-made crunchy rolls.

After eating, she had to open the gifts before they let her cut the cake. She was touched by the assortment of tiny clothes and blankets and layette outfits.

"Thank you all so much," she said when she was at last finished. "This was such a surprise, a wonderful one, and I love everything. I can't wait to use it all—"

"Except the diapers," Lily said, wrinkling her nose.

"Where is your baby?" Jenna asked Lily.

"Asleep, I hope, at home with her daddy." She glanced at the clock. "It's time I got back. It's almost time for a feeding." She gave her friend a hug. "Eric would make a great father, don't you think?" she whispered in Jenna's ear. With a grin, she sailed out of the room.

Jenna looked anywhere but at the part of the room where Eric chatted with another doctor. She was afraid her thoughts would leap into her eyes for all to read.

Lily's teasing words sizzled in her head like the stamp of a branding iron. Eric as father to her son?

Don't even think about it, she warned herself. She **had** gone into this alone and with her eyes wide open to the difficulties of single parenthood. She could handle it.

"Time to get back to work," the E.R. nurse said with a groan and then a laugh.

Jenna looked at all the stuff to clean up.

"Go on," Eric told her. "I can handle this. I'll load the gifts in my SUV. It's bigger than your car. I can bring them by tonight when you get off."

"Th-thanks," she said with an involuntary stammer.

The other E.R. nurse looked at her and waggled her eyebrows. "Something between you and Dr. Thompson?" she asked in a friendly, teasing manner on the way back to their duty station.

Jenna shook her head. "Not really. He was... helpful after I had the accident."

"Honey, if I weren't married, I think I'd see just how helpful he could be."

Their laughter was cut short when they entered the

Emergency Room area. Two people were being brought in on stretchers. "Fire," the medic with the emergency medical team told Jenna. "Their house caught on fire. They tried to save their pets and were overcome with smoke. The firemen pulled them out of the burning house."

Jenna went to work, directing the EMT medics to put the victims in two cubicles and instructing a nurse to call in a specialist on burn treatment. She checked the IVs started by the medics and prepared a special wash to start cleaning the inflamed skin as they removed charred clothing from the man and woman.

Eric and the burn specialist arrived at the same time. The specialist instructed Eric on what to do for the first patient while he started on the second one. Jenna listened and made sure the supplies were at hand, anticipating each request from the doctors as they all worked for the remainder of the shift and into the next.

"You need to get off your feet," Eric told her when they at last walked outside into the cool night breeze. He was frowning in his serious way as he looked her over.

Jenna checked the time. "It's only a little after eleven. I thought it was later."

"You've had a long day."

It was obvious he thought she'd overdone it, but no one could predict emergencies and no one walked out while dealing with one. "I'm fine," she assured him.

"Huh," he said. "I'll follow you home."

She started to protest, then remembered he had all her baby stuff in his vehicle. He probably wanted to get rid of it so he wouldn't have to do it tomorrow. "Okay."

He raised his eyebrows at her acquiescence, evidently expecting an argument. She gave him an impish smile, then unlocked her car and drove home with him a safe distance behind her car.

At the condo, he carried in most of the stuff and, under her direction, stored it in the guest room where the baby crib, sanded and painted, waited to be reassembled.

"I need to tell my father he has to come up and put the crib together," she told Eric. "I took it apart, but I can't remember how it goes back together."

"I'll put it together for you over the weekend, if you like."

"That would be very nice." Her heart bumped around her chest like a demolition derby car. She took a fortifying breath. "Did you do that when you and your wife were expecting?"

He put the last pile of boxes on the floor next to

the wall, then turned and looked at her. His face was grim. "We hadn't bought furniture yet. We thought we had plenty of time for the house to be finished, then we would get it."

"Oh, that's right," she said, recalling the information. "You had a new house built a little farther out from the hospital. The land was advertised as five-acre estates. Are you pleased with it and the house?"

She kept her manner friendly but bland as she led the way downstairs. She pretended not to notice his frown or the dark memories that filled his eyes. He had to talk about it sometime in order to get over the pain. Now was as good as any, she decided.

"The place is okay," he finally answered in forbidding tones. "I don't stay at the house much."

She laughed. "You're always at the hospital," she scolded. "You're worse than Scrooge as a work-aholic. I need something to eat. How about a ham and cheese omelet?" she asked, seeing the left-over ham on the counter.

When he didn't answer, she glanced over her shoulder. His gaze was on her in a way that started the blood to pounding, driven by the tom-tom beat of her heart.

"Eric?" she said, her voice going breathless.

"Fine," he said. "That'll be fine."

˙ She prepared the food, aware that she was hungry after the long evening of work, but knowing the hunger extended past the need for food. She sensed the same need in him as he stood at the half wall that divided the living from the cooking area and watched her work.

When they sat down at the table, silence prevailed during the quick meal. "Would you like a cup of tea?" she asked upon finishing. She named the various kinds she had when he indicated he would.

Carrying the cup, she led the way to the porch chairs. Although the night air was chilly, the porch sat in a protective alcove and was pleasant. The soft darkness seemed soothing to her taut nerves.

"It sometimes takes me a while to wind down, especially after an emergency such as we had tonight," she said. "I like to sit out here and listen to the quiet. The constant roar from the highway becomes white noise. I no longer even notice it."

"I do the same at my place," he admitted. "Where I live, there's no traffic sound at night. You can't hear the freeway because there's a hill between it and the house."

"Mmm, that must be nice."

"Yeah." After a minute, he added, "But it can be lonely, too. Some of the at-home wives complain about that."

"Is that why you stay at work? Because you find the house too lonely now that your wife is gone?"

He didn't answer for a long time. She was slumped down in the chair so her head rested on the back. She now rolled it to the side so she could study him in the faint light coming through the pleated shades at her windows.

When he looked her way, she couldn't read his expression. He was probably trying to think of words to put her in her place.

"Maybe it's the guilt that haunts me," he at last said.

"Guilt because she chose to drive off in a huff when you quarreled?"

"Guilt because she was right," he said, his voice low so she had to really listen to hear. "She was angry because I'd worked late. Again. She'd wanted to go check on a new shipment of furniture. It was time to furnish the baby's room, she said."

"Didn't she understand that as a trauma specialist, you had to stay for emergencies? Like tonight, that wasn't something one could predict or schedule. People have to be fair in picking their arguments. You have to be fair with yourself, too, in taking or ascribing blame. My dad says it takes to two to make a marriage...or to break one."

She heard Eric let out a long, slow breath. She

shouldn't be saying these things to him. His life was none of her business.

Liar, a part of her whispered. She wanted very much to be part of *his* business. She wanted him…in very basic and elemental ways. It was startling, but there it was.

"It does," Eric agreed. "Both partners have to consider the other in marriage. That's what I didn't do. I didn't call when I was going to be late. I thought she should understand that I was working and that it involved lives."

"She didn't see it like that," Jenna concluded.

"No. She said I could spare a moment to let her know what was going on. She wanted me to tell her about the cases when I got home."

"But you were tired and didn't want to talk about anything," Jenna guessed.

"Yes."

"I'm that way, too, sometimes. At times, when I get home, I can't make another decision, not even about what to eat. It just seems too much. If I had to be nice to another person, I'd probably explode."

"That's why it's easier not to date or see anyone." He met her gaze in the dim light. "Is that why you chose an anonymous donor for your baby?"

She shrugged. "I'm not sure. I haven't met anyone who fit my ideals, I suppose."

"Maybe your standards are too high. No mere mortal can live up to them."

She had to laugh at that. "I don't think that's the problem," she said, using his dry twist of humor. "Perhaps we see too much of the human condition at the hospital to be willing to put up with it at home."

He hesitated, then chuckled. "You may be right."

Their eyes met again. The laughter faded and the silence grew...and grew...

Arcs of electricity flew between them, dazzling in their brilliance. Liquid gold poured through her veins instead of blood, heating her from the inside out.

"I want you," he said, so low she almost didn't catch the words. "I want to kiss you."

"Then do it."

She dared him with her gaze. Inside, she thought she would melt at his feet if he didn't move, didn't catch her before she slipped from the chair like a rag doll.

When he stood, she did, too. He laid his hands—his long-fingered, magical hands—on her shoulders. A shiver of anticipation ran over her. She lifted her face and leaned into his lean, powerful frame. He wrapped her in his arms, holding her securely, but delicately, as if she were as fragile as a flower.

"Jenna," he said, a groan that spoke of needs he couldn't voice.

She heard them all and understood them, because the same ones were in her. Lifting her arms, she let herself cling to him. The warmth between them increased. She felt his breath touch her forehead, her cheek, her mouth.

Then it was his lips touching hers.

The kiss spun out of control at once. She luxuriated in the feel of his masculine body against hers and the way his hands slid down her back and cupped her hips so that they fit together perfectly. She arched into his embrace, the hunger erupting like a storm that had no build-up, gave no warning to the unwary.

She moaned low in her throat, demanding more from him, wanting everything he could give...

"Jenna, I...this is crazy," he murmured, strewing a thousand kisses along her neck.

"I know. It's the hunger. I didn't know it could be this way, this strong." She gasped when he left a trail of fire along her neck to the dip between her breasts.

His mouth moved to the side and he bit gently on her nipple. It contracted with painful suddenness.

"Come inside. I want to see you...have to..."

At his murmured phrases, she nodded and followed him into the house. He closed the door behind them. She heard the lock click into place. Hand in hand, they went up the steps and into the bedroom.

His hands went to her top, then paused. "If you don't want this—"

"Shh," she said, laying her fingertips over his mouth. "I do. I've never wanted anything so much in my life." She gave him a rueful smile when he peered deeply into her eyes. "Sometimes things are that way, I think."

"Sometimes," he agreed.

When he observed her with a troubled frown, as if unsure that she knew what she was doing, she smoothed the lines away from his brow, then let her hands drift to the buttons on his shirt. She unfastened one, then another, and then another…

His chest lifted. He caught her against him in a fierce, but careful embrace. "I can't go this slowly," he warned, a second before deftly pulling her top over her head and disposing of her slacks in the next instant.

He cupped her breasts and studied the darkened nipples through the thin material of her bra. Slipping his hands behind her, he unfastened the hooks, then slid the bra down her arms and tossed it aside.

"Beautiful," he murmured, his eyes sexily dark

and appreciative of her charms. He bent and laved each breast with liquid fire.

"I'm going into meltdown," she warned him, holding on to his forearms as the room spun dizzily.

He laughed, stripped the covers out of the way and laid her on the bed. When his hands moved to his clothing, she sat up and silently insisted on helping. Her breath caught in her throat when she gazed at his masculine strength, fully unclad before her.

She laid a hand on his thigh. The hair was thick and dark on his legs. She liked running her hand over it. When she touched him intimately, he, too, caught his breath, then he pushed her hand aside and stretched out beside her. Their legs meshed as naturally as vines wrapping around each other, forming one perfect whole.

Leaning forward, she planted kisses over his chest. The hair tickled her nose, making her laugh. She pulled it with her lips.

"You'll pay for that," he told her. He flicked her nipples playfully, then bent to her mouth.

They kissed hungrily, like starving castaways stumbling upon a feast on some exotic shore. It was too much. It wasn't enough. "I want...oh!" she said, feeling his shift in weight, then feeling his legs making a place for themselves between hers.

She felt the smoothness of him against her and the

moist readiness of her body where he rubbed seductively. It took only a smallest movement to deepen the embrace.

"Not yet," he whispered. "Not quite yet."

He stroked down her body, paying attention to her breasts, then her waist and the rounded curve of her abdomen before gliding lower until his touch made her writhe in ecstasy. "Eric," she whispered, a demand.

"Easy." He moved against her, tantalizing her with the promise of fulfillment.

As the hunger rose to unbearable pleasure, she cried out and bit lightly at his lips, his throat and chest, wanting more from him.

"Yes, yes, yes," she said as he thrust the tiniest bit.

"Yes," he echoed.

When she wrapped her legs around his hips, he rose, positioned himself and thrust slowly, deeply until they were merged completely.

She opened her eyes and gazed into his, caught by the emotions that spun like golden threads between them. She couldn't define the feelings in her or in him. Stroking down his sides and onto his hips with her hands, she pressed upward with her hips, bringing them just a fraction deeper, more intimately connected.

Still gazing into her eyes, he began to move smoothly and rhythmically. She caught her bottom lip between her teeth and closed her eyes as the flood of need became a roaring storm tide, ripping through her until she bucked and plunged wildly beneath him.

Eric held her securely and sipped the passion from her lips, absorbed it from her body as tremors raced over her. She sobbed his name as the tempest rolled through her and caught her in its peak and held her there…

"Yes," he said in deepened tones, his own need now desperate and wild. "Yes."

The storm surge took them both and deposited them on a faraway beach. He never wanted to return. Reality could never be as good as this….

Chapter 7

The problem with tomorrow, Jenna thought when she woke on Thursday morning, was that it always came. And with it, all the troubles of the previous day.

She lay still with her eyes closed and enjoyed the tactile sensation of a very masculine leg thrown over hers and an arm lying across her waist. Moving slowly, she rubbed up and down his leg, liking the sensation of warmth from his skin and the enticing brush of the short wiry hairs against the sole of her foot.

The muscles of his arm flexed, then he turned his

wrist and cupped her breast. She snuggled closer. Against her hip, she felt his erection surge to life. It added to the excitement building in her body. She stroked her hand over his shoulder and turned her head to nuzzle his collar bone.

"Mmm," she murmured, a demand in the sound.

His lips moved over her throat, then down to her breast. The morning, she mused, was off to a perfect start.

"Shower?" she suggested.

He helped her up and they went into the master bath. It wasn't until she adjusted the water, then stepped inside the large shower and turned to him that she became aware that his silence indicated more than early-morning lassitude.

His eyes were on her abdomen, the pain and remorse in those dark depths plain for her to see.

Following his gaze, she looked at her body, seeing it as he did—the thrust of her breasts, larger now than they used to be, and the nipples circled by a pink aureole that was darker than before the pregnancy. Her abdomen was a plump mound.

"I look as if I've swallowed a soccer ball," she said, laughing to dispel the tension she sensed in him.

"You look beautiful," he corrected, his voice hoarse and strained.

Realizing the magic of the night was definitely behind them, she managed a smile. "Thank you, kind sir."

Standing under the spray, she let it wet her hair, her shoulders and back. She didn't push him to join her, but instead closed her eyes and lifted her face to the stream.

Hands touched her tummy and slid gently over the curve of the baby. She felt the child kick. Opening her eyes a slit, she observed Eric's expression as he lingered at the spot where the baby tapped against his hand. He looked so unbearably sad, it made her ache, too. The heat of the moment had left his body, she saw.

"Let's hurry," she said. "I'm hungry."

She showered quickly while he stayed carefully out of her way. When she stepped out, he moved into the stream and soaped up. She finished quickly, dressed and, pulling her damp hair into a ponytail, went down to the kitchen.

When he came down, she had cereal and toast ready. They carried plates and cups to the little porch and ate outside.

"It's okay," she told him when they'd finished eating and were sipping the coffee while watching the ducks on the tiny lake. "Last night wasn't a commitment to anything."

His eyes met hers. Her ego was slightly bruised at

the relief on his face. Ah, well, worse things had happened.

"I don't want to start something that has no place to go," he said in his solemn manner.

He tried to play fair. She appreciated that about him. "I understand." She managed a wry smile. "Let's chalk it up to moon madness and let it go at that. Perhaps we can still be friends?"

He didn't answer right away. When she glanced at him in question, she found him studying her intently, as if looking for flaws or hidden motives.

"We can try. Truthfully, I'm not sure about that. Once sex has entered the picture, things tend to get…out of hand," he ended, after an obvious struggle to find the right descriptive words.

Huh. If he only knew how right he was. Her reaction was to leap into his arms and make him forget his scruples. She didn't, of course. Like him, she had to play fair.

"I think we can control our wild impulses." Her heart rattled around her chest as if in protest. She had to laugh.

"What's funny?" he asked, looking both perplexed and annoyed about the whole thing.

She couldn't help it. She laughed harder. "Us," she tried to explain. "One night of passion isn't a lifetime commitment. Consider it a minor trauma, doctor. We'll get through it the same as we do at the hospital.''

He set the cup down and frowned at her.

"What?" she said.

"You."

She shot him a questioning glance.

"It can't be this simple. Women don't take things in a simple fashion." He looked at his watch. "I'm due at a meeting in thirty minutes."

"You'd better go home and change," she told him. "Thanks for your help with the baby shower gifts."

"I think you've thanked me enough."

She tensed. Then she saw he was smiling, a tiny, wry smile, but a real one. "You're teasing me," she murmured. "The stern Dr. Thompson knows how to joke. Wait till I tell the other nurses," she said in exaggerated wonder.

"Make sure that's all you tell them," he ordered sardonically, still smiling.

With a wave, he headed down the sidewalk to his SUV, parked in a guest parking slot.

On the hiking path, two of her neighbors walked briskly and chatted. Jenna saw them pause as they spotted Eric on the walk, then her on the porch. Other than him, no one had spent the night at her place since she'd moved here over two years ago. His appearance obviously surprised them.

Join the club, she thought wryly. It had surprised her most of all.

Eric used the electric razor, then changed to a fresh shirt and suit. He was aware of his body in a new way. There was a bounce to his step when he returned to his vehicle for the drive to the hospital meeting of department heads.

He'd slept better last night than any other night he could recall in recent history. In two years, he admitted.

The smile left his face. Jenna had made it easy for them to return to friendship…or to a strictly professional relationship, if necessary. Was it merely her training or perhaps the years they'd worked together?

Pulling into his usual parking space at the hospital, he counted up the time. It must have been seven or eight years ago that she'd completed advanced training in trauma and moved to E.R. He'd noticed her skill on the first case they'd worked on together as a team. As time passed, he'd come to depend on her calm manner and smooth functioning.

She was like a second pair of hands connected to his brain, he thought. Last night had been similar, except he'd been the one who'd known instinctively what she'd wanted from him during their passionate lovemaking.

He waited for the guilt to hit him in a hot tide of remorse. It did, but to his surprise, it wasn't nearly as strong as he'd thought it would be. Odd, that.

Overlaying the regret for the past was a new set of emotions, far more complex than he could define at present. Balancing the heaviness of spirit was a lightness he hadn't felt for…mmm, years. Hunger pinged through him as he recalled the night. A pleasant sensation rolled over him.

Going into the hospital, he smoothed his hair, tousled by an impish breeze, and assumed the role he was accustomed to and comfortable with—that of the physician.

Do no harm.

That was the creed he tried to live by. Jenna was doubly vulnerable at the moment although she didn't seem to realize it. First from the pregnancy, then from the accident.

He hoped he hadn't hurt the relationship between him and his favorite trauma team aide by answering the passion that had sprang into being like a phoenix rising from the ashes. He would never forgive himself if he had.

* * *

Shortly before ten that night, Jenna finished bandaging the knife wound that she had cleaned and sutured while Eric observed the patient's vital signs.

"He's stable," the doctor said. "Let's keep him overnight and let his doctor look him over in the morning."

Following him into the supply room, she stripped gloves, mask and gown and tossed them in the proper bins while he did the same. "I'll write it up."

A hand caught her wrist. She glanced at Eric in surprise. Electric tingles rushed up her arm. No surprise there. She'd reacted to the slightest brush of his arm against hers the entire shift.

It had taken stern discipline to ignore the feeling when she'd first arrived at one that afternoon. Several emergencies had taken all her attention as day slid into evening, so things had become easier. However, since she wasn't comatose, she had still been acutely aware of him.

Slipping back into friendship wasn't as easy as she'd made it sound that morning. She almost groaned aloud as hunger thundered throughout her body, a reminder that she hadn't nearly had enough—

"You're going home," Eric continued, breaking into her thoughts which were becoming more wanton by the second. "You missed dinner and your rest breaks, too. I'll handle the paperwork."

"You've been here since this morning," she protested.

A half smile curved his mouth. "Are we going to fight about it?"

Meeting his gaze, heat flushed through her so strongly it caused perspiration to bloom over her face and neck, right down to the tingling points of her breasts.

He glanced down at the beaded tips visible under her E.R. uniform, then back to her eyes. His eyes darkened. With a low curse, he turned away and strode out of the room.

Jenna inhaled deeply and exhaled slowly, letting the need dissipate. Eric needed more than passion. He needed a friend, or at least a confidante, with no strings attached.

Yawning, she gathered her belongings, made sure the third shift was fully staffed, then headed for her car.

"Wait up," a masculine voice ordered.

She couldn't help the smile that sprang to her lips. "Saving my life doesn't mean you have to be responsible for me the rest of my life," she told Eric.

"Maybe not, but as your supervisor, I am concerned that my best nurse get home safe and sound."

He made sure she was locked inside her car before stepping back and letting her go on her way. She saw him standing in the same place as she stopped before pulling onto the street, his eyes on her car as she departed.

The phone was ringing when she arrived home. "Jenna, what's going on?" Rachel demanded.

"What do you mean?" she replied cautiously.

"Well, Dr. Thompson's car was seen at your place last night. And this morning."

Jenna sighed. "He brought the baby shower things over for me." There, that was the truth, but it didn't give anything away.

"It took all night to carry the stuff in?" Rachel's soft laughter followed on the heels of the question. "Lily and I will meet you for lunch tomorrow. Eleven-thirty at the deli across from the hospital. Okay?"

"No!" Jenna realized she'd spoken too quickly, too sharply when silence ensued. "That is, I, uh, will be busy in the morning. Errands and things, you know."

"You still have to eat," Rachel said firmly. She laughed. "Besides, I smell romance in the air. Bryce agrees. Lily and I want to know all about it."

"Rachel," Jenna began, then fell silent, not sure how to word her doubts.

"Yes?"

"How did you know it was love when you met Bryce?"

"So, it's like that," Rachel said, immediately jumping to conclusions. "I'm so thrilled for you."

"No, no," Jenna denied the assumption. "Eric and I are just friends. He isn't over his wife yet. I think a person needs to talk about the past in order to put things into perspective, don't you?"

Rachel's relieved sigh came over the phone. "You're asking my opinion," she said happily. "That means you've truly forgiven me for the episode with Michael—"

"There was nothing to forgive," Jenna interrupted. "He was the one at fault, not you."

"Yes, but Lily and I put you in the middle of our problem. That wasn't fair, but neither of us was seeing very clearly at the time. Now that our love lives are straightened out, we want to help with yours."

Her laughter was warm and affectionate, reminding Jenna of their long friendship and shared experiences. "I have no love life," she lamented, making an effort at keeping her tone amused.

"I think you could change that," Rachel told her. "From what I know about him, Eric is a very responsible person. He wouldn't run out on someone who needed him."

"I think you're right," Jenna said. "However, a liability isn't exactly what I had in mind."

"You're thinking more along the lines of the love of his life?"

"Well," Jenna joked in her usual lighthearted manner when things were getting too serious, "the love of the moment was more what I envisioned."

"Don't be afraid to fall in love," Rachel advised seriously. "It's the most wonderful feeling."

Laughing, Jenna said good-night and prepared for bed. The smile disappeared as she thought of Eric and her strange relationship with him. It would be easy to fall in love with him, but not with the specter of his first marriage hanging over them. She would try to help him with that. Then they would see what happened next.

In bed with the light out, she couldn't stop her thoughts from returning to the previous night and the bliss she'd experienced in his arms. He'd been the most wonderful lover she'd ever met, but was he meant for her?

Not unless he was over the tragedy of his past, some wise part of her advised.

Chapter 8

"Can you believe this?" Lily asked, gesturing toward the other two, then at herself.

"Believe what?" Rachel asked, taking a seat at the table with her friends.

Lily shook her head reflectively. "Last year we were all so unhappy...well, I was. And Rachel. Jenna was okay until we pulled her into our troubles."

"Mr. Louse," Jenna murmured, recalling the two-timer who had almost destroyed their friendship.

"Yeah," Lily and Rachel said together, then glanced at each other and burst into laughter.

Love, Jenna thought. Her friends were so much in

love, they glowed. Their newly found happiness had erased the last bit of hurt and anger between them.

Envy sliced through her. The three had done everything together nearly all their lives. Why couldn't she find the ideal man as her friends had?

Images flooded her inner vision—Eric helping her after the accident, Eric bringing lunch, Eric touching her in the most gentle, intimate of caresses…

"Look at her," Rachel, the most introspective of them, said softly.

Jenna realized her friends were observing her and tried to look nonchalant. "What?" she demanded.

"Your eyes," Rachel continued, "are those of a woman in love. You've really fallen for Dr. Thompson."

"Eric," Jenna said automatically, then felt heat sweep over her as Lily and Rachel grinned.

A tiny sound, like that of a very new kitten, caught their attention. Lily leaned over the baby carriage where her daughter had been sleeping. With the skill gained in her career as a pediatrics nurse, she scooped the precious bundle into her arms.

"I was wondering when you were going to wake," she mock-scolded the infant. "Mama needs relief."

Jenna felt her own breasts contract as Lily discreetly nursed the baby. She laid a hand on her abdomen where her own child rested safe and sound, waiting until the proper time to make his appearance into the world. Glancing up, she saw Rachel doing the same. They smiled at each other.

"I know," Lily said, catching their misty-eyed emotion. "It's like a miracle, isn't it? The three of us with babies..." Her voice trailed off as her gaze went misty, too.

Jenna blinked rapidly and took a deep breath. "Well, I've got to run. It's almost one."

"Take your breaks," Rachel advised, giving her a stern, motherly glare.

"And prop your feet up as often as you can," Lily continued the advice. "Eric can be a slave driver."

After paying for her lunch, Jenna headed over to the hospital. No cars or ambulances were parked at the emergency-room portico, so maybe it would be an easy Friday night.

Going inside, she stored her purse in a drawer at the receptionist desk, locked it, then joined the day-shift staff for a rundown on the day's happenings. Eric was already there.

Her heart did its racing act, but she smiled calmly, nodded to him, then listened to the report. There were three cases being seen at present, but no true emergencies. People without insurance had no choice but to come to the Emergency Room for treatment.

"That's it," the head shift nurse told her, closing the folder on the last patient. "Have fun. There's a rock concert on for tonight. That usually brings in business."

Jenna grimaced. After the others left, she went over each case again, noting symptoms and treatment. All was under control. She was aware of Eric standing close by as if waiting for something from her. She concentrated on the files until she'd read every word.

"I want you to take it easy tonight," Eric said when she finally looked up. "You should sit every chance you get. You need more rest."

He scooted the desk chair behind her knees. She sat down. He pulled a stool over. She recognized it as one they used so patients could climb up on an examining table.

"It's from supply," he assured her when she frowned. "I didn't steal it from a cubicle."

"Do you read minds?" She tried to keep a modicum of humor in her tone, but truthfully she felt snappish.

"Only yours. Excuse me."

He went into his office and answered the phone while she started her nightly inspection of supplies. When she went to dinner at five-thirty, she saw his office was dark. Good. He needed to rest more, too.

At that moment he strolled into the cafeteria, looked around, spotted her at the staff table and came over.

"I'm leaving now," he said. "I'll be over in the morning. Is nine too early?"

Her glanced at him in surprise. "Why?"

"To put the baby furniture together."

"Oh, that's okay. I'm sure I can figure it out. I'll go to a baby store and examine the cribs they have set up. First thing Monday," she added when he didn't look appeased.

He studied her for a long twenty seconds. "You're well into your fifth month."

"Well, duh," she said to that piece of information.

His sudden smile made her blood go all frothy like a bottle of soda pop shaken vigorously. The bubbles rose to her brain and made her dizzy.

"You should be prepared," he told her.

Her answering smile disappeared. "If the baby came now, its survival would be pretty risky."

"I meant…I didn't mean…" He stopped, his eyes going dark with emotion she couldn't read. "You're strong and healthy. So is the baby. There's no reason you won't carry to term, but you should be getting everything together so you won't have to worry about it when the time comes. I thought I could help."

He walked away. The automatic doors slid open, and he left the hospital.

After a tense couple of minutes, Jenna leaned back in the chair and relaxed. She wasn't sure how she felt about Eric's offer of help. Maybe it would be better if she didn't get more involved with him.

On the other hand, maybe it was better for him if he did help her. Working on the baby bed would force him to face the loss of his own child and perhaps accept that it hadn't been his fault.

She sighed, not sure where her concern for him ended and where her desire to see him began. Things were already hopelessly tangled between them.

Later, on her break, she called and left a message on his home phone. "Nine would be a good time to come over," she said. "I'll have breakfast ready."

For the rest of the shift, she worried about her motives and the way her insides tightened at the slightest thought of the handsome E.R. physician.

Jenna glanced out the window for the tenth time in ten minutes. The coffee and omelets were ready to be served. The patio table was covered with a pretty floral tablecloth and a fresh bunch of roses she'd filched from the bushes beside the sidewalk.

Holding her hand up, she studied her trembling

fingers and sternly reminded herself that Eric was coming over as a friend, nothing else. Remember that.

It was no use. She thought of him as a lover. Closing her eyes, she pressed her fingers to her temples and blocked out the pictures of him and her together—

A tap on the front door broke up the erotic vision. She wiped her hands down her tan maternity slacks, pasted a smile on her mouth and called out, "Come on in. It's open."

His entry brought the scent of his aftershave and the freshness of the outdoors to her. Her heart pounded so fiercely she had to steady it with a hand to her chest.

"You okay?" he asked, his eyes taking in every detail.

She nodded. "Breakfast is ready. I thought we'd eat on the patio."

That way, they wouldn't be inside. Alone. With the bedroom a short distance up the stairs. And she wouldn't be tempted to drag him up there and have her way with him.

A wave of passion spread over her entire body as she retrieved the food from the warm oven.

"The biscuits look good. It's been ages since I've had some. My mother used to make them." He picked up the basket of warm bread and the pitcher of orange juice.

"Mine, too. I hope I didn't leave any ingredients out. I can't remember the last time I made them. Oh, yes, I do. It was when my dad brought up the baby furniture. He wanted gravy and biscuits made the old-fashioned way as opposed to popping them out of a can."

They carried the food outside and sat at the small table. The neighborhood was quiet. People slept in on Saturday morning, if possible.

"My favorite time of day," she said. "I like having the mornings to myself."

"What are you going to do when the baby comes?"

This seemed like a good time to mention her plans. "I want to take six months off, then I'm thinking of working part time for a year."

"With three twelve-hour shifts, you would get full benefits and still be free most of the week."

"Well, I want to nurse Stevie for the first..." She let the words trail off as he gave her an odd stare. "What?"

"You're going to name the baby Steve?"

There were emotional undertones present in the question that she didn't understand. Was that the name he and his wife had chosen? If she remembered correctly, the child was to have been a girl. But then, people gave kids all kinds of names nowadays, no matter the gender of the baby.

"Steven Alexander. After my father," she hastened to add, in case he thought...well, she didn't know what he thought as he continued to study her.

"My middle name is Steven," he said softly.

"Oh." Confusion swept over her. "I didn't know. Really. I don't think I've ever heard your whole name. I mean, at work, it's always Dr. Thompson. And you sign the forms with your initials, which nobody can read. I mean, you sort of run them together." She stopped before the hole she was digging for herself got any deeper.

The tension drained from his face, and he smiled in a thoughtful, but natural manner. "Steven Alexander. I like that. It's a fine name for a fine boy."

She was relieved. He liked the name. He really did. His expression was sincere, his body relaxed. Also, he'd spoken of her baby without past memories darkening his eyes. That was good. Her idea of forcing him to talk about family life seemed to be working.

"Eat up," he coaxed. "I want to get the bed together before dark."

"I have to go to work at one," she reminded him.

"That's four hours. It'll be finished long before then," he promised.

All the things they could do in that length of time danced through her mind like an endless chorus line. "Well," she said, flustered by the passion and his nearness, "let's get to work."

Chapter 9

Jenna held the side of the crib against the end piece while Eric bolted them together. The task went quickly.

"It's amazing how fast work goes with someone who knows what he's doing," she remarked as they finished.

"Stand back," he said.

When she let go, the baby bed stood on its own. "Wow, success. I can't stand it."

"Do you have a mattress?"

"Yes, over here." She moved boxes aside. "I bought one on sale a month ago." She struggled with stuff her father had stacked on top of the mattress.

"Let me do that," Eric said in scolding tones.

She observed while he unearthed the mattress, then removed the plastic wrapping. He easily lifted it and fitted it into position in the crib.

"Ah, perfect," she said, bending over the boxes once more. "Dad brought all the baby stuff my mother had saved. I don't know if it's any good now."

Eric nodded. She noticed his expression had changed, becoming more somber as he used a pocket knife to split the wrapping tape on the six large boxes. She found crib sheets, blankets, towels, tiny washcloths and drawstring gowns in one box. In the others were clothing of various sizes, both for girls and boys. The scent of lavender, thyme and moth-balls wafted around them.

"This was my brother's," she said, holding up a playsuit in bright red. "They aren't faded or moth-eaten." She gave the material an experimental tug along the seams. "They look fine, don't they?"

"Yes."

She glanced at Eric. His voice had been husky, almost hoarse-sounding. He wasn't looking at the romper set, but at her. Gazing into his eyes, she recognized the hunger. An answering passion flared in her.

"Eric?" she said, a question and an invitation.

He shook his head slightly, then reached out and cupped his fingers behind her neck. His thumb traced a fiery outline of her lips.

"I don't know why I thought I could come over here and be around you and not react. It's impossible."

"I know," she said softly, a glow starting inside her. His light touch felt so right. She laid her hands on his chest, wanting to melt into him as their combined heat made her legs weak.

"Stupid," he murmured. "I shouldn't have come."

She stopped herself from leaning into him as the words penetrated the haze forming around her. "Why?"

A frown settled on his brow as he took a quick, harsh breath. "Because I can't be around you and not want you. It was foolish to think we could be friends. Or go back to a casual basis after…after…"

"After we made love," she supplied.

"I didn't want involvement," he told her, so sweetly earnest she wanted to kiss him. "I didn't want the responsibility for another person's happiness. Then there was the accident. I was worried about you. What I didn't expect, didn't figure into the equation, was the passion."

"I know. It shocked me, too. A little," she added

truthfully. "So where do we go from here? Do you want me to transfer to another hospital?"

"No," he said sternly.

"Then what?"

"I'm not sure. I think we both need time to think this through and make sure this is where we want to go."

She wanted to argue that she was sure, but looking into his eyes, she kept silent. The twin pits of hell were again reflected in those dark depths. "You're right. Let's give each other some space, then—" She shrugged.

"Then we'll see what comes next," he murmured, brushing her lips once with his thumb, then releasing her.

He stared intently into her eyes for another second, then he stepped away from her. With a troubled frown, he walked out.

In the silence that followed his departure, she considered the implications of their conversation. One thing she knew—being with her didn't open the possibilities to a glorious future for him as it did for her. It only reminded him of all he'd lost.

The atmosphere was strained in the E.R. when she went in at one that afternoon. The usual Saturday mishaps arrived via ambulance or private vehicle, usually driven by wild-eyed relatives or friends.

Jenna found that she and Eric worked together as competently as ever, no matter what their emotional stress might be. The other nurses were nervy around him, she noticed. The very grimness of his expression was enough to silence any unnecessary chatter.

"This is the third time you've been in this year," Eric said to a seven-year-old. "Isn't it time you learned not to pick up stuff off the floor in a store and eat it?"

The boy gazed at him with big brown eyes that would soften a polar bear's heart. "It looked like candy."

"You had no idea what it was," the doctor said. "You're a smart kid. Don't be stupid in the future. You'll make plenty of other mistakes without repeating this one. I don't want to see you in here again, understand?"

The mother looked rather offended, but the child nodded. Jenna kept her expression neutral as she labeled a specimen for the lab, then cleaned the stomach pump and related equipment.

The mother and son left. Eric took the paperwork to his office to finish, and she went to the cafeteria for her dinner break.

"You look tired," a feminine voice said.

Jenna glanced at her friend. "Rachel," she said warmly. "You're working rather late yourself."

The other nurse nodded and settled into a chair with a carton of juice. She covered a yawn. "This has been a hard day." She sighed.

Jenna didn't ask if there had been a death. Oncology was a difficult field, worse than trauma cases in some ways.

"We're making enormous strides in fighting cancer," Rachel murmured, "and we win some cases, but we also lose."

"Some losses hurt more than others. Who was it?"

Rachel massaged her temples. "A sixteen-year-old boy. Cancer of the bone. It had spread to his spine. He loved baseball. He wanted to make it to the majors."

Jenna listened as her friend spoke quietly about the youth. He'd shared his dreams with Rachel. He'd introduced her to his girlfriend.

"He was bright, talented and friendly, a good person," Rachel finished, grief clouding her eyes.

"That's his legacy then," Jenna said. "Years from now, perhaps at a class reunion, his girlfriend will think of him and her memories will be sweet."

Rachel squeezed her arm. "Time for me to get home. Thanks for letting me talk it out. That helped.

Come over tomorrow for lunch. Are you free, or is a certain doctor demanding all your time?''

Jenna managed a careless smile. ''No such luck. I'd love to have lunch with you. Will Bryce be there?''

''No, he and a friend are taking part in a golf tournament for a local charity. The nursery is finished, and I'm dying to show it off to someone.''

After Rachel left, Jenna ate her balanced, healthy meal and pondered Life with a capital *L*. Fate could be unkind, but people survived...most of them...

Tears gathered behind her eyes as a sense of sadness came over her. Her child would never know a father. Would he feel this as a loss in his life? Would he see her as selfish to want a baby without providing a complete family to help raise him?

Still in this sentimental mood, she returned to the E.R. Things were quiet. Eric's office was closed and dark. He'd gone home for the day. She worked steadily until ten, then drove home and let herself into the silent condo.

''We'll get a dog,'' she promised the baby as she went up the stairs and prepared for bed. ''Will that work as a father substitute?''

She realized it was a bit late to be thinking of that. Lying in the bed where she'd experienced such bliss, she knew why her thoughts were haunting her. She wanted Eric as the father for her son. She wanted him as her lover. She wanted him as her love.

Sunday dawned clear and bright. The air was fragrant with the scent of spring flowers. Jenna watered the pots on the patio, picked a few dead flowers off the shrubs around her place, then freshened up for lunch with her friend.

Driving to Rachel's new home, the impressive Armstrong mansion, she felt a few pangs of envy. Not for the house or the Armstrong money, but for the love Rachel and Bryce had found. He behaved as if the child Rachel carried was his.

Suppressing the feeling, she put on a smile for her long-time friend and actually had a thoroughly enjoyable visit. The baby's room, done in pink and gold with genuine antique furniture that had been in the Armstrong family for generations, was perfect for the girl Rachel was expecting.

Driving home later that afternoon, Jenna was truly happy for her friend. She sighed contentedly. Maybe one couldn't have everything, but she had plenty of good things—friends, a father who would be a wonderful grandparent to her son, a job she loved. Who was complaining?

At the next street, she noticed the sign and the elegant rock garden planted at the entrance to an expensive subdivision. Eric lived in here, she recalled. On an impulse, she slowed and turned in. She just wanted to see the area.

At the last house on a winding street, she spied his SUV. Her heart lurched when she saw his familiar figure in the yard, which looked freshly mown. A riding lawn mower was visible through the open door of a three-car garage.

His eyes met hers. She slowed at the curb and stopped.

"Hello," he said, coming to the street and speaking when she rolled down the passenger-side window.

"Hi." After a brief silence, she added, "I happened to be in the neighborhood. I had lunch with Rachel." The excuse sounded terribly lame.

"Come in," he invited. "I'll give you the grand tour."

She turned off the key and got out when he came around and opened her door. They walked up the long drive made of pavers and lined with lush landscaping.

"Did you have a professional do this?" She gestured toward the flower beds and the paths between them, all laid out for minimum water usage and maintenance.

He opened the door so she could enter the house.

"I used a computer program to lay it out, then had a friend who owns a nursery put in the plants."

The house was cool and completely silent once they were inside with the door closed. They were in a den with a large-screen TV and leather furniture at one end and a reading chair with a table and lamp beside it at the other. The wall was lined with book-shelves.

"Do you read a lot?" she asked, peering at the many volumes on the shelves.

"The decorator selected most of the books. I've read all of them," he said, leading the way into a dream kitchen of light cherry cabinets and stainless steel appliances and tile floors in warm tones of slate.

"This is lovely. Even I could probably cook a gourmet meal in here," she joked.

He took two tall glasses from a cabinet and filled them with ice from the refrigerator dispenser. After pouring tea in, he handed one to her. He watched her while he took a long, cool drink. "Come on," he said.

She followed him from room to room, each one perfectly furnished and immaculate. It reminded her of the model homes used by builders to showcase their work, beautiful but devoid of the little things that meant someone lived there.

"This is my office," he said, escorting her into a

room in the back of the house. Unlike the rest of the home, the room was messy. The desk was littered with papers and files. A pair of jogging shoes had been pulled off and left in front of the French doors to the patio. "I'm cleaning out a bunch of old stuff, tax records and such."

"I see." She walked to the double doors. There was a grassy backyard, just right for croquet or a game of badminton, or just tossing a ball back and forth. Beyond the lawn was a fenced area filled with grasses and wildflowers.

"My wife planned on having a pony for the kids."

She nodded. Kids. Plural. They'd wanted more than one. For a second, her throat closed up. She nodded again while she fought for control. Using skills learned in her work, she forced air into her lungs, one breath, another, then another, until she was calm.

"There's a guest bedroom down here," he continued, "and four upstairs, each with its own bath." He laughed. "I grew up in a house with one bathroom for six people. My grandmother lived with us, and she metered the time each of us three kids spent in the shower. I learned to bathe in five minutes flat."

"Sounds like plenty of time to me," she quipped, giving him a smile. She lifted the glass, saw it was empty and wondered when she'd drunk the tea. She had no memory of it.

"Here, I'll get you a refill."

Before she could protest, he took her glass and left the room. In the silence, she could hear a clock ticking.

Glancing around, she spotted a grandfather clock against the wall behind the desk. Going to it, she examined the precision pendulum and weights that kept it going for a couple of weeks. Her father had a similar one. She'd always found its steady ticking a comfort in the days after her mother had passed away when she was alone in the house, doing homework and waiting for her father to come home.

Turning from the clock, she smiled at the papers on the desk. Clearing out old stuff was a good sign, a step in the right direction, in her opinion.

A letter caught her eye. A pen lay on the page as if the writer had stopped while in the middle of it.

A shock rippled over her when she recognized the name at the top. Unable to refrain, she leaned over the desk chair and read the swiftly written lines in which he'd poured out his grief and sorrow to his deceased wife for hurting her with his neglect, his wish that they could have had another chance. It ended in despair…

I know life goes on and that a person must move on, too. I've met someone, slept with her, but I'm not sure I can ever love again or share what we had. I'm not sure I want to.

The letter stopped there. It was one of remorse, but more than that, it was one of love, a deep, abiding love that had never died. It was a letter to the woman who filled his heart.

That woman wasn't her.

Jenna heard his steps in the kitchen. Panicked by emotions she couldn't contain, she rushed out the elegant doors, around the house and down the drive. She was in her car when Eric came out the front door. He called her name, but she didn't answer.

"Jenna, it isn't what you think," he called, running toward the street.

She'd left the keys in the ignition, so it took only a turn to start the engine and speed away, leaving him looking concerned as he watched her leave. It wasn't until she was back on the main county road to town that she could think again. Tears kept clouding her vision so that she had to continually blink in order to see.

He couldn't possibly know what she thought. She didn't know herself. Except that she'd been a fool to think she could make a difference in his life. And stupid to fall in love with him.

As she rounded a sharp curve, she blinked again, but the scene didn't change. Two cars were barreling side by side down the two-lane road, racing each other.

There was a shallow ditch and stone wall on either side. Having no choice, she swung the wheel hard to the right and planted both feet on the brake pedal. She managed to cut the wheel back to the left just before impact with the wall and hoped it would be a glancing blow.

A tree loomed in front of her. She wrapped a protective arm across her abdomen. "Please," she whispered. "Eric, we need you."

It was the last thing she remembered.

Chapter 10

Eric got a call from the emergency-room reception-ist just as he sat down on the back patio with a cool beer. After Jenna had taken off, he'd showered and changed in order to give both of them time to think things through before they faced each other again. He knew he had to be certain about what he wanted to say. It would affect their future. And that of the child.

"Thompson," he said into the receiver.

The news stopped his heart for a second, then sent it into overdrive. He listened, asked a few questions then hung up. Jenna had been run off the road by two guys who were drag-racing. She'd bounced off a stone wall and crashed into a tree. She was in surgery to rejoin a cut artery and close a wound in her leg. She'd lost a lot of blood.

Dear God.

Grabbing the keys off the kitchen counter, he hurried to his car. In less than a minute, he was on his way to the hospital as history repeated itself, only this time it was Jenna who'd been in the accident.

At least she was still alive. Not like the other time. He forced the thought at bay.

After parking in his usual spot, he ran inside. "Which O.R.?" he asked the older woman at the desk. She was the one who'd thought to call him.

"It's finished," she said.

His heart stopped, literally stopped.

"She's in recovery now," the receptionist added.

He glared at the woman who'd handled the emergency-room admittance forms almost as long as he'd been born. She smiled serenely at him and gestured toward the swinging doors. He turned toward them.

Composing himself, he went down the corridor to the surgery recovery area. Three beds were occupied in the rooms surrounding the nursing station. Jenna was in the first.

He went inside, his gaze automatically taking in the readings on the monitoring equipment. Then he bent over the protective railing and looked into her face.

She had the pale, waxy appearance of someone who'd just gone through a major trauma, someone near death.

He took her wrist, needing to feel the beat of her pulse for himself. For a second he couldn't find it. A ripple of anguish ran through him.

His eyes went to the monitor. Her heart was steady. He found the pulse and counted. The oxygen monitor showed full saturation. So, all the signs were good. The relief was almost as painful as the fear had been.

A second monitor showed the baby's heart rate. It was fast, but not alarming. The child may have been bumped around, but he was still nestled securely in the cradle of his mother's body.

"Good," Eric said aloud, feeling the tension seep from his neck. The phone rang beside the bed. He picked it up. "Yes?" he said, not ready to talk to anyone.

"This is Rachel. Is Jenna all right?"

His impatience evaporated. Jenna had loyal friends who loved her. Something, his heart or soul or whatever, swelled until it filled his chest to the bursting point. "She's fine. So is Stevie."

"Stevie? Oh, the baby," Rachel said. "Yes, she's

fine,'' she said to someone in the room with her. ''What happened?''

He explained all that he knew. He'd no sooner hung up than the phone rang again. This time it was Lily. He went through the facts again. After four more calls from friends and co-workers, he recorded a message and routed calls to the voice mail.

Then he waited.

The night passed, hour by slow hour. Jenna didn't wake or move. When he held her hand or touched her forehead, she was cool, as if she were made of wax.

But her signs were steady, and at last he fell asleep in the chair, his dreams strange as he ran through a maze, but couldn't find his way either to the center or to the outside.

''Eric?''

Jenna narrowed her eyes and studied the man whose hand rested on top of hers. He had a growth of beard on his face. She'd seen that twice...the morning after he'd spent the night on her sofa and the one after he'd spent the night in her bed.

He opened his eyes and stared into hers. Then he smiled, a slow, sexy smile that stirred up things in her heart. ''Hi.''

"What are you doing here?" She looked around. "I'm in the hospital. The wreck—"

Panic hit her. She slipped her hand away from his and laid it on her tummy.

"He's okay," Eric said. "He probably didn't like the jouncing around, but he's not hurt."

"My leg hurts."

"A piece of metal sliced through an artery. It's been repaired, but you'll have to stay off your feet for a few weeks until it heals."

She checked the monitors. "It's kind of odd to observe your own heartbeat and everything. I suppose that's better than the alternative, like not having one to check."

"Stupid young punks," he said fiercely. "You could have been killed, you and Stevie."

His eyes were stark with anger, she saw, but there was more. She just didn't know what it was.

"We weren't," she reminded him softly. "Have you been here all night? You should go home and rest," she said without waiting for his confirmation.

He took her hand. "Not unless I can take you with me."

For a second she was dazzled by the possibilities, then she remembered the letter. The glow faded, leaving grief in its place. "You're not responsible for me or the baby. You don't have to take care of us." She managed a smile.

"I want to," he said.

He smiled, too, and she was close to being dazzled again. She took a firm hold on her emotions as she shook her head in a scolding manner. "You'd better watch what you say, doctor. You know how patients can take things wrong."

He took her hand and gently squeezed it. "Then I'll be very clear," he promised, "because I want you to take things right."

She saw his chest lift and fall in a deep breath. She did the same, preparing herself for his words.

"The letter you saw wasn't written recently. I wrote it over a year ago after a night with a friend, a widow who, like me, tried to get on with life. It didn't work for either of us. We weren't ready. Or maybe the person wasn't the right one."

Jenna nodded. Her heartbeat stayed the same on the monitor. She was proud of that.

"Yesterday," he continued, "I was restless. For some reason, I started cleaning out my desk. I realized it was time to clear out the past, because I want a future." He lightly touched her abdomen. "With you and our children."

The heart monitor went into double-time. The blood pressure indicator zoomed into the red zone.

An alarm went off. A nurse hurried in. She paused at the foot of the bed in confusion, her eyes going from the machine to the patient, then to the doctor who calmly sat and held the patient's hand and didn't look worried at all.

Footsteps sounded in the hall. The surgeon entered, another nurse on his heels. "What's going on?" he asked, shutting off the alarm, then giving Eric a mock-stern glare. "Doctor, are you interfering with my patient?"

Eric checked the monitors. Jenna's heart and blood pressure were dropping into the high normal range. "If you can get her stabilized, I'd like to ask her to marry me."

The alarm went off again.

"Jeez," the surgeon said, hitting the reset button, "can't you wait until she's out of recovery?"

Eric gazed into wide blue eyes. "No," he said softly. "I can't wait another second."

"Well, go ahead," the other doctor ordered, "while we're here to resuscitate her." He grinned.

"Jenna Cooper," Eric said solemnly, "will you marry me and make me the happiest man on earth?"

The heat rose to her face, but she decided this was no time for an attack of modesty. "Are you sure?" she asked.

Eric knew what she was asking. He nodded. "Life

can be cruel, but it can also be kind, giving us a second chance even though we don't deserve it. I want that chance with you.''

He waited while Jenna stared into his eyes, uncertainty in hers. Opening his heart, he tried to let her see all the way to his soul, all the way to the overwhelming love that filled him, love that she had brought to life.

''I love you,'' he said simply.

''And I, you,'' she whispered.

Tears filled her lovely blue eyes. He wiped them away with a tissue, then unable to resist, he bent forward and kissed her. Her lips were soft against his. And warm.

When he raised up, they were alone in the room. The vital signs were all in the normal range, he saw.

Jenna's eyes closed as she rested again. A smile lingered on her delectable mouth. A hint of color warmed her pale cheeks. A great happiness flooded his heart, and he was content.

Epilogue

Rain splashed against the window, but inside, a fire flickered over gas logs and the guests were cozy.

Bryce Armstrong, their host, lifted his cup of egg nog, which of course had no alcohol due to the nursing mothers, and proposed a toast. "To our beautiful wives."

Jake and Eric called, "Here, here," and drank to the three women, who smiled and nodded graciously.

"To friends noble and true," Bryce continued.

They all sipped from their cups.

"And to the holidays and the new generation now sleeping—thank heavens—in the nursery."

The three couples laughed, the merry sound covering the howl of the wind as a storm blew in from the Pacific Ocean.

Jenna glanced at Eric and found his gaze on her. The darkness was gone from his eyes. Only the glow of love, freely given and received, lingered there now. Looking around the pleasant room and counting her blessings, she saw her two best friends doing the same.

They exchanged smiles.

"Love," she said, raising her cup.

"Happiness," Rachel said, raising hers.

"Forever," Lily added and took a sip when the other two did. "By the way, Jake and I have decided we, uh, want to increase our little family as soon as possible."

The other two women stared at the couple.

"That sounds like a challenge to me," Eric said. "How about you?" he asked Bryce.

"Yeah," the other man agreed. He gave Rachel an assessing perusal, then waggled his eyebrows at her.

"Not for a year," she declared firmly. "At *least* a year."

Eric glanced at Jenna, his eyes warm with laughter. "Steven is barely three months old. I think we'll give it some time," he said, "then we'll see about a sister for him. And maybe a brother after that."

"I'm thinking we need enough to field a baseball team," Jake said, looking very serious.

Lily opened her eyes wide in alarm.

"Well, I'm game if the rest are," Jenna stated. "After all, we can't let the team down, can we?"

That brought on more laughter. They had drawn names and now exchanged presents, opening them before the evening grew too late. In a quiet moment, Eric drew Jenna into his arms and kissed her briefly but tenderly.

"Your love is the best gift of all," he told her. "I was almost afraid to accept it. When you were in that accident, I thought I would die, too, if you didn't make it. I realized life was giving me another chance at happiness. I nearly let fear ruin it."

"I'd given up, too," she said, smoothing a dark lock off his forehead. "Going to the clinic to conceive a child was my way of avoiding a relationship. We were lucky that fate intervened."

"Yeah, lucky," he agreed.

Their laughter brought chuckles from their friends. It was a sound to delight the heart.

* * * * *

*Don't miss the next story from
Silhouette's* LOGAN'S LEGACY:
*TO LOVE AND PROTECT
by Susan Mallery.
Available June 2004.*

*Turn the page for an excerpt from this
exciting romance...!*

Chapter 1

"**I** need a man with good hands," Liz Duncan murmured to herself as she studied the sketch, then the beautiful blond female model she'd hired for the afternoon.

"Don't we all?" Marguerite said as she adjusted the baby she held, then tossed her long hair back over her shoulder. "That's why they wrote a song about it."

Liz tilted her head. Something wasn't right. The proportion, she thought. With a man holding the baby, the image would be more powerful and evocative. Marguerite's fingers were too delicate, her palms too narrow.

"A song about what?" Liz asked absently.

"Slow hands, honey. Get with the program. If you're going to get a man, get a good one. Make sure he knows what he's doing."

Liz glanced at the tall, slender nineteen-year-old. "I'm talking about work."

"I'm not."

"You never are." Liz flipped through her sketches, then shook her head. "You can put her down. We're done."

"Sure, boss." She carefully placed the sleeping baby back into the bassinette and lightly touched her cheek. "Thanks for the good time, kid." She looked at Liz. "You really done with me?"

"Sure. I'll let the agency know I changed my mind about the assignment, not that you didn't work out."

"I appreciate that."

Marguerite collected her large tote bag and walked out of the room. Liz crossed to the bassinette and stared at the sleeping baby. The infant's tiny features stirred her heart.

"I wouldn't mind taking you home with me, little one," she murmured. "Too bad this is all about work."

After wheeling the baby back to the nursery, Liz wandered the halls of the Children's Connection, the non-profit adoption and fertility center that had hired her to do the artwork for their new brochure. She'd been on manhunts before, but never in connection with her work.

"I should give myself hazard duty pay," she murmured as she rounded a corner and began checking out offices.

She found nine women, three guys over the age of fifty, a hunky guy about thirty, but no strong, masculine types with great hands. Her vision was clear—someone holding a baby. At first she'd thought that someone should be a woman, but now she knew better.

She headed toward the exit, thinking the hospital next door might be a better source. Maybe she could find an intern or resident to take pity on her. If her luck held, her baby model would continue to nap peacefully. If she could just—

A man reached the front door the same time she did. He pulled the door open and waited politely for her to exit first. Liz stumbled to a stop as she studied the strong fingers and broad palms. His hands looked more than capable—they looked safe. She could see them cradling the baby, offering shelter and security and the perfect resting place for a tired, trusting infant.

"Change your mind?" the man asked.

"Huh?" Liz blinked at him, then realized he was still holding open the door. Was he leaving?

"Wait! You can't go." Without thinking, she grabbed the sleeve of his leather jacket. "Are you leaving? Do you have a few minutes? Okay, maybe an hour, but no longer. The baby is going to wake up after that. But I've got at least an hour, if you do."

As she spoke, she looked from the man's hands to his face. He was young, maybe in his mid-twenties. Handsome. Confident. Intriguing. Brown eyes regarded her quizzically while a firm, sensual mouth curved up slightly at the corners.

"What?" she asked, aware that she might not have made as much sense as she could have.

"I'm debating between deranged and charming," he told her.

She released his jacket. "I suggest charming. It's more flattering and accurate. I'm occasionally temperamental but almost never crazy. You should hear me out."

"Fair enough." He released the door and stepped back.

As he tucked his hands into the front pockets of his jeans, Liz became aware of a subtle tension crackling between them. Not a surprise, she thought ruefully. Dark-haired guys with broad shoulders were totally her type. Combine that with an air of mystery and an easy disposition and she was almost always open to the possibilities.

"Elizabeth Duncan," she said, holding out her hand. "Liz. I'm a commercial illustrator hired by the Children's Connection to do some artwork for their new brochure. If they love my design enough, they'll start using it on letterhead and publicity materials."

"David Logan." His hand engulfed hers. "I can draw a stick figure that would make you green with envy."

She chuckled even as she ignored his slightly crooked, very charming smile and the way the warmth from his fingers made her want to purr. She was on a schedule—not just because of her deadline but because her other model—the baby—wouldn't sleep forever.

"So here's the thing," she said. "I have approval for my idea, which was a woman holding a sleeping baby. The drawing focuses on the baby, so we only see the woman's forearms and hands. But when I did a preliminary sketch, it looked all wrong." She tried to look as innocent as possible. "I need a man instead."

One eyebrow rose. "Of course you do."

"I'm serious. You have great hands, the baby is asleep. All you have to do is hold her. It's maybe an hour out of your life. Just think, if the people in charge love my design, your hands could be famous. That would help you with women.''

He chuckled. ''What makes you think I need help?''

* * * * *

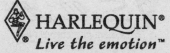

Coming in June from Silhouette Books...
more stories from the bestselling Silhouette Desire series,

Dynasties : The Danforths

Dynasties:
Summer in
Savannah

Welcome to Steam, the trendiest nightclub in Savannah, a place where temperatures and passions are sure to rise during one hot summer. Join top authors Barbara McCauley, Maureen Child and Sheri WhiteFeather as they deliver three sexy stories in this brand-new collection.

Available at your favorite retail outlet.

Silhouette®

Where love comes alive™

Visit Silhouette Books at www.eHarlequin.com   PSSIS

A determined woman searches for her past.
Will true love stand in her way...
or fulfill her deepest desire?

**Don't miss the emotional second installment of
this new continuity series from Silhouette Books**

Logan's Legacy

Because birthright has its privileges and family ties run deep.

SECRETS &
SEDUCTIONS

by *USA TODAY*
bestselling author

PAMELA TOTH

Determined to uncover the truth about her
mysterious heritage, Emma Wright went to
the Children's Connection—and straight to the adoption
agency's handsome director Morgan Davis. She expected his
help...but she didn't count on falling in love with him....

Coming in July 2004.

Where love comes alive™